LAURA
& EMMA

A NOVEL

KATE GREATHEAD

✳

Simon & Schuster

New York   London   Toronto   Sydney   New Delhi

Simon & Schuster
1230 Avenue of the Americas
New York, NY 10020

First Simon & Schuster hardcover edition March 2018

SIMON & SCHUSTER and colophon are registered trademarks of Simon & Schuster, Inc.

For information about special discounts for bulk purchases, please contact Simon & Schuster Special Sales at 1-866-506-1949 or business@simonandschuster.com.

The Simon & Schuster Speakers Bureau can bring authors to your live event. For more information or to book an event, contact the Simon & Schuster Speakers Bureau at 1-866-248-3049 or visit our website at www.simonspeakers.com.

Interior design by Carly Loman

Manufactured in the United States of America

1   3   5   7   9   10   8   6   4   2

Library of Congress Cataloging-in-Publication Data

Names: Greathead, Kate, author.
Title: Laura & Emma / Kate Greathead.
Other titles: Laura and Emma
Description: First Simon & Schuster hardcover edition. | New York : Simon & Schuster, 2018. |
Identifiers: LCCN 2017027550 | ISBN 9781501156601 (hardcover)
Subjects: LCSH: Self-realization in women—Fiction. | Mothers and daughters—Fiction. | Single mothers—Fiction. | Families—Fiction. | Domestic fiction. | BISAC: FICTION / Literary. | FICTION / Contemporary Women. | FICTION / General.
Classification: LCC PS3607.R42865 L38 2018 | DDC 813/.6 —dc23 LC record available at https://lccn.loc.gov/2017027550

ISBN 978-1-5011-5660-1
ISBN 978-1-5011-5663-2 (ebook)

To the memory of my grandmother
Victoria Parsons Pennoyer,
who untaught me everything

Someone sewed their eyes shut
with needlepoint thread
and when they speak
they make up for it
in booming tones.

—SUSAN MINOT, "BOSTON ANCESTORS"

LAURA
& EMMA

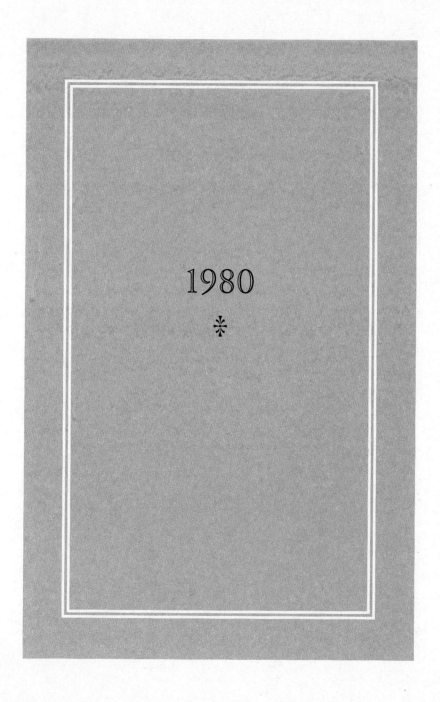

1980

✳

LAURA SOMETIMES WOKE UP IN THE NIGHT, RATTLED BY thoughts she'd never have during the day. A reoccurring nocturnal concern was that her apartment wasn't really hers. She owned it, her name was on the door, there were official papers, but this wouldn't always be the case; someday it would belong to someone else.

Looking around her bedroom envisioning everything packed up in boxes to be hauled off by movers was very unsettling. But this was the inevitable outcome of apartments—no one's really belonged to them. In a hundred years the apartments of everyone she knew would be inhabited by future generations, whose taste in music and art and films and clothes would be completely foreign to her. Not that it mattered, as she, and everyone she knew, would be dead.

It was ridiculous to worry about, but in the sobering still of the small hours these thoughts consumed her, and were she to have a husband, Laura imagined she'd wake him up to unload them. And his laughing at their absurdity. And her laughing back. And then, feeling reassured and safely contained within the walls that surrounded her bed, drifting back to sleep.

The other time Laura thought having a husband would be nice was when something broke and it was too late to call the super. If it was after nine o'clock and she discovered her bedroom window was swollen shut from the humidity, or the smoke detector started beeping in need of a new battery, she had to live with it until the morning. That was it, though; these occasions aside, Laura was getting along very well without a man in her life.

But still—it upset her, the idea that she didn't truly belong in her own apartment.

"REALLY, IT DOESN'T MATTER WHO you marry," Laura's mother had said more than once. "However *madly* in love you are in the beginning, one day you will find yourself sitting across a table from him thinking, 'Anything, anything, *an-y*-thing would be better than this!'"

Laura had never been madly in love—or even sanely in love. She didn't hate sex, but she didn't particularly like it either. The idea of being expected to do it all the time seemed exhausting. She was not a romantically or sexually inclined person. She'd heard that this was the case for some people and suspected she fell into this category. But upon turning thirty she decided to seek a professional opinion, and made an appointment to meet with a psychoanalyst.

THE OFFICE WAS ON THE ground floor of a Turtle Bay brownstone, and the analyst was comfortingly older, with a kind, intelligent face. Laura could tell he'd been handsome in his youth but in a nonthreatening way. After inviting her into his office, he took a seat behind a desk and gestured for her to take the chair across from him.

"Before we get started, I'd like to answer any questions you might have about how this works, and hear a bit about you and what brings you here."

"I know how it works," Laura told him. "I'm afraid I'm not here as a long-term patient."

Laura paused in case he was interested only in long-term patients. When he didn't say anything, she proceeded to explain her reason for coming.

Marriage had never appealed to Laura the way it did to other women. She was flattered by and appreciated the attention of men, but could do with just that. She was more than content with her life choices and current situation.

"Then what brings you here?"

"I'm not sure," Laura admitted. "I recently saw my internist for my annual appointment, and the results came back and everything looked fine, and I guess I came here hoping you could perform the psychoanalytical equivalent."

"A routine mental," the analyst said, chuckling. "You want a clean bill of mental health."

Laura smiled sheepishly.

"Well, from what you've told me, it sounds like there are no issues."

"It was probably silly of me to come," she said.

The analyst's face suddenly turned serious. He stood up and pointed to the couch at the other end of the room. "If you would lie down, we can get started."

Laura felt funny lying down in front of a stranger and asked if she could sit on the couch instead.

"Your choice. However, many people find it easier to open up lying down."

In the spirit of cooperation she reclined. Notebook and pen in hand, the analyst settled into an armchair beside her.

"Should I start with my childhood?" she asked after a minute of silence.

"If you like," he said.

Rather than sketch out her parents or brother or the general emotional atmosphere of her upbringing, she began describing a morning routine from her early childhood. It was of sitting on the toilet trying to go "big jobbie," as her nurse called it. Marge insisted that this happen every day at the conclusion of breakfast, and Laura's day was suspended until she did it. Marge would come into the bathroom afterward to inspect the evidence. Laura's digestive system wouldn't always cooperate with the schedule, and there were many lonely mornings of sitting on the toilet for hours, pushing and pushing and pushing until she was gasping for air—and having nothing to show for her efforts.

As Laura lay there reliving this, the contours of the light fixture on the ceiling went slack, and she realized she was crying. She was glad she was lying down, as it meant her analyst couldn't see her face. But then a box of Kleenex appeared and hovered above her chest. He was leaning across the space between them to offer it. Her deep breathing must have given her away.

"This is embarrassing," she said, taking a tissue and dotting the corners of her eyes.

"Not at all," he said kindly.

Laura excused herself to use the bathroom. She blew her nose and splashed cold water on her face. When she felt composed, she returned to the couch, where she resumed their session upright.

AMONG THE MISPERCEPTIONS OTHERS HAD about Laura was that she was oblivious to her looks. This was largely due to the simplicity of her wardrobe. To work she wore a white turtleneck, one of five rotating Laura Ashley skirts, and a pair of Frye cowboy boots. One year earlier, a photographer named Bill Cunningham had taken a picture of her in this outfit. Laura had been waiting at the crosswalk of Lexington and Sixty-first and hadn't known her photograph was being taken until it appeared in a series of street portraits in the *New York Times*. Her mother had been the first to spot it and called Laura to tell her. Laughing too hard to speak, she'd put Laura's father on the phone, who directed her to the page of the newspaper.

Laura had put the clipping under a magnet on the fridge. But then this struck her as egotistical, so she took it down, and with the intention of keeping it safe, she'd put it somewhere she couldn't remember.

Others in her social circle had also laughed at the photo. Of everyone they knew, Laura was the last person one would expect to see in the *New York Times* as a paragon of Manhattan style.

It was true Laura had little interest in clothes, but what people assumed was her absentminded ignorance of fashion was actually concern for the fate of the Earth. Everything she owned would one day end up in a landfill, and she avoided acquiring anything she didn't need. She'd once heard the phrase "Use it up, wear it out, make it do, or do without," and guiltily thought of it every time she bought new clothes—which was itself an ordeal, as it was difficult to find clothes that fit her. Laura was so small that most things had to be tailored, and to avoid the hassle she often found herself browsing the children's section of whatever store she was in.

One afternoon she was in the boys' department of Morris Brothers department store on Eighty-fifth and Broadway looking for a new winter parka—they were having a sale—when she felt something warm and moist against her thigh. She looked down and discovered a little boy, maybe three or four, burrowing his face into her jeans, seemingly for the purpose of wiping his nose.

"Excuse me," Laura told him, realizing he must have mistaken her for his mother, "but we're not related."

The little boy looked up at her. His face darkened and he began breathing in a husky, emotional way. With each exhalation, a green bubble of mucus protruded from his nose.

"You're not my mom," he told her, shaking his head. There was a petulant, accusatory edge to his tone, as though Laura had posed as his mother with the intention of kidnapping him.

"It's okay," Laura attempted to reassure the child. "Your mom is somewhere in this store. I'll help you find her."

She reached out to pat the top of his head, but this only made the boy more suspicious, and after batting her hand away he took a doddering step backward, lost his balance, and fell on his bottom. For a moment he sat there in silence, a confused, slightly panicked look on his face, like he was playing the part of a little boy in a movie and had forgotten his line. Then he opened his mouth and screamed.

"Joshua!" an equally loud voice shrieked from the other end of the store. A woman came galloping toward them.

"See, I told you she was here," Laura said cheerfully, and stepped aside as the mother swooped in like a bird of prey, scooped the child up with feral urgency, and began pecking his face with kisses.

As a dramatic reunion unfolded, Laura was troubled by two thoughts, the first being that this little boy had mistaken her for this other woman, who had a homely, disheveled look you often saw on the Upper West Side. Laura knew she was not a smart dresser, but she didn't like to think she was in the same category as this woman.

The second wasn't so much a thought as a sudden awareness of her irrelevance in their universe, the parameters of which seemed to have contracted so that it contained only the woman and the boy. That this hurt Laura's feelings confused and embarrassed her.

With the exception of Margaret, nearly all her contemporaries had children by now. Though a few had privately admitted to feeling initially bewildered by the little creature they'd brought home from the hospital—Edith going so far as to compare its appearance to a space alien—it was only a matter of time before they fell under the spell of unconditional maternal love. Though this seemed to be the universal trend, it still struck Laura as a roll of the dice—to allow fate to assign you a person whom you were expected to adore for the rest of your life. You did not get to choose your child, and while all the mothers she knew gave the impression of having received exactly what they would have ordered, it still seemed like a cavalier thing to do.

Also selfish. It had taken the world's population until 1804 to reach one billion, and another one hundred and twenty-three years to double. What Laura imagined people assumed would be her greatest regret—not having any children—she considered her greatest gift to the planet.

"How do you feel about money?" her analyst asked during their second session.

Laura thought it was an odd question. She wasn't sure what there was to say.

Her income wasn't much, but she had a modest trust, which generated annual dividends that her father's accountant would transfer into her bank account. This extra money allowed her to contribute to various nonprofits, such as the Natural Resources Defense Council, the New York City Commission for the Homeless, National Public Radio, and the Barnard scholarship fund. What remained of this money she hadn't earned went toward Christmas tips for her super, seamstress, the man who resoled her boots, the cashiers at her grocery store, the owner of the hot dog cart where she bought her afternoon Coca-Cola, her mailwoman, and the nice family who ran the Laundromat across the street.

She didn't share any of this with her analyst, because it didn't feel worth his time.

"Many people are uncomfortable discussing money," he said after a silence.

"I'm not uncomfortable discussing it," Laura clarified. "It just doesn't interest me. It doesn't feel relevant to what I'm doing here."

"And what would you say you are doing here?"

"I thought analysis was mostly for figuring out the emotional impact of your childhood."

"And do you think," the analyst asked, "that growing up in such a wealthy family had any kind of impact?"

The word *wealthy* embarrassed Laura. It was not a word she or anyone she was close to used, and she wished her analyst hadn't spoken it.

"There are a lot of things that are difficult for me to talk about," she said. "Things I've never discussed with anyone. Money isn't one of them."

"What about sex?" he asked.

The whole point of having the patient lie down, as Laura understood it, was to avoid seeing the analyst and thus reduce inhibition. But today the analyst's armchair was positioned at an angle where one of his shoes and a part of his leg poked into her frame of vision. He must have been sitting with his legs crossed because the foot was suspended in the air, and it bopped with a restless energy that was incongruent with his calm and measured speaking voice. As with many men, his pants rode up his calf when his legs were crossed, and his black socks only went up so far, exposing an inch of pale, hairy shinbone.

"What about it?" Laura asked him back.

"Well"—the foot bopping picked up with the speed of a dog's wagging tail—"do you ever masturbate?"

"I'M GLAD YOU ENDED IT," said Margaret, Laura's oldest friend and confidante. "The whole thing is a racket. Think of all the people we know who are going. Do any of them seem to be getting better?"

Laura pondered this.

"New Yorkers are so susceptible to these things," Margaret continued. "The other day I overheard a woman in Bloomingdale's talking about primal scream therapy." Margaret paused for Laura's reaction. "That's the kind where you pay a hundred dollars for the privilege of sitting in a so-called doctor's office and screaming at the top of your lungs."

"I've heard of it."

"Apparently it's supposed to take a year of weekly appointments to do the trick, but this woman claimed it cured her in a single session. Or *saved her life*, as she put it." Margaret laughed. "Have you ever heard anything so ridiculous?"

"The poor neighbors," Laura said.

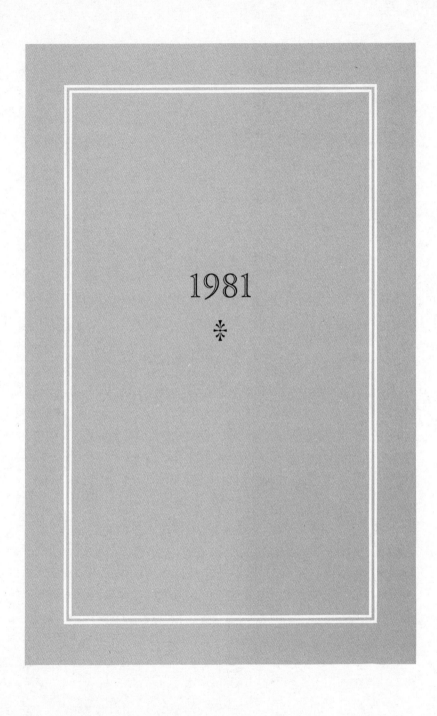

1981

✳

MARGARET HAD ONCE CONFESSED TO FEELING SIMILARLY IN-different to intercourse, but this didn't stop her from marrying Trip, a boy they'd grown up with who had a reputation for a voracious and often indiscriminate sexual appetite, among other vices.

As a teenager, Trip had once gotten so tipsy at a cotillion ball that he'd vomited and a string bean had come out of his nostril. Though this had happened over half a lifetime ago, Laura still had trouble looking at him without this image coming to mind. Evidently this was not the case for Margaret, who, upon their being declared "husband and wife," thrust a triumphant fist into the air, like an Olympian mounting the pedestal after receiving the gold.

Following the ceremony there was a reception at the Carlyle. A fleet of London Towncars had been rented to chauffeur the guests, but Laura decided to walk. It had rained earlier and the late April air was ripe with freshly fallen petals and the loamy odor of wet concrete. Puddles reflected quivering images of the blossoming pear trees that lined Madison Avenue. The sun on the sidewalk radiated warmth; it felt like the city was waking up from a nap. Laura could've walked all afternoon, but eventually she arrived at the Carlyle and felt obligated to go in.

The reception was a tedious marathon of thirty-second conversations with people she knew but didn't really know. None of the toasts mentioned the string bean incident, especially not hers, which, Laura realized—halfway into it—focused exclusively on the earlier years of her friendship with Margaret, and offered nothing in the way of the woman Margaret had become, nor of Margaret-and-Trip, which was what wedding toasts were supposed to do—especially when you were the maid of honor.

When it was time for the bride to toss the bouquet, instead of haphazardly chucking it into the throng of little girls who stood on the dance floor waving their arms above their heads, Margaret (who happened to be very coordinated) threw it in such a way that it soared up and diagonally across the dance floor and landed at Laura's feet.

All eyes on her, she had no choice but to pick it up. The girls flocked over, and she handed it to the youngest of them, who squealed over her prize.

THE LIBRARY, ONCE THE PRIMARY residence of Laura's great-grandfather, was now a museum that was also used for private events. Originally this was a privilege extended just to corporate members and institutional donors, but the Library's endowment was limited and, a decade ago, the board decided to make the venue available for rent to the public. Its tastefully renovated period rooms and marble banquet hall made it a popular wedding spot, so a new position was created: wedding coordinator. Laura, having just graduated from college with a degree in English, was initially reluctant to take the job. She wasn't particularly ambitious, but she wanted to get involved in larger issues—do something that made a positive impact. But then she'd found the apartment. Though her parents would be helping her with the monthly maintenance regardless of her employment status, it didn't feel right to own an apartment if you didn't have a job. She accepted the position, and she remained there a decade later.

She knew it wasn't like this for everyone. Those plucky, brave souls who moved to New York City on their own and had to start a life from scratch.

Laura recalled telling her parents she'd been taken off the wait list for Barnard. "That's terrific," her father had said, while her mother had groaned, "I suppose this means we'll have to have what's-his-face and his dreadful wife over for dinner."

Laura was envious of others' accounts of struggle, which were recalled with a certain fondness. It had been an adventure, the thrill of the hustle; they'd chased a dream against the odds, and now they were living it. She could only imagine the pride of being personally responsible for everything one had—professional success, friends, apartment—and being able to trace all this back to hard work. Knowing that everything in their lives wasn't a given, that it could have all gone a very different way.

Laura had never even read the classifieds. There'd been no reason. Everything came to her through direct channels, and if her immediate network didn't provide it, someone knew someone who could help. When deadlines were missed or obstacles encountered, a person of power or influence intervened on her behalf. Often this person didn't know Laura: it was a friend of the family, a former classmate's neighbor, the stepfather of a cousin-in-law—it didn't matter. Phone calls were made; exceptions were granted; she was put on the top of the list.

Many of the brides Laura worked with were unaware of her personal affiliation with the Library, and she preferred it that way. Nepotism aside, Laura was ashamed of her great-grandfather, whose legacy of shrewd business dealings earned him a full page in her tenth-grade American history book in the section *Robber Barons*. Her mother bemoaned the fact that she hadn't inherited a dime of his money (everything had gone to her uncle, his firstborn son), but Laura was glad this was the case. She did not want to be the beneficiary of the man who'd founded a bank in his name and had once been photographed with a dwarf on his lap.

And yet she was aware of experiencing a flush of something resembling pride upon hearing his name invoked by people who had no idea she was his great-granddaughter—the pride of moral superiority, suspecting that were they to share her ancestry (which also included the mayor of the original *Mayflower* community and the founder of the country's first insurance company), they would seize every opportunity to let it be known.

LAURA DIDN'T LIKE VACATIONS OR travel, though come August she often relocated to 136, the four-story brownstone on East Sixty-fifth Street where she'd grown up. Her parents spent the month in Europe, so she had the place to herself.

There was a garden out back where she could lie in her bikini, something she'd never felt comfortable doing in Central Park. Laura loved sunbathing. She knew about the studies saying it was dangerous, but she kept doing it anyway. She wasn't a drinker, a smoker, an overeater, or a consumer, but she was a sunbather; this was her one vice, and she'd made peace with it.

One Sunday night, after a weekend of reading and sunbathing at 136, Laura lay in bed on the verge of sleep when she heard the carpeted creak of someone coming up the stairs. There had been a string of burglaries on the block that summer, and she'd half been expecting this. She lay still as a corpse, which is what she'd heard you were supposed to do in these situations. So long as the intruder didn't think you'd seen him, he had no reason to kill you.

To mitigate the terror she made a mental inventory of all the people she'd known who'd lived through these situations to tell the story at a dinner party. Then she started imagining how she would narrate her own story of surviving a break-in. Typically Laura became nervous when telling an anecdote to a group, and often held back for this reason, but this would be too good not to relay. She was at the part of the story that coincided with the present, and was waiting for what happened next, when she heard the toilet flush, followed by the sound of an electric toothbrush, and she realized that it was just another one of Nicholas's friends.

Her brother, Nicholas, occasionally let out-of-town friends stay there. Laura didn't mind; she felt safer knowing another person was sleeping in the house—but it would've been nice for Nicholas to have called to let her know of his guest in advance.

THEY CROSSED PATHS IN THE kitchen the next morning.

"Jefferson," he said, offering his hand.

"Laura," she said, shaking it.

She made herself a cup of tea and sat down to read the *Times*. There was apparently a new kind of cancer that, for reasons that remained a mystery to the medical community, afflicted only New Yorkers and people who lived in San Francisco. The article made her anxious, and she was relieved when she got to the end and it said that no cases had been reported outside the homosexual community or in women. She was annoyed the journalist hadn't thought to put this fact in the beginning.

After making some eggs, Jefferson joined her at the table and took a section of the paper. At one point he spoke: "Evolution is happening, and I'm excited about where it's taking us." Laura didn't know what to say to this, so she made a concentrating expression and pretended not to hear.

JEFFERSON DIDN'T INITIALLY STRIKE LAURA as handsome, but she saw how women might find him attractive. He had charisma and swagger and joie de vivre. Though he was not especially large in stature, there was something substantial about his build. He had a certain density that gave the impression of bearing more weight than the space he took up. He moved through the rooms with proprietary ease and had no qualms helping himself to anything he wanted. That his comfort in the house she'd grown up in surpassed her own might have irked her had she not found him so amusing.

When asked how he knew her brother—they'd been roommates at St. George's—Jefferson seemed momentarily taken aback, perhaps mildly hurt to realize that Nicholas had never mentioned him. Hoping to spare his feelings, Laura explained that Nicholas rarely volunteered anything about that chapter of his life.

Over the course of the week they spent cohabitating, Jefferson regaled Laura with descriptions of pranks the two boys had undertaken at St. George's: short-sheeting their dorm mother's bed, covering the headmaster's car with shaving cream, releasing a box of crickets in the chapel during morning prayers. "We had the best time," Jefferson punctuated each account. Laura was surprised and relieved to hear this.

Five years older, Laura had been a mother figure to Nicholas when he was little, reading books to him, teaching him how to spell his name, tie his shoes—how to identify the different kinds of birds that passed through their back garden. As a child, Nicholas suffered from a terrible case of eczema and a mild but pesky stutter, which had made things difficult for him at school. To make up for it, Laura would always intentionally lose at pick-up sticks and jacks and checkers—which they played a lot. For the first decade of his life Laura had tended to Nicholas's needs, and he had basked in her attention and gestures of affection without any embarrassment. If he'd had a bad dream, it was Laura's bed he came to in the middle of the night.

When it was time for Laura to apply to college, the prospect of abandoning Nicholas at 136 made her feel so guilty that she decided to forgo her dream of a quaint New England campus and chose a school in New York City. This had been for naught, however, as Nicholas ended up being sent off to boarding school. It would toughen him up, had been their parents' reasoning.

The sensitive boy who had turned to Laura for everything came back from his first year at St. George's a remote and surly adolescent. He did not want to visit the Natural History Museum, go to the movies, get a hamburger at Jackson Hole, or do any of the things the two of them used to do together. Laura's attempts to rekindle their closeness continued to be rebuffed in the ensuing years. Even their mother had noticed the change, grimly speculating to Laura and her father that something must have happened to Nicholas at school.

"You think he's being teased or bullied?" Laura had asked.

"Everyone gets a bit of that at boarding school," her father responded.

"I mean something worse than that," Laura's mother said. "A sexual violation of some sort."

Jefferson's jolly narrative of her brother's life at boarding school put such sinister fears to rest. It was a comfort to know that Nicholas had been one of the boys, making mischief, having a good time.

THE EVENING SHADOWS OF THE trees outside danced across the walls with the languid quiver of plants in a fish tank. Laura lay supine on the ancient sofa by the window. With each breath she sank deeper into the silky give of its bosomy cushions, once rose-colored, now faded to a pearly pink. She was reading an advance copy of a book that a friend who worked in publishing had sent, thinking it would be up her alley. It was actually the kind of book Laura avoided, pure fodder for insomnia, but now that she'd begun it, she felt obligated to finish. Between turning pages her free hand absently stroked the distinctly distressed spot by her side, where Mr. Baggins, a beloved childhood corgi, had once nestled.

When Jefferson came into the room she sat up, scooched to the far end of the sofa, and drew her knees to her chest. Now her free hand rested on the arm, plucking and strumming the strings of its threadbare surface, releasing a homey musk of aging upholstery, her father's pipe tobacco, and subtle undertones of other dearly loved, long-deceased pets.

After a few minutes of silence, Jefferson made a *pssst* sound, as one would do trying to get someone's attention in a library. He lay on the chaise perpendicular to Laura, ankles crossed, hands clasped behind his head.

"Have I told you lately that you're beautiful?"

"Thank you," Laura responded, attempting to hold the book in a way that obstructed her face from his gaze. She could feel the corners of her mouth twitching; it was such a silly thing to say to someone you'd known for a week.

"I wouldn't have thought something called *The Fate of the Earth* was a funny book," Jefferson said.

Laura ignored his comment and drew the book even closer to her face.

This worked; Jefferson stopped talking. But she had trouble regaining focus, too aware of his presence in the room. And then of his absence.

After listening to his footsteps bounce down the stairs, Laura tried to imagine what he was doing in the basement. Eventually he trotted back up with a bottle of red wine from her father's collection. She agreed to share it with him.

She wondered why she didn't drink more often; she was less shy, and it was a wonderful feeling.

"You have a nice figure," Jefferson said, pouring her a second glass. Laura was often told this, and normally her response was to complain about her height—five-foot-two—and say she wished she were taller, but tonight, she said, "I know," and fingered the stem of her glass.

"You don't act like it," he said.

Laura shrugged and leaned over to pluck a sprig of dried lavender out of the arrangement on the table. After discovering it had no scent, she twirled it in her fingers for a bit, then tucked it behind her ear and pretended to go back to her book—knowing that Jefferson knew she was pretending and would remain there staring at her for as long as it took for her to give up the act.

It wasn't lust, but rather vanity that made her agree to take her clothes off, and from there on it was a feeling of obligation that made her carry through with the rest of it.

What transpired was not unlike all the other times, and it did not undo Laura's conviction that something was different about her, that her experience of sex wasn't what it was for others. But as she lay there afterward, his arms tethered around her as though she were a precious thing he'd just caught and now might run away—"Soft little fucker," he'd murmured, stroking her shoulder—that part she liked very much.

SHE HADN'T BEEN PREPARED FOR this, and the next morning Laura went back to her apartment to retrieve her diaphragm, then she made an appointment to get her legs waxed, and then she found herself circulating the aisles of Bloomingdale's, trying on different scents.

Laura had slipped out before Jefferson had woken up that morning and hadn't left a note; she liked the idea of his waiting and wondering when she'd come back. By the time she set out to return to 136 it was already evening. The sky was a benign shade of lavender, but soon it would erupt into a violent riot of pinks and reds.

August in New York often gave Laura a sad, left-out feeling, but this evening she felt different. It was a time of day, during a time of year, when no one was in a rush. The sidewalks belonged to a procession of couples gratuitously strolling. Men took off their jackets and held them with two fingers behind their backs, the other arm draped around the waists of their companions.

At one point Laura got caught behind a couple with a young child who walked between them, one hand in the mother's, the other in the father's. The trio took up the width of the sidewalk, and every few steps the parents would chant, "One, two, three, *wheeee!*" and swing the child up off the ground. The child loved this and would laugh with excitement each time, and upon being set back down would immediately demand to be swung again. "More! More!" it would plead.

Jefferson did not come running to the door after Laura let herself in. She called his name but he didn't answer. She went upstairs and he wasn't in any of the bedrooms. The kitchen and living room were also empty, as was the dining room. He wasn't in the garden or basement either.

She called Nicholas.

"Who's Jefferson?" he asked.

When she reminded him Jefferson had been his roommate at St. George's, Nicholas said, "I lived in a single."

THE WHOLE THING LEFT LAURA perplexed—and ashamed. Not only did she have no idea who he really was, but who was *she*, to have been so easily seduced? *Soft little fucker*—it made her shudder. She vacated 136 after the episode, and spent the remaining days of summer in her own apartment.

*   *   *

LAURA AND NICHOLAS SAT ON a bench outside the restaurant waiting for their parents, who had returned from Europe that morning. A reservation had been made for seven. At seven-twenty, Laura speculated that perhaps they'd lain down for a nap and hadn't woken up.

"So you think they're dead," Nicholas said dryly.

"Of course not," Laura said, though she knew he was kidding. "I mean maybe they were so exhausted from the trip that they slept through their alarm."

Finally, a cab pulled up. "Yoo-*hoo!*" trilled their mother's voice through the back window. Their father emerged from the other side of the vehicle and walked around to open the door for her. Bibs wore a lime-green shift dress and her hair pulled back in a headband in a way that looked French. She accepted Douglas's hand when climbing out of the cab, but once on both feet, she batted it away, making a dramatic show of struggling to maintain her balance as she headed toward the curb.

"Don't worry, I'm not tipsy," she said giddily. "I'm feeling the swells from the boat! Everything's still rocking!"

Upon reaching her children, Bibs clutched Laura by the shoulders like a rag doll, kissed her firmly on each cheek, then turned and did the same with Nicholas.

"Good to see you kids," Douglas said, giving Laura a single kiss on the cheek and patting Nicholas on the back as he ushered them into Claude's.

A mirror hung on the wall behind their table. Catching a glimpse of herself, Bibs straightened her shoulders and elongated her neck. "Thank goodness for dim lighting," she said to no one in particular.

A busboy materialized and filled their water glasses. Bibs dabbed the corner of her napkin into hers and used it to wipe her husband's brows.

"This is a new routine we have," Douglas said, when Laura asked what she was doing. "Apparently, there's a problem with my eyebrows."

"They're going rogue," Bibs said gravely. "It happens to men in old age."

"I don't know what she's talking about." Laura smiled at her father.

"I'm talking about how a bird could lay an egg in them," said Bibs.

Nicholas lowered his menu to have a look.

"I discovered my first few gray hairs," Laura volunteered, wanting to take the heat off Douglas.

"Oh, don't worry about that," Bibs said. "Jean-Paul will take care of it. Let me make you an appointment with Jean-Paul. I'll be seeing him first thing in the morning."

"I'm not coloring my hair," Laura said. "It's only a few, but if they start to proliferate, I'm going to let it happen."

"But you're too young for that, darling. Much, *much* too young." Bibs looked at Douglas for support. "Don't you agree, dear? Don't you think she's too beautiful to let that happen?"

Douglas, who looked embarrassed by the question, ignored it. "Nicholas just told me he's getting a promotion."

"That's exciting," Laura said. "What does your new position entail?"

Nicholas addressed his father while delivering a long-winded, tangential explanation. Douglas sat listening with his hands clasped, periodically lowering his eyelids and nodding rapidly to indicate he understood—no need for Nicholas to elaborate in such detail. It was a counterproductive gesture, as each time he did this, Nicholas, who was very sensitive to their father's opinion, experienced a momentary relapse of his childhood stutter, and it took him that much longer to wrap up his point and move on to the next. Laura knew her father wasn't a cruel man, but she couldn't understand how he could be so clueless. Nicholas had not inherited their father's unflappable confidence and placid demeanor, but he strived to project such an image, and it was painful to see him unravel before the person he most wanted to impress.

Their food arrived, and as Nicholas paused to catch his breath and take a bite of pork chop, Douglas said, "And when do you start?"

Nicholas's gaze fell to the table and his fork went slack as he considered the question. "I don't know the t-t-t-timeline because nothing is set in stone yet." Picking up his knife, he began cutting a baby potato in two. "I'm one of several in-house candidates they're considering. I th-I think-I *thought* I mentioned that."

"No," Douglas said, catching the attention of a passing waiter and pointing to his empty scotch glass. "No, you did not mention that."

Bibs was looking in the mirror again, but this time she was fixated on Laura's reflection. The intensity of her stare was unnerving, and Laura cocked her chin so that a curtain of hair obstructed her face. Bibs reached out and tucked the hair behind Laura's ear. She leaned over and whispered, "Gray hair isn't always a bad thing—occasionally it can be quite beautiful. But instead of committing to it out of principle, I think you should have a wait-and-see approach, because you never know what shade of gray you're going to get. It could be a beautiful, silvery shimmer, or it could be that moldy off-white, yellowing lampshade, dog-peed-in-the-snow . . ." She lowered her eyes and gestured with her chin at a woman at another table.

"I'll keep an open mind," Laura whispered back.

The waiter brought the bill. Douglas placed his American Express card inside the check holder without reviewing the charges.

"Oh, I almost forgot!" Bibs said with excitement. "Someone broke into the house while we were gone. We've been *burglarized.*" Bibs held out her fingers and frowned in concentration as she recalled the list of missing items. "A box of silver cutlery, two fur coats, a pewter tea set, some first-edition books, and a few other things I can't remember. The most bizarre items, don't you think? What would a *crook* want with a *tea* set?"

"To sell it for cash," Nicholas said. "You should file a police report."

"The Henrys are taking care of it," Douglas spoke up.

"Shhh!" Bibs gave him a stern look. "I'm not done. You'll ruin the story."

"He went to the Henrys next," Bibs proceeded. "They were out of town and their cleaning woman, that crazy Albanian, she came in and found him just sitting in the kitchen eating breakfast, wearing Mr. Henry's robe. He'd spent the night in their bedroom. Claimed to be a nephew. The Albanian didn't buy it. Smart cookie. Picked up a frying pan and chased him out of the house and down the street."

"And was he apprehended?" Nicholas asked.

"He got away." Bibs grinned. "Lucky man, she might have killed him."

"And how are you certain it was the same person?" Nicholas asked.

"They found two suitcases in the closet of the Henrys' master bedroom, full of our things."

The waiter returned with the bill. Laura twirled a loose cuticle on her thumb until it came off in her fingers. Now that the full scope of her foolishness sank in she felt oddly numb. So long as nobody knew about it, it could be as if it had never happened.

"So you got everything back?" she asked.

"It was all in the suitcases," Douglas confirmed as he signed the receipt.

"Everything was recovered," Bibs reiterated. "Except, of course, for Mr. Henry's slippers and robe."

IT WAS NO COINCIDENCE THAT all of Laura's doctors were male. She'd had a few encounters with female doctors over the years, and in each instance they'd attempted to engage her on a personal level, asking questions that went beyond her medical history. They weren't prying, merely trying to establish a friendly rapport, but that wasn't what she went to the doctor for. Male doctors, in Laura's experience, had no trouble with boundaries, and so she was flustered and irritated when Dr. Newman's response to her current symptoms—dizziness, loss of appetite, fatigue—included questions about her love life.

No, she was not seeing anyone.

Yes, of course that meant she was currently celibate.

How long had it been since her last relationship? Laura recalled her brief courtship with Alan, a British journalist she'd met at Edith's wedding. About three or four years, she told him. She knew what he was thinking and she resented his pity. She wished she could think of something clever or sassy to say, like Mary Tyler Moore would in this situation.

Dr. Newman suggested she eat more red meat. It sounded like low iron, but just to rule out anything else, he would like to take a blood test.

SHE WAS AT WORK WHEN Dr. Newman's office called. Laura's iron levels were low, but that wasn't the reason for her symptoms.

MARGARET SUBSCRIBED TO A CERTAIN set of rules and lacked the imagination to consider another perspective. Hers was a black-and-white view of the world, and when filtered through this narrow lens, there was no problem that didn't present an immediate, logical course of action. Which was what Laura wanted right now: not to make a decision, but to be told what to do.

But Margaret, who typically reveled in presiding over the private lives of others—who gladly dispensed unsolicited critiques when Laura violated some unspoken social protocol, like wearing espadrilles to Janet's wedding, bringing her own cloth napkin to restaurants that provided only paper, or pointing out an adorable baby rat poking its head out of a flowerbed on the curb of Madison Avenue—recused herself from weighing in on the matter, telling Laura it was too personal an issue; a decision a woman could only make for herself. Even more unhelpful, she was uncharacteristically philosophical about the ethical dimension of it, saying things like "no one knows, exactly, when life begins."

Laura wasn't looking for comfort, but she was struck by Margaret's tone, which felt coldly detached and ever so slightly judgmental that Laura would find herself in such a predicament. And then the brusque way she'd ended their call: "We'll have to continue this, my husband just got home."

My husband.

It was a little early for Trip to arrive home from the office, Laura thought, as she put the phone down.

Five minutes later the phone rang and it was Margaret. She might have sounded a little curt, she told Laura, and she was sorry if that was the case.

"Is everything okay?" Laura asked, because Margaret rarely apologized, and her voice sounded a little muffled, like she'd been crying.

After a moment of silence, Margaret burst into tears.

"It's not so easy to get pregnant. Some happily married couples spend months and months trying to conceive, only to be told it's not in their cards." Margaret blew her nose. "So for it to happen so easily for you—from a *one-night stand* with some *con man*, and you don't even want it . . ."

"I'm so sorry, Mags," Laura said. "I had no idea."

THE MORNING OF HER PROCEDURE, Laura woke up to discover a bird in her bedroom. A sparrow. The heat had been set too high the night before and she'd slept with the window half open. Now she opened it all the way, but the bird was too agitated to find its way back out.

Laura waited twenty minutes before calling the super, who didn't like to be bothered before eight. His wife answered the phone. She always seemed put out. Today she told Laura that Tony was in New Jersey, and when Laura asked when he'd be back, she said, "If he knows what's best for him, not anytime soon."

A little unprofessional, Laura thought, but she was afraid of Italians. "Okay," she said, "thank you," and hung up the phone.

The bird continued to fly around her room in a skittish tizzy. She would need to catch it herself and let it out. Each time it landed on a surface to rest, Laura would gingerly approach, but the bird was terrified of her and would resume flight.

The routine continued. Soon it was eight-thirty. Then it was eight-forty-five. She thought about calling her ob-gyn's office to ask them to tell the hospital she might be a little late—but what a ridiculous reason to be late for something like this.

At ten past nine, Laura lost her temper. "Fuck you," she cursed at the bird. "I'm just trying to save your life and you're going to make me late to my abortion."

Speaking these words restored Laura's calm. She was doing her best; she could only keep trying.

Another ten or forty minutes passed, Laura lost track, it no longer mattered. She'd resigned herself to the situation. She wasn't going anywhere until she caught that bird.

When it finally happened, there was a rush. Time stopped, then rapidly accelerated, before resuming to normal. Mission accomplished, Laura shut the window and looked at the clock; she would be late to her appointment, but if she got a move on, only ten or fifteen minutes.

The feeling of the bird lingered as she took a taxi across town. For all the trouble it had given her, she was left only with the skin-touch memory of its weightless warmth, the swollen curve of its downy breast, the delicate tremble of its beleaguered heartbeat as she'd carried it to the window.

As she'd leaned out her window over Lexington, there was a moment after she'd unclasped her fingers before the sparrow had taken off.

FOR NOW MARGARET WAS THE only person, besides her doctors, who knew. Margaret was a good friend. She called Laura at least twice a day, just to check in, make sure that she wasn't overexerting herself, and had remembered to take her vitamins. Sometimes she would demand to know everything Laura had eaten that day. Occasionally she lit into her for accidentally ingesting something on the list of dangerous foods, such as Brie or prosciutto.

When Laura quoted Edith as saying she'd lived on Brie while pregnant with Jack, Margaret quoted Janet as saying she'd always wondered if Maxwell's slightly malformed earlobe was the result of the occasional cocktail she'd allowed herself.

"When you're educated about these things," Margaret said, "and have the means to eat only what's healthy and safe, I find it hard to fathom why you would take any chances. In fact, I find it completely selfish and unconscionable to do otherwise."

Laura took Margaret's criticism in stride, knowing it was related to her anxiety of not being able to monitor the daily routine of the woman whose child she would be adopting.

"Seventeen, Caucasian, Staten Island," Margaret said. "That's all the agency will tell me."

LAURA WAS READING THE *Times* when she came across an article with the headline "Mothers Who Don't Marry."

"Even in the era of the 'supermother,'" went the first paragraph, "they stand out from the pack: ostensibly independent women who elect to become mothers out of wedlock, maintaining their careers while raising children in households without fathers or any talk of marriage."

The article interviewed over a dozen of these "supermothers." Several of them had had A.I.D.—artificial insemination by donor.

"A.I.D. FOR SHORT," LAURA ADDED as her parents and Nicholas absorbed the news.

"I've always wanted to be a mother," she continued after a puzzled silence, "and as I'm not getting any younger, I decided to make arrangements to do this on my own."

Her parents nodded. Nicholas stared into his glass. Their waiter approached—then, intuiting a sensitive conversation, politely retreated.

"To hell with husbands," Bibs declared. "I think it's wonderful. Hip hip hooray!"

Douglas raised his glass. Nicholas blinked rapidly as he mimicked his father's gesture—on both their parts, an earnest attempt to convey something along the lines of congratulatory approval.

"And who is the donor?" Bibs asked.

"It's completely anonymous," Laura told him. "He's twenty-five, in good health. That's all they'll tell me."

"But he's—of European descent?" Nicholas asked.

"Yes," Laura said, and then, because it was the first country that came to mind, "Swedish ancestry."

"So the baby will be *Swedish*," Bibs said with a smile.

As a child Bibs had had a Swedish nursemaid, Sofia, to whose influence Laura attributed her mother's lifelong infatuation with the Swedes—*the most beautiful people in the world*.

"Half," Laura said.

"And she doesn't wear a lick of makeup," Laura had overheard someone say of her once. The comment pleased her because it was true. Most of the women she knew used only a little makeup, but she wore absolutely none.

She did, however, get her eyelashes dyed. The results were subtle yet noticeable. Following her appointments, people would often remark that Laura looked especially pretty, and Laura would shake her head when they asked if she'd done something: had she gotten a facial or a haircut—was she wearing makeup? "Eight hours of sleep, maybe," she'd say with a shrug. It didn't feel like a deception; the dye only accentuated Laura's naturally long, thick lashes, which had once caught the attention of a transvestite on the Lexington Avenue subway who had wanted to know where she'd "bought" them.

The dyeing process required Laura to lie down and close her eyes for twenty-five minutes. If she opened her eyes, the dye could get in and blind her. Because of the danger, New York State had recently outlawed the procedure, but Sufrina, the Russian woman who'd been doing Laura's eyelashes for over a decade, continued to see clients in the back room of her mother's psychic parlor on Sixth Avenue.

After Sufrina applied the dye, she set the egg timer, turned off the light, and left the room. Normally soft classical music played in the background, but not today. As Laura lay there alone in the quiet, she had a disturbing thought: What if the building were to catch on fire? Would she be able to feel her way out to the street with her eyes closed? Doubtful. Could she squint, enough to see a little bit, without the dye getting in? Her choices were blindness or third-degree burns—the consequences of an illegal beauty procedure. It seemed like a modern-day fable.

The twenty-five minutes passed and there was no fire. Sufrina returned, removed the excess dye, and all was well. Laura was on her way out the door when Sufrina's mother intercepted her.

"I see something you should know," she said, tugging Laura behind a pair of velvet curtains into a purple room that smelled of incense. She pointed to a chair and instructed her to sit. Laura, who had to be back at work for a meeting, reluctantly obeyed.

"You are with child," the woman said, taking Laura's palm in her own.

Laura wasn't sure if she was supposed to act surprised by this information, which had clearly been relayed to her by Sufrina, whose eyes, Laura had noticed, had unabashedly appraised her little belly when she'd lain down on the table in the back room.

"Eleven weeks," Laura responded.

"It's a boy," the woman said. "You are having a son."

Laura smiled, as her instinct had told her the same thing.

"A boy needs a father." Sufrina's mother shook her head grimly. "Father is no good."

Laura wasn't sure how to respond. When the woman's scrutinizing gaze shifted from her palm to her face, her discomfort became irritation. She had not signed up for this. The incense made her nauseated; she needed to get back to work.

"You are afraid," the woman said. "Don't be afraid."

Laura nodded, hoping to move things along.

"There will be another man," she pronounced solemnly. "*He* will be father."

OF THE CITY'S MANY VISUAL blights—the FDR, the Midtown Tunnel, Penn Station, the interior of Grand Central (to say nothing of the filth, soot, grit, grime, and dog shit that one encountered on a daily basis)—it was the glass-and-steel high-rises that most upset Laura.

Buildings of this sterile aesthetic had begun springing up in the sixties, but unlike the Chrysler and Empire State Buildings, they were utterly devoid of charm and character. That was the point: to forgo stylistic features traditionally associated with New York City architecture to achieve a generic, universal look. "International Style," it was called. If that was the look of the future, Laura was glad she wouldn't be around for it. More than merely mar the skyline, the proliferation of these phallic protrusions obstructed the light, casting the city in an ever-expanding shadow of corporate greed and consumerism.

Even if people were to come to their senses and resume constructing buildings that were attractive to look at, the damage would be done, Laura thought sadly every time her sights snagged on the World Trade Center, which had now been there for a decade but which she would never get used to. Bibs agreed.

"A pair of glistening pricks in the sun," was her description.

Nicholas had a more favorable opinion of the towers, and was very excited when his investment firm had relocated to the forty-seventh floor of one the previous spring. Proud of his view, Nicholas invited Laura to pay a visit to his office, for the first time, to catch the sunset—*you must be curious to see where I spend my days.* Laura was touched that Nicholas cared to impress her. She felt bad for him when she arrived and it was drizzling and overcast.

He was waiting for her as she stepped off the elevator. "Perfect timing," he said, glancing at his watch. "Four-eighteen. Sunset's in twenty-six minutes."

"Do you think we'll be able to see it?" Laura asked, following him down the hall. He walked briskly, several paces ahead of her.

"It'll clear up," Nicholas said, opening the door to his office. "Have a seat." He pointed to a leather armchair parked by the window.

It had stopped raining, but there was still no trace of the sun.

Laura sat and Nicholas wheeled his desk chair over so that it was adjacent to hers.

They quietly waited.

"I'm sorry—would you like something to drink?" Nicholas asked. "Coffee?"

"A cup of herbal tea would be nice," Laura answered.

Nicholas walked out to the hall. He returned empty-handed.

"It's coming," he said, settling back into his chair.

"I'm excited," Laura said. "But if it doesn't clear up on time, I'll come back another day."

"I meant your tea." Nicholas glanced at his watch. "Nineteen minutes until the sunset."

They resumed staring out the window in silence.

The door opened and a woman a few years younger than Laura entered with two mugs. Nicholas thanked her.

"Hey, Kim," he called as the woman turned to leave, "if you're free right now, you should make yourself a cup of tea and join us."

The woman seemed caught off guard by his invitation. "Thank you, but I'm a little busy," she said, slipping out to the hall.

After a prolonged silence, Nicholas spoke. "You need to tell me if somebody did this to you and isn't doing the right thing." He was looking straight ahead as he said this. "I would like to know who that person is."

"That's not what happened," Laura responded. "I did this. This is something I wanted. Something I'm excited for.

"A *happy* thing," she added, when Nicholas didn't return her smile.

The phone rang. Nicholas went to his desk to answer it. "He told you *what?*" he groaned into the receiver. "Mark my words . . ." He pinched the top of his nose. "Mark my words . . ." Whoever he was speaking to must have been cutting him off, because Nicholas kept repeating the phrase.

Wanting to give him privacy, Laura stepped out to the hall and shut the door behind her.

Kim walked by. "Restroom's right there," she said, pointing.

"Thank you," Laura said, realizing she did have to go. When she returned, Nicholas's door was open. He was still on the phone.

"Full of shit," he was saying now. "Guy is *full* of shit." He sounded less agitated than vindicated. Seeing her standing tentatively in the doorway, he waved her in and gestured to the window.

A swath of bronze light had penetrated the canopy of clouds, alchemizing a portion of the East River and refracting off the windows of the buildings in its path, which glittered like rows of sequined evening dresses. Taken as a whole, there was a slapdash elegance to the skyline's irregularities—sharp angles punctuated by the slope of a domed roof here, a potbellied water tower there. The variations felt random yet majestic, like trees in a forest. Even the mysterious gaseous matter that perpetually spewed from the smokestacks of the city's industrial outskirts looked less menacing from this vantage point, vaguely celestial, drifting toward the atmosphere in crisp white plumes.

Shifting her gaze south, Laura could see all the way to New York Harbor, where the boats came in. She could see the Statue of Liberty and those enchanting little islands that sat like crumbs in the East River, home to squirrels and birds and the foundations of abandoned buildings, former hospitals and municipal outposts, whose lovely brick ruins, among the feral terrain, looked like something out of a fairy tale.

"If he *thinks* for one *second* we're going to bend over and *take* it," Nicholas said into the phone, "he's got another thing coming. Another thing coming." Nicholas laughed the way he had as a child when winning a game.

Laura knew very little about Nicholas's job, beyond that it involved the stock market and helping rich people get richer, but she could see that it made him happy. This was the most animated, self-possessed version of her brother she'd seen in years. He was in his element up here in his little stall in the sky.

In another minute the sun disappeared and the vista darkened. Laura tapped Nicholas on the shoulder. "I should be going," she whispered.

"Hang on a sec," he told the person he was speaking to. Holding the phone in the crook of his neck, he fished through a drawer in his desk.

"I know it's a little early," he said, handing Laura a box wrapped in tissue paper.

"Thank you, Nicholas," Laura said. "Is it all right if I open it at home?" She was afraid she might tear up. She was genuinely touched; her brother was not a present-giver.

Nicholas nodded and went back to his phone call. "Tear him a new one," Laura heard him say as she closed the door behind her.

The present, Laura discovered at home, was a toddler-size T-shirt with the name of Nicholas's boarding school emblazoned across the front.

LAURA'S MIDSECTION BEGAN TO SWELL but the rest of her remained slender. This continued to be the case as she entered the second trimester of her pregnancy, but as a precaution she purchased a leotard and a copy of Jane Fonda's pregnancy video. Every morning she would wake up and make a pregnancy milkshake that consisted of two heaping tablespoons of Ovaltine, whole milk, and a raw egg in a blender. Then she would put on her leotard and do the exercises in front of a mirror.

As the weeks rolled by the bump grew more pronounced. New technology made it possible to see the fetus, and her doctor was always trying to get her to have a look. Laura wasn't sure how she was supposed to respond to the extraterrestrial image on the screen with its chicken-bone limbs.

When her doctor asked if she wanted to know the baby's gender, she said no. She knew she was having a boy, but still, she wanted it to be a surprise. She felt proud walking around, thinking of this person inside of her who would one day grow up to be a man.

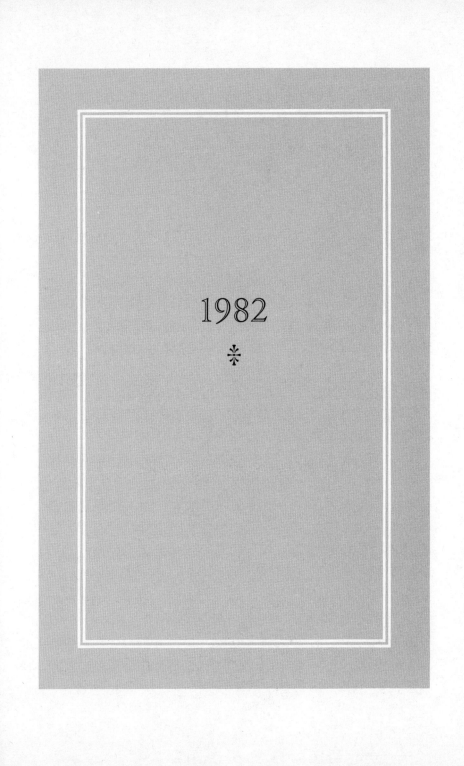

1982

*

LAURA REFUSED TO HAVE A BABY SHOWER, BUT MARGARET WAS very much looking forward to hers. The morning it was supposed to take place the adoption agency called: the birth mother had checked into the hospital with contractions. She was three weeks early, it could be a false alarm—they would know more soon. Margaret took a car to Staten Island Hospital and sent Trip in her place.

Trip arrived looking anxious, confused, and disheveled. His hair was damp and a small piece of toilet paper clung to a spot on his cheek where he had evidently cut himself shaving.

"Are you sure she doesn't want to reschedule?" Janet, who was hosting the shower, asked as she let him in.

Trip looked intrigued by this option then shook his head. "Just following orders here."

Trip had never attended a shower before, and they had to explain to him how it worked: he sat in the middle of the circle and opened all the presents. Though he clearly had no interest in baby things, Trip made an effort to feign enthusiasm for each item, and everyone would *ooh* and *aww* as he held it up for them to see.

Some of the items were unfamiliar to him.

"It's a baby monitor," Janet called out as Trip smiled dumbly at the box in his lap.

"There's two of them," Trip said. "Maybe Laura would like one?"

"Actually, I gave it to you," Laura said. "And you'll need both. One for the baby's room, one for yours."

"Do you know what a baby monitor is, Trip?" someone asked.

"Don't bother," said Margaret's mother, who was writing everything down. "We've got a lot more to go, let's move on to the next."

With the opening of each new present, the routine felt more tedious. Then something remarkable happened that changed the atmosphere of the occasion.

Trip had identical twin sisters, one who lived in Connecticut, the other, London. There were polite gasps when Trip held up the first twin's present (a silver spoon from Tiffany's), and everyone took a breath and prepared to make the same manufactured sound as he opened up the second twin's present. However, this time the gasps were for real, as Trip held up *another* silver spoon from Tiffany's. Identical twins, opposite sides of the Atlantic—the same present! Excitement took hold of the room as everyone marveled at how such a thing could happen.

"I've heard that twins have the same thoughts," someone said, and the twins did not dispute this fact, adding that this wasn't the first time something like this had happened.

"They have ESP," Trip told the group, and proposed his older sisters demonstrate this by playing a game they'd made up as children. It worked like this: one of the twins would stand in the hall and the group would pick something in the room for the remaining twin to think about. Once this object had been determined, the other twin would come back into the room and guess what it was.

"This is the most fun I've had at a baby shower," someone said, and others echoed the sentiment. Everyone was enjoying themselves— even Trip—whom Laura saw in a new, more endearing light.

The joviality was cut short when the phone rang and it was Margaret. Everyone fell silent as Trip got up to take the call. He nodded soberly and made affirmative noises into the receiver. "Okay-okay-okay," he said, putting the phone down.

"Does anyone know the fastest route to Staten Island?" he asked the group.

They all shook their heads; no one had ever been there.

LAURA'S DUE DATE ARRIVED, BUT the baby did not. Another two weeks passed before she finally went into labor. Laura hadn't wanted any drugs, but she quickly changed her mind. She pushed and pushed but nothing happened. When eighteen hours of contractions yielded no results, Laura heard the doctor say: "Fine, you don't want to come out? I'll reach in and get you."

"Don't worry!" The nurse smiled reassuringly. "He'll use forceps."

HOW STRANGE THAT THERE WAS no test you had to pass or license you had to acquire to be a parent, Laura thought when the infant was first lowered into her arms.

"Hello, hello, hello," she cooed, smiling and opening her eyes as wide as they would go. She felt self-conscious with the nurse standing there watching.

After some fussing, the baby fell asleep in Laura's arms, its curly purple fingers occasionally twitching and extending in a vaguely arthritic way.

She had a daughter.

*　　*　　*

Two rooms down the hall a famous Hollywood actress was recovering, having also just given birth to her first child. The staff of the maternity ward was very excited about this, but they were even more excited about Laura's baby, who, at ten pounds, eleven ounces, was among the largest they'd ever delivered. All the more remarkable having come out of such a tiny woman!

Other doctors who were not her obstetrician came to look at the baby and marvel at her size. "It's like a terrier giving birth to a Labrador," one of them said.

When her parents learned the baby's name was Emma, Bibs closed her eyes and held a hand over her mouth. A moment later she opened them and smiled. "You're just teasing," she said.

Laura shook her head. "You don't like it?"

"How could you do this to me?" Bibs threw up her arms and left the room.

"Her sister-in-law," Douglas explained.

"She thinks I named the baby after Percy's wife," Laura said, understanding. "Which makes no sense. We're not even in touch with them. It's been years since I've even seen that woman."

"It's a beautiful name," he said. "She'll get over it."

Margaret, whose baby was also a girl, had chosen the name Charlotte. For weeks after bringing her home from the hospital, Margaret had refused to take Charlotte outside. A car could jump the curb, a crane could collapse, a pigeon might shit.

"Just you wait until yours arrives," she'd told Laura. "You'll be the same."

Laura's neuroses concerned the quality of New York City air. Was it safe for an infant to breathe? Emma arrived in the final week of May, but it wasn't until the second week of June that Laura took her out for her first morning stroll.

"Here we go," Laura said, one hand pressing the elevator button, the other gripping the handle of Emma's pram, which she'd bought last-minute in the basement thrift store of a church in Gramercy. It had looked so sweet and old-fashioned when she'd spotted it among the clutter of antiques, but now it embarrassed her with its extravagant girth and imperious red velvet canopy.

As she waited for the light to turn, some pigeons picked at the remains of a sandwich someone had discarded in the middle of the crosswalk. Laura got nervous when she heard the flatulent rumble of an ancient garbage truck making its way up the street—with the menacingly slow but unwavering determination of a tank—but the pigeons remained unfazed, flapping out of the way only at the last possible moment. The city was just waking up; soon would come the manic wails of sirens, the violent drilling of cement, and the increasingly unsubtle odors of urine and garbage.

The baby slept for the first part of the walk, but on their way back she began to stir.

"Hello, hello, hello," Laura cooed and made a kissing sound.

The baby began to cry. It was not happy to be there, and she didn't blame it. It was a filthy, concrete island they lived on. Laura lived there for no other reason than it was where she was born and had grown up, and the prospect of attempting to move somewhere else and start a whole new life from scratch was too much. And now the cycle was continuing.

* * *

LAURA'S WALKS WITH EMMA GOT longer. One afternoon they were at Sixty-eighth Street when Laura realized she needed to use the bathroom. Rather than turn around to go back to their apartment, she continued walking south toward 136, which was closer.

As Laura fumbled around her purse for her keys, Sandra, her parents' housekeeper, opened the door.

"Bambina!" she sang, scooping Emma up from her pram.

"Would you mind watching her while I quickly use the bathroom?" Laura asked as Sandra took Emma into the kitchen.

Her mother was home—Laura could hear her talking to someone on the phone while she was in the bathroom.

Bibs was a loud phone talker. "Sperm donor," her voice bellowed through the wall. "It's different from a test-tube baby . . . Yes, well, everyone's curious but too polite to ask, and I'm sure there's quite a bit of scuttlebutt, so I figure just come right out and tell them. The donor was Swedish. Emma's half *Swedish*."

"Betsy Cornwall sends her best," Bibs said when Laura walked into the living room.

Laura mustered a halfhearted smile.

Bibs gave her a scrutinizing glance. "You're upset with me," she said.

Laura didn't say anything.

"Darling," Bibs said with a frown, "if you don't tell people these things, they make all sorts of assumptions."

"I don't feel obligated to explain to people how I had Emma," Laura said. "But if people are going to gossip, I agree I'd rather the truth be out there, so you can go ahead and tell people I used a donor. But as far as the specifics of her paternity, that's no one's business."

"But everyone loves Sweden," Bibs protested.

"It's not anyone's business," Laura reiterated. "And when she's older, I don't intend to tell Emma where her father is from, either. I don't want her speculating about him at all." She looked at her mother.

"Fine," said Bibs. "Let her grow up thinking all she has is boring old British blood."

LAURA DID NOT ENJOY NURSING. She found it tedious and she worried about the irreparable damage it might be doing to her once-perky breasts. She envied her mother and all the women of her generation for having given birth before nursing was something you were expected to do. "You're not missing anything," she told Margaret.

Laura had been granted a six-month maternity leave. She'd never spent so much time in her apartment and began to feel different about it, especially on days the phone didn't ring. It was no longer a sanctuary; it was a pen.

The chair she nursed in faced a window with no view, just the shaft between her building and the next. When she moved the chair so that it faced the window overlooking the street, she became preoccupied with a plastic bag snarled in the branches of a tree. Each time a breeze came through, it seemed as though the bag would unsnag and blow away. She began to think of the breeze as a friend to the bag. At the same time she was aware that the breeze was responsible for the bag's predicament in the first place. Weeks passed and the bag was still there.

A new sensation would strike out of the blue. It was physical: a leaden feeling in her chest that would gradually seep through her limbs, settling deeper and deeper into her bones, until she was so swollen with the weight of it that she felt paralyzed. And whatever she'd been doing at that moment she couldn't bring herself to finish. Dishes piled up and the trash overflowed.

Laura needed Emma to offer some indication that she wanted to be there, and she wasn't getting it. Emma was a colicky baby. One night when the crying wouldn't stop, Laura had a sinister thought: how little it would take to accidentally kill the baby. It passed as quickly as it had come on, but the shame and horror of it lingered.

The next morning she packed a bag for the two of them and got in a cab.

LIFE WAS MUCH EASIER AT 136. Dinner was prepared, the house was cleaned when she wasn't looking, she could pass Emma off to Sandra when she needed a break. After a week, Laura decided that it made sense, at least while Emma was a baby, to stay there, and she put her apartment on the market.

THE PLAN HAD BEEN TO stop nursing when she went back to work. But Laura worried that the baby would no longer be interested in a relationship with her, especially as she'd now be spending nearly all her time with Sandra, so she continued to nurse in the mornings and after returning from work.

One evening she arrived home to a funny odor.

"Do you smell that?" she asked, taking the baby from Sandra.

"I just change diaper," Sandra said.

"It's not that," Laura said. "It smells like burning rubber."

"I know *nutheen*," Sandra said, putting on her coat. "But your ma-der is crazy, you know." She walked out the front door for her evening break.

Laura headed toward the stairs then realized no one was home and decided to nurse in the living room. She had just begun when the front door opened.

"Yoo-hoo!" her mother's voice called from the hall.

Laura jumped up and slipped through the swinging door that led to the kitchen, where Bibs rarely set foot. She didn't like to nurse in the same room as her mother, who made no attempt to hide her disgust and fascination with it. "It's just so mam*mal*ian." She'd once gawked upon walking in on Laura doing it, and then did a mean impression of the baby's mouth in action with exaggerated sound effects.

The baby fell asleep in the middle of nursing. Laura laid her in the pen in the corner of the kitchen and made herself a cup of tea as she waited for Sandra to come back and take over. The front door opened, but she could tell from the heavy footsteps it was her father.

"Hello," he said, shuffling into the kitchen.

"Hello," Laura said, picking up a section of that morning's paper.

"Smells funny." He headed toward the liquor cabinet.

"I agree," Laura said. "Not sure what it is."

After pouring himself a whiskey, Douglas disappeared through the swinging door into the living room, and before it swung shut her mother slipped in, a nervous, giddy look on her face.

"I did something naughty," she whispered.

"What did you do?" Laura asked.

"Something I should've done a long time ago." Bibs fingered her pearls, glancing skittishly at the swinging door.

"Where's the TV?" came Douglas's voice from the living room.

After covering her mouth to silence a giggle, Bibs composed herself and shouted back, "I threw it out!"

"I did," she whispered to Laura. "I really did!"

Her father came back into the kitchen. "You did *what* with it?"

"Sandra and I carried it out to the curb," Bibs said. "Also the VCR. A sanitation truck hauled them away."

"And why, exactly, did you throw the television away, dear?"

"I hated being lied to and told what to do—*don't change the channel, we'll be right back*," she said. "After umpteen commercials they'd be back!"

Douglas looked unamused.

"That's not all," Bibs said. "There was also another reason. I found a tape in the VCR. I tried to burn it on the stove, but Sandra had a fit and the smoke alarm went off. Anyhoo, I think you know what it is."

Douglas made the throaty noise that signaled he was about to speak.

"Uh-uh!" Bibs wagged a finger. "You don't need to say anything. Just look in the mirror, give your head a little shake, and we won't speak of it again."

Wearing a poker face, Douglas turned to leave the room. "Tell me, dear." He paused by the door. "How am I supposed to watch the evening news?"

"You can read a newspaper," Bibs said, and hurled a section of the *Times* in his direction. It unfurled midflight, landing on the floor beside

Emma's pen. The commotion woke her up and she lay there looking startled, her eyes darting about. When she saw Laura, her face puckered like an overripe tomato and she began to cry. As soon as Laura picked her up, the crying stopped.

"I think you're a faker," Laura said in an animated voice. "My soft little faker."

Laura drummed her fingers atop the summit of Emma's belly, which trembled as Emma let out a spastic infant cackle. Laura, who'd hated being tickled as a child, felt a little bad doing this, but oh, she loved that sound. And she could tell, by the expectant gaze on Emma's face when she pulled her fingers away, that Emma liked this—that she was waiting for it to happen again. The little space between her nose and upper lip dimpled in anticipatory excitement; she fixed her eyes on Laura's and followed them like liquid magnets. Laura's love felt like a bird in her chest, beating its wings against her rib cage.

And then Sandra returned, and Emma's arms shot out in her direction and she let out a despondent wail, which stopped the moment Laura passed her over.

"Thank you, Sandra," she said. "I'll be in the next room if you need anything."

"Thank your *father*, he pay me," Sandra responded, bouncing the baby on her hip.

LAURA HAD NO DOUBT WHAT was on the VHS tape her mother had discovered, and she was relieved when there was no further mention of it. She wondered how her father had acquired such a video. Had it come in the mail? Had he gone into one of those awful little stores in Times Square?

As a child she had discovered her father's stash of dirty magazines in the back of the linen closet. She couldn't remember how old she'd been—young enough not to think anything of the fact that she enjoyed looking at the photos. And she had periodically returned to the linen closet to look at them again. This had gone on for a while—a few years, maybe. Then one day Nicholas had been caught in the library with a pair of binoculars, peering out the window that overlooked the garden.

"What are you looking at?" their mother had asked.

"Nothing," Nicholas said. He returned the binoculars to the shelf and abruptly left the room.

Bibs walked over to the window. "Well, at least we know he's normal," she said, giggling.

When her mother had left the room, Laura went over to the window to have a look. In the adjacent garden a woman lay sunbathing. She'd peeled the top part of her bathing suit down and her breasts were exposed. A hat covered her face.

When Laura next found herself in the linen closet, her mother's voice popped into her head: *At least we know he's normal*. After that, she stopped doing it.

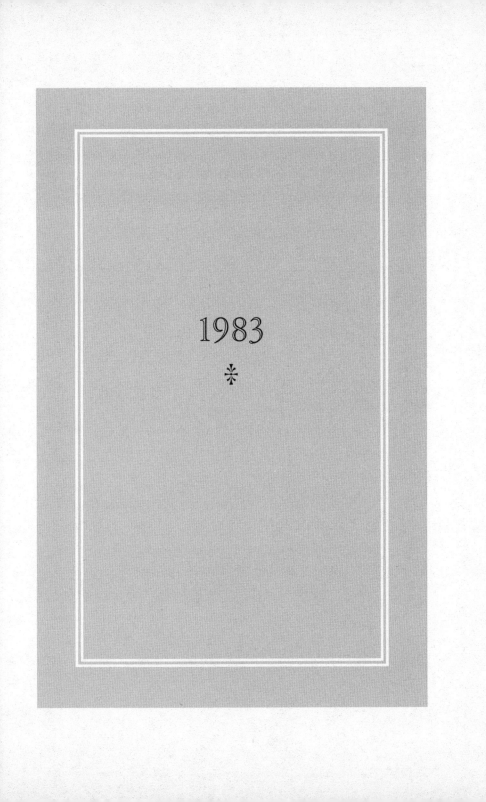

1983

❊

EMMA, AT THE TOP OF THE CHARTS FOR WEIGHT AND HEIGHT, was behind when it came to physical milestones. To encourage her to crawl, Laura used butter, which she loved, as a lure. She would put Emma down on one side of the room, a stick of butter on the other. Working her arms like flippers, Emma would pull herself across the kitchen floor toward it. Her legs, too thick to bend or separate, dragged behind like a single useless appendage. Cries of excitement, grunts of exertion, and the sound of her rubbery palms smacking linoleum ended in tears of frustration when, just as the butter was in reach, it was taken away.

The pediatrician assured Laura that there was nothing to worry about. Dr. Brown was short for a man—only a few inches taller than Laura—and had a boyishly slender physique. He wore round tortoise-shell glasses, a bow tie, and impeccably polished shoes. He had a gentle, soft-spoken demeanor, but when he found something amusing, which he often did, he was quick to laugh. It moved her to think of a man who didn't have any children of his own spending his days taking care of other people's.

Laura was surprised to learn Dr. Brown wasn't married—he was so kind and easy to talk to. Then again, most of the women she knew were fools when it came to choosing husbands.

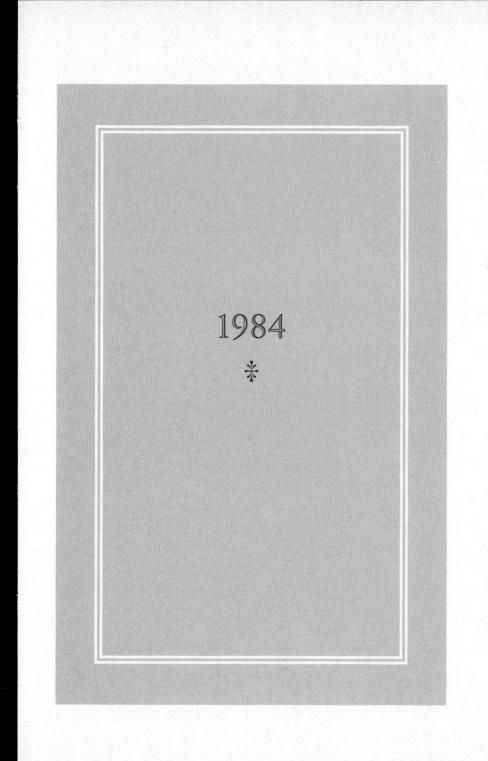

1984

✢

NICHOLAS WAS CONSTANTLY TRYING TO PROVE HIMSELF. THIS was how Laura made sense of his girlfriends over the years, all of whom looked like they'd stepped out of the pages of a magazine. Stephanie, the latest one, was the first who was an actual professional model. Nicholas had told them something vague, that she was an assistant of some sort, but during the meal it came out that she was really a model, albeit for clothing catalogs they had never heard of and newspaper circulars. Laura had no interest in the fashion industry, but did her best to pretend otherwise as she asked Stephanie questions about her work. Stephanie had just started to tell them about her latest shoot when Nicholas aggressively steered the conversation toward President Reagan's "Star Wars" missile-defense plan, of which he was fully in favor. A two-way conversation between Douglas and Nicholas ensued.

"You know what I think of the current political situation," Bibs interrupted. She waited a beat to make sure she had everyone's full attention. "I think it's boring."

After Nicholas and Stephanie left, Bibs stood before Laura and Douglas in the living room, a confrontational glint in her eye.

"*So* she grew up in *Florida, so* she loves Princess Diana, so *what*," she said. "Don't be such a snob!"

Laura glanced across the room. Her father either hadn't heard or was refusing to validate the accusation with a response.

Bibs disappeared and returned a moment later holding the pastel-blue carnations Stephanie had brought, which she'd put in a vase.

Setting it down on the table with a thump, she repeated the charge. "Don't be such a snob!"

"I don't know what you're talking about," Douglas finally said from behind his copy of the *Times*. "I thought she was lovely."

"I wasn't talking to you," Bibs responded. "But of course you did. You couldn't take your eyes off of her—I think everyone noticed *that*."

"But Laura was very polite to her," said Douglas. "She made a real effort."

"I saw the way you were looking at her nails," Bibs said. "And I saw your face when she said she'd never heard of Edith what's-her-face."

Douglas peered over his paper to offer Laura a sympathetic eye-roll.

"I thought Stephanie was very nice," Laura said. "I'm happy Nicholas has someone."

"*Very nice!*" Bibs scoffed. "Do you *ever* say how you really feel?"

"And how, exactly, do I really feel?" Laura asked.

"Since you're the expert," Douglas added.

Her father's coming to her defense buoyed Laura—but only for a moment, as Bibs shook her head, more in disappointment than condemnation, it appeared, and left the room.

"Don't worry about your mother," Douglas told her. "You were perfectly appropriate with Stephanie."

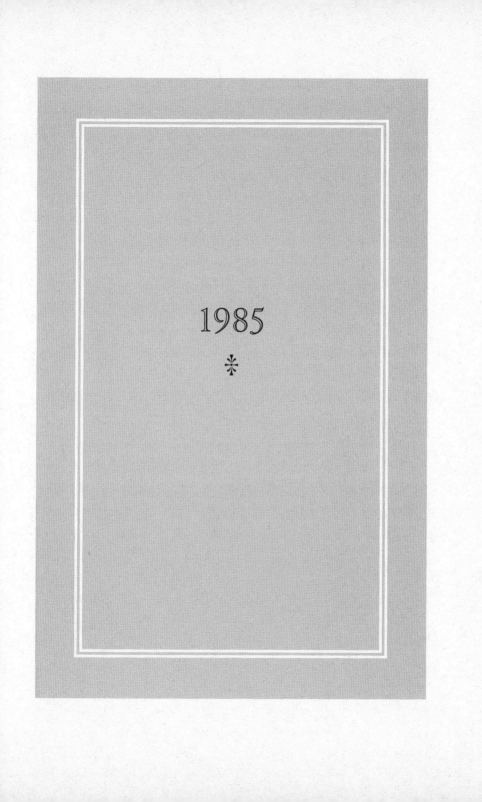

1985

*

EMMA WOULD BE TURNING THREE IN MAY; IT WAS TIME TO MOVE out of 136 and into an apartment of their own. Laura was hoping for something near the park, close but not too close to her parents. "A sunny two-bedroom with a working fireplace on one of those shady streets between Madison and Fifth would be ideal," she told Joan, a former classmate, now a real estate broker. Joan said no such thing existed in the price range Laura quoted, not between Madison and Fifth. But there was an apartment between Lexington and Third: a prewar penthouse. It had two and a half bedrooms, a terrace, a view of the Empire State Building, and a wood-burning fireplace. It had just gone on the market and would get snatched up any minute, so they'd have to act fast.

It sounded too good to be true, and then Joan revealed the exact street address.

"Harlem," Laura said. "That explains the price."

"*Across the street* from Harlem," Joan corrected her.

LOCATED ON THE SOUTH SIDE of the street, thus placing it officially on the Upper East Side, 166 East Ninety-sixth was the only high-rise on the block. All four sides of the building were jarringly exposed, giving it a certain primitive look: sky, street, building. Randomly perched atop this structure, like the afterthought of a child's crudely simplistic, precariously tall tower of blocks, was the penthouse.

The apartment was small for a penthouse. Surrounded by a terrace of potted plants, it felt separate from the rest of the building. Taking Laura outside to admire the unobstructed view, Joan said, "Unlike other penthouses farther south, you have complete privacy up here."

The interior had casement windows and original hardwood floors. The bathroom fixtures and appliances had not been updated in some time, which Laura liked.

"I don't know about you," Joan said, "but I feel like I'm in a cozy brick cottage on the edge of a cliff in the English countryside in the nineteenth century."

On their way down, the elevator stopped on the fourth floor. An African-American man stepped on carrying a hamper of laundry and pressed B, for basement.

"He's the only one in the building," Joan whispered when they got off in the lobby.

Laura wished she hadn't said that, or had at least found a better way to phrase it than "the only one." Not knowing how to respond, she just nodded slightly, as if this information couldn't have mattered less to her.

"The washer-dryers were all replaced last year, by the way," Joan added brightly.

IT WAS DIFFERENT, LIVING SO high up in the sky; it would take some getting used to.

With the views came a greater awareness of Manhattan and the rhythms that governed its chaotic pulsing sprawl. At the end of each day the city slowly wound down as hot dog men packed up their carts, metal grates rolled down over the mom-and-pop shops, curbs accumulated freshly bagged trash, and people disappeared from the streets into the warrens of the subway system. Following this came a brief lull in noise and activity, during which their apartment felt like a peaceful, cozy place to be.

Like watching a soap bubble emerge from a wand only to see it pop, upon being registered this precious pocket of tranquility was immediately punctured by the rip of a motorcycle, the shriek of a siren, a whoop here, a whoop there, gradually forming an off-kilter chorus of unwholesome sounds as packs of hoodlums began swaggering about, marking their territory with gobs of spit and booming voices, while cars of bombastic proportions bounced through the streets blasting music that buzzed the windows and rattled the foundations of apartments as high up as the seventeenth floor.

NOW THAT IT WAS JUST the two of them, Laura would need someone to watch Emma while she was at work. A perk of having an extra half bedroom, Margaret had pointed out, was that Laura could get a live-in au pair: a European girl, young and well educated, eager to live in America, full of light and energy. "An incredibly good bargain," she'd added, explaining room and board were considered part of their salary. Indeed, Laura was shocked to learn how low the going rate was.

She contacted an agency and began interviewing candidates, all of whom seemed highly competent, warm, and enthusiastic about the job. This final quality perplexed Laura, who couldn't imagine leaving some picturesque European village to move to filthy-crowded-loud

Manhattan and essentially become an indentured servant. They were all lovely in their own way, but Irene especially so.

"I'm the eldest of eleven, so I grew up with little ones," she told Laura in her Irish brogue. "A little one in m'bed, a little one on m'lap, the house was crawling with 'em."

Her soothingly brisk, cadenced manner of speaking was punctuated by a quick, familiar laugh. Whatever she said had an amusing, musical quality, as if she were reciting the lyrics of a naughty song or reading from a book of nursery rhymes.

Emma was immediately smitten, tugging her down the hall into her bedroom.

"Missy, you're a funny one, aren't you," Irene said, when Emma tried to push Laura out of the room and shut the door.

When it was time for Irene to go, Emma threw a tantrum. After pacifying her by putting on *The Sound of Music*, Laura called the agency to let them know she'd made other arrangements and wouldn't be needing their services after all. Her contact there asked if something was wrong with the girls they'd sent over.

"They all seemed great," Laura said. "I've just realized that a live-in au pair is a bit out of my price range."

JACK, THE LIBRARY'S DIRECTOR, REJECTED Laura's proposal to modify her schedule to part-time hours. "I'm sorry, Laura, I'm sympathetic to your situation, but this is a full-time position," he explained.

"I understand," Laura said, privately balking at taking the next step. Jack was a kind boss and she hated the idea of undermining his authority. Conflicts made her second-guess herself. Was she being selfish or unreasonable? Taking advantage of her familial relationship with the institution? Asking too much?

"Absolutely not," Margaret assured her. "You're a single mother—don't be ridiculous."

So Laura approached the board, and the trustees got involved and a new contract was drafted—and it was even more generous than what Laura had originally asked for. Not only would she be a part-time employee (her hours corresponding with the hours Emma spent in preschool), but she would also maintain her full-time salary and benefits.

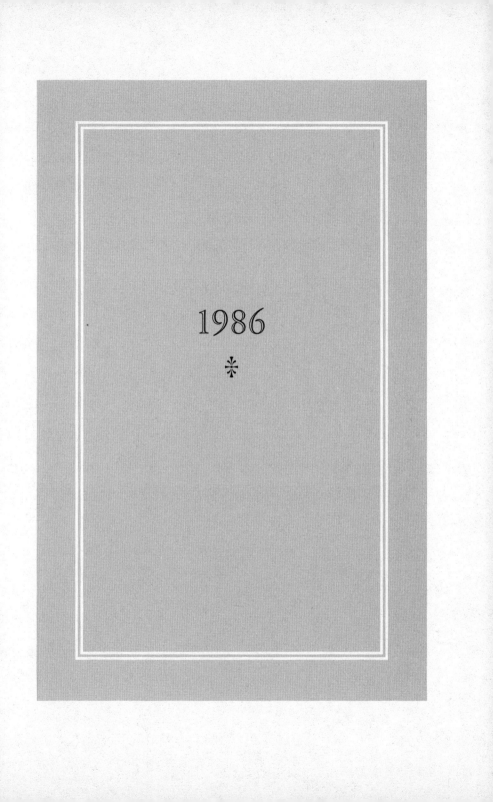

1986
✳

THE ROUTE TO EMMA'S PRESCHOOL, PARK AVENUE PROTESTANT, included one of Laura's favorite blocks in the city, Ninety-fifth Street between Lexington and Park. The brownstones were beautiful, but it was the trees that did it for Laura. They were old and tall and healthy, and in the summer months their leaves formed such a dense canopy that it almost felt like walking through a tunnel. Margaret had grown up on this block and so had a few other people Laura knew, and they all called it Goat Hill. And so Laura and Emma called it that, too.

"Do you want to know why it's called Goat Hill?" Emma asked one morning as Laura pushed her stroller up its sloping sidewalk.

"Sure," said Laura.

"Because in the olden days, New York was the country and this is where the goats lived."

"How interesting," Laura responded.

"Wanna know how I know that?"

"How do you know that?"

"'Cuz I used to live here."

"No, you used to live on Sixty-fifth Street," Laura corrected her. "But they look a little similar. I could see how you might get them confused."

"I wasn't talking about that!" Emma snapped. "I was talking about my *old* life—when I was *Wendy*."

"I thought Wendy lived in a tree house in the woods—or was it a houseboat."

77

"No, *Mabel* lived in a tree house, *Matilda* lived on a boat."

Emma twisted around and looked up at Laura, her face scrunched in contempt.

"Oh, yes," Laura apologized. "Of course! So many previous lives to keep track of."

"We are poor," Emma said as they approached the end of Goat Hill.

"Why do you say that?" Laura asked.

"'Cuz we have to live on Ninety-six Street between Lex and Third, which is not our neighborhood!"

"What's our neighborhood?" Laura asked, curious to hear Emma's answer.

"A neighborhood is where you see people you know and go into stores!"

"I know what a neighborhood is," Laura said. "My question is, what is *our* neighborhood?"

"This!" Emma said, waving her arms as they emerged onto Park Avenue, where the sidewalks were hosed down each morning, and again in the afternoon, and the concrete had the slick, pristine look of the shoreline moments after the tide retreats.

Laura didn't say anything because she had to agree. Their neighborhood began on Goat Hill and went all the way to Central Park. This was where they saw people they knew and conducted their business. Once they crossed Lexington Avenue onto their block, it was a whole different world.

THEIR BUILDING DIDN'T HAVE AN elevator man, or even a doorman, just an elderly super named Frank. Most supers stayed behind closed doors and kept to themselves. Not Frank. A cat-collecting, chain-smoking religious fanatic who spent his days painting pastel portraits of Jesus Christ in various ethereal settings, Frank—and these extensions of his identity—were a part of the atmosphere of their lobby.

To the left of their building was a long brick wall featuring the colorful scrawl of local graffiti artists, and Laura braced herself for the day Emma would be able to sound out F-U-C-K, S-U-C-K, C-O-C-K, and P-U-S-S-Y, among other vulgar words on that wall.

There was no hosing down of the sidewalk outside their building and it was speckled with pieces of gum that had been spat out, smooshed into the cement, and caked with soot and grime. As you approached the subway entrance on the southeast corner of Ninety-sixth and Lexington, the constellations grew denser.

On the adjacent corner a store called Kwik Stop advertised twenty-four-hour cash-checking services. Next to this was a row of condemned tenements. The buildings were supposedly vacant, but there was definitely some sort of activity going on in them. At night you could hear dogs barking, and during the day a collection of men hung out on the stoops, occasionally stepping out to the street to lean into the passenger windows of idling cars, their dangling chain necklaces catching the light. Laura wondered if they had guns. It gave her the creeps to live so close.

On the northeast corner of Ninety-sixth and Lexington was a grocery store called Associated Value. From the outside it looked grungy and depressing, possibly even dangerous. It had never even occurred to Laura as an option. But one evening when they were out of milk, rather than trekking all the way over to Madison, she mustered the courage to venture inside.

It didn't smell great; the aisles were narrow and congested with people taking a lot of time to consider their options; the checkout lines were long and moved slowly as customers handed over coupons and, occasionally, food stamps. But apart from this, Laura discovered it was pretty much a normal supermarket. You could find anything and everything you'd need, except it was all significantly cheaper.

Laura began doing her grocery shopping there, and she couldn't believe how much she was saving. "People think New York City is so expensive," she started telling people. "It's not—you just have to know where to shop."

The aisles of Associated Value were difficult to navigate with a stroller, and as Laura got more comfortable shopping there, she would park Emma by the store's entrance, right beneath a collage of Polaroids featuring the distressed faces of all the people who'd ever been caught shoplifting there. Emma was fascinated by these photos.

Because they were among the only white people who regularly shopped there, Laura and Emma became minor celebrities among the staff, who loved to tease them and called them snowflakes. Laura felt cozy filling up her cart at Associated Value. It reminded her of the stores of her childhood, before her neighborhood was overtaken by fashion and pretension, when there were small, practical, family-run businesses and people had charge accounts and the shopkeepers knew your name.

EMMA WAS A FEW DAYS shy of her fourth birthday when she began asking about her father. The questions didn't concern his identity or whereabouts, only his absence, which she'd apparently conflated with nonexistence. Why didn't she have a dad when everyone else did, she wanted to know. Not everyone did have a dad, Laura countered, some families just had a mom. As an example of this she named Grace, a child they knew from the playground.

This didn't answer Emma's question.

Laura knew this day was coming, but she hadn't expected it to come so soon. It didn't seem like the kind of thing one consulted the pediatrician about, but Dr. Brown was so nice. He always called back right away, and was so patient and kind, no matter how small the issue was.

"I'm a proponent of telling children the truth," he told Laura over the phone.

"The truth," Laura repeated, realizing Dr. Brown was referring to the story she'd told him four years earlier: that she had conceived Emma using a sperm donor. It was the lie she'd had no reservations telling her parents, her brother, and various acquaintances, but she regretted having told it to Dr. Brown, of whom she'd come to grow quite fond. If there was anyone she trusted more, she couldn't think who.

"Children are surprisingly able to understand science," Dr. Brown said, "if you use the right words."

THE FOLLOWING MONDAY, DR. BROWN'S secretary called to say that there was something at the front desk for her to pick up when she had the chance. Laura stopped by after dropping Emma off at school.

Dr. Brown was talking to his secretary when Laura arrived. He took a manila envelope from behind the desk and invited her into his office. The envelope contained a booklet that managed to explain the alternatives to conventional conception in terms that a child would understand. It addressed the basic facts of the human anatomy without embarrassment. While breaking things down in a straightforward way, there was also a reoccurring metaphor of a flower growing in a garden. Lovely, whimsical pencil drawings offset the hand-lettered text, which rhymed.

"*A Very Special Baby*," Laura read the title. "This is perfect. Where did you find it?"

"Being a doctor wasn't always my plan," Dr. Brown said. "Growing up, I wanted to be an author."

"You mean you *made* this?"

He blushed.

Dr. Brown soon usurped Margaret Wise Brown as the author of Emma's favorite bedtime book.

"A baby grows in her mother's tummy, where she gets everything she needs," went the first page. "But a baby's not how she starts out— she starts out as a . . ."

"Seed!" Emma would recite, reaching out to turn the page.

"BUT HAVE YOU TWO GONE on a trip yet?" was Bibs's response to Nicholas's announcement over dinner at Claude's. "They say you shouldn't marry someone you haven't traveled with."

"You mean he didn't *tell* you?" Stephanie said with sunny incredulity. "He took me to Bermuda—the Coral Beach Club! That's where it happened, where he *proposed*. There was a gorgeous sunset and—"

Nicholas put a restraining hand over hers.

"Well, congratulations," Laura said, raising her water glass to initiate a collective clinking of glasses. "We're all very happy for both of you!"

After setting his scotch down, Douglas addressed his wife from across the table.

"You've got it wrong, dear," he said. "I believe it's, 'You shouldn't travel with someone you're married to.'"

They all laughed at this, Bibs the loudest. Other patrons turned to look as her cackle ripped across the room.

"Shouldn't travel with someone you're married to!" she repeated several times.

THERE WAS A CERTAIN KIND of woman Laura noticed more and more of in *their neighborhood*. They were tall, tall, tall, and rakishly thin, and the delicate features of their Oil of Olay faces were dwarfed by over-size dark glasses. They wore miniskirts and high heels and fur coats. Their jewelry was not subtle. Nothing about them was. They spent their days traipsing up and down Madison Avenue, pausing to take in the window displays of luxury boutiques, which had proliferated. Where had these women come from and what possessed them to feel so at home here?

Laura was pushing Emma home from preschool one afternoon when one of these creatures popped out of Laura's old deli on Madison and Ninety-third clutching a frozen fruit Popsicle. The temperature was below freezing and the woman was wearing leather gloves, which made it difficult for her to remove the wrapper. As she stood there trying to do this, she and her voluptuous fur coat blocked the narrow strip of sidewalk between the store's entrance and the row of

Christmas trees for sale along the curb. She may have been oblivious to Laura's standing and waiting—though it was also possible she was indifferent. When the woman finally managed to remove the Popsicle from the plastic, the wrapper clung to her glove. Transferring the pop to her other hand, she shook herself free of it. It fluttered for a bit then landed sticky-side-down on the sidewalk. Wanting to set an example for Emma, Laura bent down to pick it up.

"Litterbug," Emma said, pointing at the woman's back.

"That's right," Laura said.

"Litterbug!" Emma repeated, this time more a shout. But her little voice was lost in the hiss of oncoming traffic, which was a good thing, because when the offender stepped off the curb to hail a cab, she removed her sunglasses, and Laura realized it was her most recent client—Emma's aunt-elect, her soon-to-be sister-in-law.

WHAT MADE LAURA GOOD AT her job was that she was careful not to make her clients feel delusional or demanding. "We've never done that before," she'd say. "The logistics might be a little challenging, but I'll look into it."

This was important because, for many women, planning a wedding became something much more: an opportunity for the universe to make good on all the ways in which the bride felt she'd been short-changed in life. Stephanie wasn't the worst client Laura had dealt with, but she was definitely in the top ten.

Their meetings went like this: Laura would present Stephanie with the options and Stephanie would cut Laura off and say, "I'm imagining . . ." and then describe something that wasn't on the list. Her most ridiculous request—which fell outside the domain of Laura's typical responsibilities, as well as jurisdiction—was to wear the wedding dress that had been worn by Laura's great-grandmother. While owned by the Library, it was currently on loan to the Museum of the City of New York.

"We—our family—has never done that before," Laura told her. "I'll look into it."

The dress was scheduled to be returned to the Library well before the date of the wedding, but the Library's trustees declined to grant permission for it to be worn, even only for the ceremony.

"I think this is for the best," Laura told Stephanie. "It's seen its best days, that dress—it's yellowed, it smells a little funky. To be honest, I thought it might look a little Miss Havisham."

"Miss *who?*" Stephanie asked, clearly miffed by the trustees' decision.

"Charles Dickens," Laura told her. "*Great Expectations*. The point is, I think you'll be happier in a new dress."

The wedding day arrived. Emma was the flower girl, the first of the bridal party to process down the aisle. She took her time scattering petals, and Laura was relieved when she finally reached the altar and took her place off to the side, as she'd been instructed to do at the rehearsal. There were bridesmaids—Stephanie's sorority sisters, with whom she was still close—and one after another they kept coming out, as if from a clown car, and then finally the bride. The ceremony commenced; pews creaked as everyone took a seat.

"If I speak in the tongues of men or of angels," thundered the minister's voice from his pedestal, "but do not have love"—here he lowered his voice and paused for dramatic effect—"I am only a resounding gong or a clanging cymbal." Now his voice picked up its former volume and urgency. "If I have the gift of prophecy and can fathom all mysteries and all knowledge and if I have a faith that can move mountains, but do NOT HAVE LOVE"—another theatrical pause before proceeding in a whisper—"*I am nothing.*" Loud again: "IF I GIVE ALL I POSSESS TO THE POOR . . ."

Laura hated Corinthians. It was one thing to celebrate love, another to sanctimoniously demean the existence of those who did not have it. How was it in the spirit of Christ to tell people who were alone in the world that whatever else they had going for themselves— spirituality, wisdom, a virtuous heart—none of it counted because, at the end of the day, no one loved them?

Laura was so deep in this thought that it took her a moment to notice Emma had left her spot at the margins of the bridal party and was now standing at the center of the altar, facing out to the congregation, as though this were a show and she was about to break into a solo.

And then she did. Not a whole song, but a line from a song: "The sun, has gone, to bed and so must I." After singing these words she lay down on the floor and shut her eyes, pretending to go to sleep.

There were a few titters, but for the most part the church was silent. Laura knew what this was: a reenactment of her favorite scene in *The Sound of Music.* Laura figured Emma was imagining this scene would unfold similarly and that a bridesmaid—or, better yet, the bride herself!—would walk over, pick her up, and carry her off while the congregation sang the good night chorus.

Shortly after lying down, Emma stood back up, curtseyed, and returned to her place. The whole interruption had been no more than a minute, but it felt like the longest minute of Laura's life.

The ceremony concluded and everyone spilled outside the church. There was some milling about on the sidewalk as people waited to get into the cars that would take them to the reception. The bride and groom would be traveling in a horse-drawn carriage, which had yet to arrive.

When Laura was done speaking to her, Emma looked chastened. Sandra took her hand and began leading her down the block, away from the crowd.

"I don't know why she's in trouble," Bibs said, blowing her grand-daughter a kiss. "I thought it was *adorable*, the best part of the cer-emony."

"It was completely inappropriate," Laura told her.

Stephanie hovered by the church's fire exit, enshrouded by the bridesmaids. She was crying, Laura realized. Nicholas stood off to the side, looking uncertain if he should join the effort to console his bride.

Spotting Laura, he walked over. "She's upset with Emma's little performance," he said.

"That's understandable," Laura responded.

"Well, are you going to apologize?" Nicholas asked.

"Of course," she told him.

The bridesmaids nervously dispersed as she approached. "I'm so sorry, Stephanie," Laura said. "I don't know what got into her."

Stephanie's cheeks were streaked with mascara. "Isn't she old enough to know this was a religious ceremony, not a beauty pageant?"

"You would think." Laura shook her head in remorse. "I told Sandra to take her home for a time-out." Borrowing the language of Emma's preschool teacher, she added: "She's considering her ac-tions."

"I've been imagining this day for my whole life." Stephanie's eyes brimmed with fresh tears. "You get one chance to stand at the altar."

"Not necessarily," Bibs murmured from a few feet away, shamelessly observing the interaction.

HAVING A CHILD DIDN'T STOP men from noticing Laura, and she enjoyed the occasional vanity rush of recognizing this was happening. When Emma was with her, she was all the more flattered, as she figured the men assumed she was married and thus had no agenda; they were just admiring her for the sake of admiring her, perhaps thinking *what a lucky man.*

To further the impression of being a taken woman, she moved a ring she'd inherited years ago from her right index finger to her left. This generated disapproving comments from various female friends and relations, who were all the more adamant she find a husband now that she had a child. They continued to try to fix her up, and occasionally Laura cooperated and agreed to meet the man.

She always regretted it. If Laura even had a "type," it was not the kind she was set up with now that she was a thirty-six-year-old single mother: at least a decade her senior, divorced (acrimoniously so), disgruntled, cynical, and politically apathetic or Republican. The dregs of the Upper East Side dating pool.

One evening Laura was duped into having dinner with a business associate of Trip's who turned out to be an unabashedly outspoken member of the NRA. As she sat across the table from this Republican lobbyist lunatic, she thought of what her mother had said of marriage: *Anything, anything, anything would be better than this.* That's how others viewed her current situation as a single mother, she realized. How else to explain their rationale in matching her with such maniacs? They saw her and Emma as incomplete, stray people, a free-floating fragment; the goal was to make them whole and *anyone, anyone, anyone* would be better than no one.

1987

✳

"WHEN YOU WERE PREGNANT WITH ME WERE YOU SCARED I'D have brown hair like you?"

Emma stood before the full-length mirror in the front hall closet. She'd removed the rubber bands that had secured her two braids, and now she was running her fingers through her hair, untethering the sections. She took her time doing this, admiring her reflection.

"Scared?" Laura laughed. "Why would I be scared you'd have brown hair?"

"Because blond is better." As she spoke Emma's breath fogged the glass, obscuring her image.

"I don't know where you got an idea like that," Laura said.

"It's true." Emma wiped the condensation away so she could see her face. "Everybody knows it."

"Bath time," Laura said.

"Maybe she's *born* with it," Emma sang as she bent over, so that her hair fell forward covering her face. "*Maybe it's Maybelliiiiine.*" She flipped her head back up, teasing her hair into a poof.

"Bath time," Laura repeated.

Emma held up a peremptory finger in her mother's direction. "Good night, dah-ling," she said, and leaned in to kiss her reflection.

WHEN LAURA WAS A STUDENT at Winthrop, things were a certain way, and when a student's conduct deviated from this standard, she was told, "That's not the *Winthrop way*." Significant cultural changes had taken place in the intervening decades, but from what Laura observed on the tour for prospective parents, the *Winthrop way* had persevered. The day still began with Prayers, in which students sang hymns and recited Bible verses. The girls were no longer required to wear blazers and berets upon exiting the building, but wore the traditional lime-green tunics and seemed to carry themselves with the same deferential air.

The hunched spine that afflicts so many women as they age had not touched Miss Gardner, who stood more erect than ever as she emerged from her office to greet the parents on the tour. Though Miss Gardner's stiff decorum now registered as more quaint than imperial, Laura still found herself intimidated by her former headmistress, who recognized her instantly.

"So wonderful to see you," Miss Gardner said, giving Laura's hand an extra-long shake.

In the middle of the tour, one of the couples began quietly bickering. They also had a child at Park Avenue Protestant, though she was in a different class from Emma. Things gradually escalated, and as they filed into the auditorium, Laura heard the husband say: "How dare you talk about my kid like that!" Everyone heard the wife respond, "First of all, she's *our* kid, secondly, what's wrong with being average!"

Realizing all eyes were on her, the wife burst into tears and dashed into the hall. The husband dutifully lumbered after her. There was an awkward silence before Mrs. Olsen, director of admissions, smiled and continued the tour without them.

A few days later, Laura ran into the wife on the steps of Park Avenue Protestant. They'd both arrived early for pickup, and after exchanging hellos, the poor woman felt obligated to address what had transpired on the tour. Their daughter had scored in the thirty-ninth percentile on the preschool admissions test, and they had been told Winthrop was a long shot and not to even bother. "But you know fathers," the wife said, rolling her eyes. "If it's their kid, she's got to be a *genius*."

Laura nodded sympathetically and, wanting to make the woman feel better, told her that her own daughter had scored in the thirty-seventh percentile, though this was a wild guess—she hadn't bothered to find out Emma's results.

Hearing this number, a look of irritation flashed across the wife's face, followed by a hostile smirk. "And of course *you* have nothing to worry about," she said. "You're an alumni, your daughter's a shoo-in."

School let out, for which Laura was grateful, as she felt herself flushing. She'd tried to be nice to this woman, and she'd responded by shaming her for her background, making it sound like anything Emma achieved or would achieve—and by extension, anything *Laura* had achieved or would achieve—was only the product of their privileged family, that on their own they would amount to nothing.

Alumn*a*, Laura thought as she watched the woman greet her daughter. She had taken three years of Latin.

Janet, who'd attended Winthrop with Laura and whose two boys were enrolled at St. Christopher's, thought Laura was making a mistake in deciding to send Emma to the Day School, the progressive alternative to Winthrop. She didn't come right out and say it, but conveyed her opinion in her typical Janet way, which was to start to say something she knew Laura didn't want to hear, and then stop short of saying all of it, eliciting Laura's curiosity and forcing her to tease the rest out.

"I'm not sure about the Day School," Janet was saying. "The atmosphere is a little *I don't know*."

"A little *what?*" Laura asked.

"A little hippie-dippy.

"As for the quality of the education," Janet continued, "I can't speak to that, but I have heard things about their approach that would give me pause."

"Such as?"

"That it's a bit loosey-goosey."

"Can you give me an example of what you mean by that?"

"Apparently they let students learn to read at their own pace. In the meantime, there's an entire unit devoted to teaching students how to make their own *shoes*," Janet said. "It's a bit artsy-fartsy, if you catch my drift."

"I see your point," Laura said. "But these are all the reasons why I think it would be a good fit for Emma. She's a spirited little girl. Let's face it, Winthrop's a little hoity-toity."

"If you really want my honest opinion, Laura dear, and I say this as one of your oldest friends, it's *you* I don't see fitting in at the Day School."

"Well, I won't be the one going," Laura pointed out.

"Yes, but you'd be surprised how much parents are expected to be involved these days."

According to Janet, there was a middle school puberty unit at the Day School where parents were expected to come into the classroom, sit in a circle, and say the names they called their private parts.

Laura laughed. "They would never do that—it's the most ridiculous idea I've ever heard!"

"It's absolutely true. It's supposed to make kids feel more comfortable about their bodies."

"*More* comfortable?" Laura laughed even harder. She didn't believe it, but this didn't stop her from conjuring the scenario, and the dizzying, dry-mouthed, anticipatory panic of her rapidly advancing turn.

DAISY CANCELED AN HOUR BEFORE Laura had to be at the Library to receive a late shipment of flowers for a wedding taking place the next day. Although Laura didn't normally trust her mother to babysit Emma, she had no other option.

The delivery kept getting delayed. Finally, at six o'clock Laura headed to 136 to pick up Emma.

The house was quiet. "Hello?" she called, letting herself in. "Hello?" she tried again. She walked through the dining room and into the living room, which was also dark and empty. "Hello? Anyone home?"

She thought she smelled something cooking and poked her head into the kitchen. A pot boiled on the stove and Sandra sat at the kitchen table, flipping through a tabloid.

"Oh, hi!" Laura smiled warmly. "Wasn't sure if anyone was home! Have you seen Emma and my mother?"

"I just get here," Sandra said, licking an index finger to turn the page.

"I see. Thank you, Sandra."

"Thank your father, he pay me."

Laura nodded and forced another smile. She wished Sandra wouldn't say that. She could never be sure if it was a cultural thing or if there was some hostility.

"Hello?" Laura called, walking upstairs. "Emma? Bibs?"

The second-floor hall was dark, but she noticed light from beneath the door to her parents' bedroom. She knocked lightly. When there was no response she knocked louder, and then she opened the door.

"*Shhh*," Bibs hissed from across the room.

There they were in bed, Emma sprawled like a frog across her grandmother, body rising and falling to the rhythm of Bibs's breaths. A half-eaten carton of melting rainbow sherbet rested on the bedside table beside two cans of ginger ale and a plate with the remains of toast with smoked salmon. Bibs ran her fingers through Emma's unbraided hair, which cascaded across her shoulders.

"How long has she been out?" Laura asked.

Bibs shot her a fierce look. "You'll wake her!" she whispered sternly.

"Yes, that's my intention," Laura said. "Naps aren't good. It means she'll never fall asleep at her bedtime."

She put her hand on Emma's back and gently shook. "Emma. Time to go home."

"Don't want to," Emma said drowsily.

"Let her stay!" Bibs said, wrapping her arms around her defensively.

"You two." Laura stood back and folded her arms and chuckled. "I wish I had my camera right now."

Her amusement was short-lived, however; it was getting late and she was tired. After a few futile minutes of trying to rally Emma, she'd had enough.

"Fine," she said. "It's not a weeknight. You two want to have a sleepover, go ahead."

Laura paused by the door and blew Emma a kiss. "Call me if you need anything!"

When Emma didn't object to her exiting the room, she continued downstairs, considering the possibility of carrying through with the threat. It felt irresponsible to just walk out the door, but why? Sandra was here, her father would be getting home soon—what was the danger? It wasn't often that Laura had a night to herself: she could see a movie, sit at the bar of a restaurant with a book, order mussels and a glass of red wine. She could go back to the apartment, get takeout, and watch PBS. She had many options and they were all things she enjoyed and wished she were able to do more often, so it didn't make sense to her that now that the opportunity had presented itself, she didn't want to do any of them.

LAURA WAS HURT WHEN IN March of that year a letter arrived from the Day School rejecting Emma from their incoming kindergarten class. Wasn't a progressive school supposed to be non-exclusionary— weren't they supposed to take everyone?

Laura called her mother, who shared her outrage.

"They're idiots," Bibs said. "Absolute idiots."

Emma, on the other hand, couldn't have been more excited to learn she'd be attending Winthrop.

"I get a uniform! I get a uniform! I get a uniform!" she sang.

* * *

LAURA'S EIGHT-WEEK PAID SUMMER VACATION, a component of her part-time work schedule, meant that the Library could no longer offer weddings during the months of July and August. Summer weddings had been a significant source of revenue and Laura felt guilty about this, but she felt even guiltier imagining Emma's spending the summer in sweltering, stuffy Manhattan—and so at the end of every June they packed up the car and headed up I-95.

Ashaunt was a finger of land that jutted out into Buzzards Bay, Massachusetts. Laura's paternal great-grandparents had bought the land at the turn of the century, building a summer cottage at the tip of the peninsula. In the ensuing decades, more houses had been constructed to accommodate their descendants. None of the houses were winterized, and for nine months they sat empty. In June, station wagons began to arrive, and by July the place was teeming with relatives—Laura's first and second cousins, their parents and spouses and children. Ashaunt was too rustic for Bibs's taste, and Nicholas was allergic, so the house that Douglas had inherited was occupied solely by Laura and Emma.

"You know, we're very lucky to have Ashaunt," Laura told Emma as they pulled up to the entrance. *Ashaunt Point, Private Property, No Trespassing, Bicyclists and Walkers Please Turn Around*, read the sign. Laura rolled down the window and reached out to punch the security code into the keypad.

"Most people don't have something like this," she reiterated as they waited for the metal gate to retract. "They don't get to spend the whole summer at a nice house by the ocean with their cousins. They have to stay in the city and work."

Emma sucked the last drops of liquid in her juice box with such force that the walls of the container caved in. "*Ahhh,*" she hissed.

The road was paved, but narrow and potholed—for two cars driving the opposite direction to pass each other, one had to veer into the grassy embankment while the other inched by. After the gate it snaked through a wooded enclave before the houses began. Proximity to the water compromised arboreal fertility. As the road crept along, hearty hemlocks and matronly firs gave way to adolescent cedars, clematis, and bayberry bushes. It was too early for crickets, but the country quiet was embroidered with the quivering thrum of cicadas, punctuated by the occasional peeper, newly born and safely sequestered within lush thickets of tall grass, their starchy stalks adorned with feathered plumes, which swayed in deferential submission to the encroaching ocean and quicksilver sky.

Though the first whiff of salty sea air still evoked feelings of joy for Laura, upon stepping into the house a sense of dread set in as she braced herself for the physical discomforts of the weeks to come. To Laura's disgust but also fascination, there was a distinctly soggy spot on the old straw rug in the front hall—the result of a glass of lemonade being spilled in the early 1960s. She had been there and witnessed the accident. The scientific explanation was that, once wet, nothing ever completely dried in Ashaunt. Bedding, rugs, towels, dogs, your hair (no matter how long you spent blow-drying it): there was nothing the ocean air couldn't penetrate. Even the wood the houses were made of was soft and mossy to the touch, and if you pressed your fingernail into one of the clapboard panels it would leave an indentation.

As Laura brought their bags in, she noticed the house was disconcertingly still—then she remembered she hadn't flicked the switch in the basement that turned on the electricity. As soon as she did, the floors hummed to life with the comfortingly familiar vibrations of the ancient, avocado-green refrigerator, which, for reasons Laura always meant to ask the caretaker to investigate, in addition to a steady rumbling occasionally squawked like a bird.

After unloading the groceries, Laura rinsed the fruit and placed it in a bowl in the middle of the kitchen table. A pair of fruit flies immediately descended upon it. She fished through the pantry in search of the protective mesh dome, but by the time she located it, they'd seemingly procreated into a village. A fly swatter hung from a rusty nail by the light switch, but Laura couldn't be bothered. Like mold-speckled pillowcases and clammy sheets, fruit flies were a fact of life in Ashaunt; there was no point in trying to fight them.

Emma excavated her bike from the garage and took off to go find her cousins.

After Dustbusting the mouse turds out of their dresser drawers, Laura unpacked their clothes and stored their suitcases in the hall closet. She had returned to the kitchen to get dinner started when Emma flew in and breathlessly announced she would be eating at Holly's house that night. Before Laura had a chance to respond, she'd scampered off, the screen door bouncing behind her.

Laura picked up the phone to call Holly's mother, who confirmed the invitation. "We're having tomato salad, truffle risotto, and swordfish," Ginny said apologetically. "Is that okay? Will Emma eat that?

Tell me the truth, because I'm more than happy to make mac and cheese."

"Emma will eat anything," Laura told her. "Thank you for having her. We'll have Holly tomorrow."

Laura made a fried egg and sat down with a *New Yorker* article titled "The End of Nature." It was about the greenhouse effect, and the news was grim. She tried to commit certain facts to memory to use in future debates, though it seemed pointless. The skeptics weren't so much unconvinced as ideologically opposed to the notion that anything that made life convenient for them could be bad for the planet— they subscribed to a view of things that didn't tolerate such discord. They were almost always men. Laura knew, and was related to, many of them.

The house had a chill, and after dinner she collected some logs and laid a fire, but hesitated to light it when she heard some activity in the chimney. She made a note to call the caretaker in the morning, and in case she forgot the reason, wrote *raccoon back*.

It was almost nine and Emma still hadn't returned. Laura had slept poorly the night before and was exhausted from the drive. She wanted to go to bed. Finally the phone rang and it was Emma, calling to say the grown-ups wanted Laura to come over and play a game with them.

"A game?" Laura yawned. "What kind of game?" Dial tone. Laura put on a sweater, slipped on her flip-flops, and shuffled out into the night.

Ginny shared a house with her sister, Dinah, and between the two of them they had three dogs, four cars, and seven kids, Holly being the youngest and the only girl. Built in the seventies, theirs was one of the newer, bigger, more controversial houses on Ashaunt. It had a television, a room in the basement with electronic exercise machines, and there were rumors they were planning to install a swimming pool. A swimming pool on Ashaunt, surrounded by ocean! No one could imagine it. Laura hoped it wasn't true but, given their husbands, she wouldn't be surprised.

Ginny and Dinah had married Timmy and Rick, who'd been best friends growing up in Boston. Timmy and Rick liked sports, grilling meat, and arguing about what was the best kind of car. Laura had once heard something strange about Rick, which was that he got regular manicures for some medical reason having to do with his cuticles. Other than that, both brothers-in-law were straight out of a commercial. Unabashedly American, they were.

"Oh, great, she's here!" someone said as Laura let herself in. "We can play!"

In addition to Dinah, Ginny, and Tweedledum and Tweedledumdum (as Bibs referred to Timmy and Rick) were two additional couples at the table. After introducing Laura and the houseguests, Dinah explained the game, which was called Fantasy. Everyone was to think of a secret fantasy, write it down on a slip of paper, fold it up, and put it in a bowl. The bowl would be passed around as people took turns drawing a slip, reading what it said, and guessing whose fantasy it was.

"Remember to disguise your handwriting," Ginny said, distributing paper and pens. After a few turns, Laura quickly regretted what she'd written, which did not fit with the tone of the game. Most of the wishes concerned benign vices (*Beer turns out to prevent cancer*) and playful criticisms of one's spouse (*My husband learns how to do laundry!*). Laura wasn't sure why *My wife is insatiable* was so funny, but she pretended to find it as amusing as the others.

Laughter came easily to this group, and that their sense of humor wasn't particularly sophisticated did little to mitigate Laura's feeling of inferiority in the personality department. Stripped of the routine responsibilities of day-to-day life, a person's value in Ashaunt was his or her company—and Laura was aware hers wasn't the most fun. People *liked* her, of course, but no one went out of their way to spend time with her. She wouldn't have even been invited to this game night if not for Emma.

Laura's slip of paper was drawn by a houseguest husband. In addition to being much too earnest, the fantasy was politically awkward. She could tell by the look of this man (pink shorts, yellow polo, sailboat-embroidered belt) that he was a card-carrying Republican, and what she'd written concerned global warming, the government's restriction of CO_2 emissions, and harsher legal repercussions for companies who flouted the law, including jail sentences for high-level executives. It was a long-winded wish and took a while for the man to read.

When he was done there was a silence, broken only by Rick saying, "That one was mine," to which everyone boisterously laughed.

"I've never played this game before," Laura apologized when they'd settled down. "I'll do better next time."

"Can Emma stay for a sleepover?" Holly pleaded when Laura said it was time to go.

"Fine with me!" Ginny said.

As Laura let herself out the front door, a fresh shock of laughter shook the house and broke like a wave, spilling out onto the porch, down the steps, and onto the grass, the foamy lick of its wake seeming to chase Laura's feet as she headed up toward the road, back to her house, into the damp sheets of her bed, where the only sound was the occasional scuttling of squirrels within the walls.

WHILE THE OTHER MOTHERS WERE always complaining about how busy they were—the never-ending laundering of towels, the hosing down of sandy feet, the deticking of dogs—Laura found it a challenge to fill up her days on Ashaunt, especially now that Emma was five and no longer required constant supervision.

For kids, Ashaunt meant freedom. They roamed about in packs, barefoot, bug-bitten, and sunburned, scattering like rabbits upon spotting an approaching adult. As evening arrived, there was a gradual disbanding as the cousins returned to their respective houses for dinner. An older cousin would be charged with escorting Emma home. This reaffirmed her status as Ashaunt's lone only child—of a single parent to boot—and was an abrupt and sobering conclusion to the excitement of the day. Fortunately, the action would resume in the morning.

Eager not to miss out, Emma took off each day after breakfast, returning only to dash upstairs to retrieve something from her bedroom, change into her bathing suit, or seek Laura's permission to join another family's picnic or boating expedition to the islands. On the occasions she reported home for lunch, Emma brought guests, sometimes as many as half a dozen second cousins, whom Laura—feeling guilty about all the lunches their parents had served Emma—was more than eager to accommodate.

When she wasn't mass-producing tuna melts, Laura occupied herself with books and organization projects. Her mornings were industrious, but as the briny air had a way of eroding the houses, the sun-bleached hours of midday had a way of chipping away at Laura's resolve to keep plugging away at whatever endeavor she'd undertaken that day, which suddenly seemed pointless.

Laura was determined to keep Ashaunt's shoreline completely litter-free. Each tide deposited a fresh spattering of miscellaneous refuse—shards of glass, Styrofoam cups, buoys—so this was an ongoing project. As the summer progressed she expanded her sweeps to include the craggy tip of the point, where the rocks got bigger and bigger until they were more like boulders. It was difficult to navigate and the one area where children were forbidden to go. No one went there, in fact, and adding to the spooky feeling, the outer tip of the point had once been used as a military base during the Second World War, a lookout spot in case enemies invaded. During this time, the government had temporarily confiscated the area where her great-grandparents had built their original house, which had been torn down to make room for a makeshift command center, beneath which they'd constructed a series of underground tunnels where the soldiers had lived.

In Laura's memory of sneaking out here as a child, the iron door that led to these tunnels had always been locked. She was relieved to discover this remained the case. At the base of the entrance was a smooth patch of asphalt, and the radiating heat sent a pleasant shiver up Laura's legs. The sun felt good on her exposed skin, and she decided to lie down and get a little tan. She was completely secluded, so she took off her shorts and shirt. A few minutes later she removed her bra; when would she get the chance again? She kept her underpants on.

The boat didn't make a sound, and Laura wondered how long it had been there. Sitting up, one arm covering her breasts, she groped for her shirt. She knew the man inside the boat had been watching because he abruptly turned around and cast his fishing rod on the other side, facing away from her.

Laura left in such a hurry she forgot her bag of trash. When she went back for it the next day, the boat was there again, closer to shore than she'd remembered it being before. Before turning up toward the asphalt, Laura looked at the fisherman, and he looked back at her, and then turned to an angle where he couldn't see her.

Today Laura had worn a bikini beneath her clothes, and after stripping down to it, she sat on the asphalt, keeping tabs on the fisherman, making sure his back was to her, as she removed her top. She lay down so she couldn't see him, but she could feel that he was now watching her.

Again, she forgot the bag of trash.

So began a new secret routine. The fisherman was handsome in a weathered, man-of-the-sea kind of way, but it wasn't so much he who excited Laura as his lust for her, and the unspoken and illicit nature of their arrangement. *My fisherman*, she came to think of him.

THERE WAS A CONSTANT ANXIETY about time and the rapid passing of it on Ashaunt. "The crickets are getting louder as they are getting closer to death," an aunt had once told Laura when she was a child—and there was rarely an evening on Ashaunt when she didn't think of it. "The summer is almost over," people started saying soon after the Fourth of July. As August rolled around, the dread of September took on an existential air, and each sunset had the sensation of being the last.

While Laura looked forward to returning to the routine of their lives in New York, the feeling still got to her, and it was especially acute when she arrived at her secret spot at the end of the point and discovered her fisherman wasn't there. There had been a few days when he hadn't shown up, but this was her final afternoon of the summer.

A few hours later, their car was loaded and ready to go. Disconsolate at the prospect of leaving, Emma climbed a tree and refused to come down. After a fifteen-minute standoff, she surrendered, under the condition that they stop for a final dip at the swimming dock. The water was cold and she lasted less than a minute. Weeping and shivering, Emma climbed back up the steps. Laura toweled her off, and they were about to leave when Maggie, one of her oldest and frailest great-aunts, arrived for a swim, and Laura thought they should linger to make sure she didn't drown.

"You have a lot of freckles," Emma said between sniffles, pointing to Maggie's shins.

"Those are liver spots, dear," Maggie told her, meticulously tucking every last rogue wisp of silver hair beneath the rubbery base of her mustard-yellow bathing cap. She stood up, unfastened the belt of her towel coat, and shed it with the comfort one did a winter jacket; skinny-dipping had once been the norm at Ashaunt, and for older generations it remained the preference.

Maggie's knuckles flashed white as she gripped the railing that ran along the steps leading to the water. It was a long, slow, cautious descent, but eventually she reached the last step, arched her back, tossed up her arms, and dove in with a splash. Once she was in the water there was no trace of the prudence with which Maggie negotiated her movements on land; her body seemed transformed into a younger, stronger, more confident one. Even her breasts appeared miraculously restored to their former shape and buoyancy. As she flipped over they broke the surface of the water like pale blue moons, growing smaller and smaller as she backstroked toward the horizon.

Eventually Maggie reversed direction. As they waited, a boat appeared in the distance. Laura assumed it was Rick, who was known for driving his boat much too fast and close to the swimming dock. His proximity to Maggie made Laura nervous and she waved her hands in the air, trying to signal for him to slow down.

The boat did slow down, but Laura's relief was fleeting as she realized it was not Rick.

"Who is that?" Emma asked, as the boat approached the dock.

"We don't know him," Laura said.

"*Trespasser*," Emma muttered with a growl.

"The ocean doesn't belong to us," Laura said quietly.

Close to the steps, Laura's fisherman put the boat in neutral. It bobbed menacingly as he stared at Laura, who wanted to turn away but was afraid to do so. She'd never seen him this close, for this long, and there was something in his face she'd never observed before, an uncouth, wanton look in his eyes.

"What's he doing here?" Emma whispered.

Laura squeezed her hand but didn't speak. Her fear was laced with shame and remorse. Laura had been reckless; thinking of what she had done, she felt she didn't know herself.

"Sir!" Maggie's voice carried sharply over the water. "I would like to get out and I'm not wearing a suit. If you could please give me some privacy!"

And with that he took off, the wake of his boat unzipping the water like the back of a dress.

As Laura had anticipated, Emma struggled with the *Winthrop way*. It was only November, and the fourth time she had done something that prompted a telephone call home about behavior that was "inappropriate," a word with which she was now very familiar. Today's incident was regarding a picture Emma had drawn featuring "inappropriate content" that had left her kindergarten teacher "a little concerned."

"No need to mince your words," Laura told Miss Cole. "Let me know what it was and I'll talk to her."

"She drew a man who was—in his birthday suit."

"Oh, dear." Laura sighed. "I can explain. Last weekend, we were about to cross the street, when all of a sudden a man in a proverbial trench coat appeared out of nowhere and did his thing."

Miss Cole did not say anything.

"Life on Ninety-sixth Street!" Laura mustered a chuckle. "Anyway, thanks for letting me know, I appreciate the call, here she comes now, I'll have to have a chat with her, goodbye, Miss Cole, see you tomorrow!"

Laura hung up the phone and looked at Emma, who stood in the doorway clutching a stack of freshly dog-eared catalogs. (That Laura never processed Emma's orders didn't stop the catalogs from piling up.) At five, Emma remained in the upper percentiles for height and weight. Though her body had lengthened, she still had the distended paunch of a toddler, the bulk of which was further exaggerated by the pleated skirt of her Winthrop tunic billowing out like a tent. This belly was her center of gravity, and she carried it with a regal immodesty, letting it announce her as she entered spaces.

"Guess who that was?"

"Miss Cole?" Emma said in a baby voice.

Laura nodded. "Why do you think she was calling?"

"How am I opposed to know?" Emma's shoulders rose in a phony way.

"The word is *sup*posed. And I think you do know."

"Because my weekend update was inappropriate?" Emma timidly placed the catalogs on Laura's desk.

"Bingo."

"Bingo?"

"Yes. You're correct. That's why Miss Cole was calling."

Laura searched Emma's face for signs of remorse.

"They're called 'private parts' for a reason," Emma said, clearly repeating what Miss Cole had said to her.

"If you knew it was inappropriate, why did you draw it?"

Emma shrugged again.

"You're not a little kid anymore, I know that you understand these things. The question is, what inspires you to pretend not to know any better? Do you think it's funny? Do you think it's *cute*?"

Emma chewed the inside of her lip and looked at the floor.

"Do you know how embarrassing it is for me, as your mother, to get these phone calls?"

Emma nodded. The expression on her face was sober, if not wholly contrite.

"You don't draw pictures of penises in school," Laura said.

"You don't draw pictures of penises in school," Emma repeated.

"Or what we have," Laura added as Emma turned to go back to her room.

"Va-*gi*-nas!" Emma shouted as she skipped down the hall.

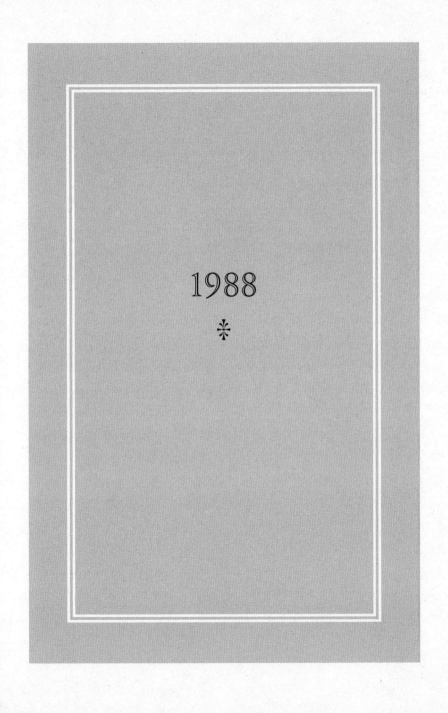

1988

✻

On the third Sunday of every month, Laura helped make dinner for the residents of a local women's shelter. Emma typically stayed home, but one evening the babysitter canceled and Laura took her along. It was here, in the kitchen, that Emma met Sylvia.

She had never met anyone named Sylvia before; it was the most beautiful name she'd ever heard. And with her pretty red hair and pink lipstick, Sylvia was the most beautiful homeless person Emma had ever seen.

Sylvia was other things Emma had never encountered before, including the only adult who hadn't been amused or flustered by the question, "Do you think God is real?" Sylvia didn't *think* God was real; she *knew* He was. She had seen Him and He had spoken to her.

Emma was equally awed by Sylvia's thoughts on Jesus: "He is the way, and the truth, and the life. No one comes to the Father except through Him."

As they were saying goodbye, Sylvia told Emma that she used to wear glasses, but after praying for God to fix her vision, one day she'd woken up to discover God had fixed her vision. Now that she no longer needed glasses, she could see everything, including things other people couldn't. Emma wanted to know what these things that Sylvia could see and normal people couldn't were, and when she asked, Sylvia said she could see that Emma wasn't like other children—that she was special.

On their way home Emma asked if Sylvia could be her babysitter the next time Laura had to go out.

"But what about Daisy?" Laura responded. "You love Daisy."

Emma shook her head. "She's doesn't pay me any attention. She's always talking on the phone."

"I'll think about it," Laura said.

"BEAUTIFUL CHILD!" SYLVIA GASPED AS Emma entered the living room in the new, floor-grazing dirndl her grandparents had brought back from the previous summer's trip to Europe.

As Emma walked across the room toward the sofa, where Sylvia sat waiting for her, she took small, delicate steps, making sure her toes didn't poke out from beneath her skirt, so as to create the impression that she wasn't walking, but floating—like the sugarplum fairies in the opening scene of the second half of *The Nutcracker*.

Sylvia was supposed to be the babysitter, but Laura stayed in the apartment the whole time. Emma escorted Sylvia to her bedroom and shut the door. She handed Sylvia a brush and requested that she do her hair to look like Marta's in *The Sound of Music*: two braids twisted and pinned above her ears. After this, Sylvia taught Emma the proper way to pray: knees on the floor, head bowed, hands clasped, lips moving but no sound coming out.

Emma prayed for, among other things, sisters and brothers, glasses, braces, a dog, a pet rabbit, a Polly Pocket, for the ozone layer to grow back, to be in the next Olympics, for Nickelodeon to come take over her school, for it to be the olden days, for Sylvia to be her governess, and for God not to punish her mom even though she didn't believe in Him.

This last wish Emma verbalized to Sylvia, who agreed it was a concern. When Laura poked her head in the door to check on them, Sylvia said, "If serving the Lord seems undesirable to you, then choose for yourself, but remember in whose land you are living."

Laura smiled and said that it was probably getting time for Sylvia to go home.

As Sylvia and Emma stood in the hall waiting for the elevator, Emma had a sinking, panicky feeling. She had an idea. She ran back inside and returned with a slim glass vial that had once held Indian beads. Removing its cork stopper, she handed the vial to Sylvia and asked her to breathe inside it. She did, Emma corked the bottle, and the elevator door opened and Sylvia stepped in.

Holding Sylvia's breath to her chest, Emma stood and watched the panel above the elevator illuminate the number of the floor she was on, 17-16-15-14-12-11-10-9-8-7-6-5-4-3-2—until it stopped at L.

"Goodbye, Sylvia," Emma said, and kissed the bottle.

GETTING OUT THE DOOR EACH morning was a production, and Emma's first report card noted that she had been delivered late to school on thirteen separate occasions. There was no mention of Laura's tardiness at afternoon pickup (she had been a bit relaxed about these), but beneath the attendance record, Miss Cole had added a personal note: "Let's see if we can all do better in the winter term."

Laura made a concerted effort to be more punctual, and she made it through January without an issue. Such was shaping up to be the case with February when tragic circumstances intervened.

She didn't know of anyone this had happened to, although most people she knew didn't ride the subway. When acquaintances learned that Laura—petite, demure Laura—braved the dangerous and chaotic New York City underground twice a day by herself, they were flabbergasted. But it was a point of pride for her, a method of transportation that was cheaper, generally quicker, and certainly more environmentally friendly than taking a cab. And there was invariably a character or two in your car. The people who didn't use it were missing out on a quintessential New York experience, never venturing out of their safe little bubble.

She was on her way to pick up Emma; as her train approached the Ninety-sixth Street station, Laura stood up to wait by the door, gripping the overhead bar to steady herself. After pulling abreast of the platform, the train stopped with a violent jerk—but the doors did not open. Five minutes passed, and the doors remained closed and there were no announcements explaining why. Subway officials were out on the track with flashlights, looking beneath the train. A few of the passengers in Laura's car tried to communicate with them via hand gestures and exasperated expressions but were ignored. Finally the conductor's voice came on over the radio and said that due to a police investigation the train was no longer in service and everyone needed to disembark.

Police had congregated on the platform. Farther down the platform, passengers who'd emerged from another car peered over the ledge at something on the track. From the expressions on their faces Laura knew what it was.

Laura felt quivery, like her knees might buckle. The poor conductor, she considered, how traumatic for him. As for the person, she couldn't bear to think of it. Had they been pushed? Jumped? Perhaps they'd been standing too close to the yellow line when a rat had come along and scurried between their feet and, being skittish, they'd accidentally leapt forward—that had long been a fear of hers.

A childish part of Laura wanted to join the gawkers at the end of the platform, but shame prevented her from indulging such morbid curiosity. Slipping her hands into the pockets of her coat, she proceeded in the other direction, away from the spectacle, toward the exit. As she headed up the steps to the street, she had to step aside for a team of paramedics. That they didn't appear in a particular rush extinguished any doubt she'd had regarding what had happened.

Laura arrived at Winthrop to find Emma standing on the front steps with Miss Cole. As she approached, Miss Cole patted the top of Emma's head and said, "Do you want to tell Mom how it makes you feel when she's late?"

"Like my time is—like *your* time is more important than me," Emma said.

The suspiciously adult language was not lost on Laura, who resented that Miss Cole would plant such an idea in Emma's head.

"Of course that's not true," Laura said. "I'm late because my subway was delayed."

"You always say that," Emma huffed.

"Well, today was especially bad. There was some sort of police investigation and they wouldn't let us off the train." Shifting her gaze up to Miss Cole, Laura mouthed the word: *casualty*.

Grinning her customary frigid grin, Miss Cole responded, "These things happen."

Laura was confused. *These things happen* was something you said to pardon someone who'd committed a minor transgression—not to the shaken bystander of a tragic accident. In case Miss Cole had failed to register it, Laura leaned over and whispered in her ear, "My subway ran someone over."

"Mom." Emma tugged Laura's coat. "Can we go?"

As they waited to cross Lexington at Ninety-sixth Street, Laura noticed a crowd of people loitering outside the entrance to the subway. Several police cars and an ambulance idled by the curb. Their timing couldn't have been worse. The light turned, and just as they reached the other side, the team of paramedics Laura had seen going down the subway steps came back up.

In her six years of living in New York City, Emma had seen a number of people on stretchers being loaded into ambulances; she was curious why this one was zipped up in a black bag.

"How can the person breathe?" she wanted to know.

"He *dead*," one of the corner boys answered.

"Hit by a train," another added, smacking his fist into his palm.

"In real life did that happen?" Emma asked as they stepped into the building. "A man got hit by a train and died in real life?"

"Of course not," Laura said. "I'm sure he's fine."

When the elevator reached their floor, it always overshot its destination by a small margin, and as it reversed direction there was a brief moment when the body recalibrated its momentum, creating a feeling of low-gravity weightlessness similar to being in a car on the crest of a hill, or a roller coaster. Emma, who usually attempted to prolong the sensation by jumping up as it happened, did not do so today.

By dinnertime she was herself again. As she squeezed the ketchup bottle, it made a wheezing, spluttery sound, and she giggled.

"Mom," she said. "Listen." She repeated the sound several times for Laura's benefit, laughing with each stertorous squeeze. "What does that sound like?"

"Very amusing," Laura said.

"But what does it *sound* like?"

"Like passing gas."

"*Passing gas*," Emma squealed, seeming to find these words even funnier than the corresponding sound effect. "It's called a *fart*, Mom."

Emma revisited the subject of mortality as Laura tucked her into bed that night.

"Does it happen to everyone?" she asked. "Every person in the whole wide world?"

Laura nodded. "Eventually."

"The good news is we all get to be together again in heaven," Emma said as Laura snapped off the light.

"Some people believe that," Laura said in a neutral tone.

"ARE THERE SOME PEOPLE WHO never die?" Emma asked Dr. Brown at her next appointment. "Like kings and queens?"

Dr. Brown pursed his lips and shook his head. "Even kings and queens die," he told Emma, resting a hand on her bare knee. "Part of life is that one day it's over. Everyone and everything that is ever alive, one day dies. Trees, plants, flowers, birds, bugs, dogs, people, butterflies—we all die. It's what makes our time together so meaningful, knowing that each moment we're alive is so precious."

Laura tried to make eye contact with him to communicate her gratitude for his sensible yet gentle response, but Dr. Brown's gaze remained fixed on Emma as she grappled with this information. His furrowed brow and periodic blinks conveyed something. Laura wasn't sure what, but it struck her as something important; something so fundamental there wasn't a word for it—something that she hadn't been offered as a child, and was hence unequipped to provide herself.

AS SOON AS LAURA HUNG up the phone, a crisis of confidence set in. Was it crossing professional boundaries for a pediatrician to socialize with the parent of a patient? Yes, Laura decided, but she had initiated it and he'd been too polite to decline and now it was too late: Dr. Brown was coming for dinner next Wednesday and there was no uninviting him.

She tried to get used to the idea of it. Visualizing the evening from Dr. Brown's perspective, it pleased her to imagine his surprise walking down their block, taking note of the grungy store on the corner, the row of abandoned tenements across the street, the wall with the graffiti, and then stepping into their building to be greeted by Frank with his cats and cigarettes. Their humble circumstances would impress and move him; they weren't at all like his other patients.

She would need to make a visit to the liquor store, but what should she get? Most men she knew drank whiskey, but that didn't seem like Dr. Brown's kind of thing. A bottle of wine seemed appropriate, though she'd have to ask him to open it. But what if he was a recovering alcoholic?

Laura took out *The Moosewood Cookbook* and *The Enchanted Broccoli Forest*. She was not a confident cook, but the books' slapdash aesthetic and casually chatty tone—*sprinkle hither and thither . . . taste to see if it wants more salt . . . bring the whole pan to the table so your eating partner(s) can see how attractive the dish looks*—had inspired her to believe it wasn't too late to become one; that it was simply a matter of allowing her culinary intuition to take over.

After giving it more thought, Laura decided it was safer to stick with her usual dinner party menu of chicken, wild rice, and peas, followed by a simple green leaf salad. Or perhaps the salad should come first; Laura had grown up eating salads after the main meal, but some people found this strange and confusing.

Laura planned to give Emma an early bath so she'd be all ready for bed when Dr. Brown rang the doorbell. She'd let Emma open the door, say hello to Dr. Brown, and then Laura would escort her to the TV room, where the VCR would be set up with *The Sound of Music*. Though Emma would likely fall asleep before the movie ended, Laura also prepared herself for the possibility of an interruption. Emma loved dressing up and making theatrical entrances. In Laura's experience, dinner guests always found this amusing. Would Dr. Brown? Yes, of course he would; Dr. Brown was very fond of Emma.

The week passed, and Laura got more and more used to the idea of Dr. Brown coming for dinner and was even excited about it. The morning of the dinner date she took the elevator down with Emma and read Frank's handwritten sign that had been Scotch-taped to the wall the last few days: *NO WATER WENDSDAY NOON–8 P.M.*

Only now did she put two and two together. It was too late to cancel. There was only one option: the dinner would have to happen at her parents' house.

DR. BROWN ARRIVED AT 136 with a flower in his hand—a single long-stemmed red rose. Laura reached out to take it, and he started to give it to her, but just before it reached her fingers, he pulled it back and said, "Is she still up?" She felt like a fool thinking it was for her, but also relieved, as receiving flowers from men had always embarrassed her.

"Douglas," her father said, offering him his hand.

"Bibs," her mother said.

"Bibs," Dr. Brown repeated. "Short for Barbara?"

"Vivien," she corrected.

"It's *Vivs*?" Dr. Brown clarified as Laura led him upstairs to say hi to Emma, who was watching TV in the library.

"*Bibs*," Laura's mother boomed from below. "Two B's, as in *bosoms*."

Emma was sitting mesmerized in front of *The Sound of Music*.

"Dr. Brown is here," Laura said as she leaned down to put the VCR on pause.

"Hello, Emma." Dr. Brown stooped down to her. "This is for you."

He handed her the rose. Emma examined it while rolling its stem between her fingers.

"What do you say?" Laura prompted.

"Thank you kindly," Emma said in her theatrical voice.

Dr. Brown laughed. "You're most welcome," he said.

"Thank you *kindly*," Laura repeated as they walked back downstairs. "I'm not sure where she picked that up."

"So," Bibs said when they were all seated for dinner. "You must love children."

Dr. Brown smiled and looked like he was about to reply when she continued.

"When Laura was little, she used to say the most peculiar things. One morning she said, 'Mummy, you're going to have to divorce Daddy, because when I grow up *I'm* going to marry him.'"

"No, I didn't." Laura blushed. She did not remember this, and found it hard to believe.

"Oh, you *did*," Bibs said with a wild grin. "And another time you were watching Nicholas have a bath and you said, 'I have one, too, and it's even better because it's hidden and no one can cut it off—'"

Douglas interrupted by asking Dr. Brown where he had grown up, but it was too late. The dinner was ruined for Laura.

"Ohio," Dr. Brown said, his face red with amusement. At least he found her mother entertaining. Laura couldn't believe she'd thought this would be a better idea than canceling.

"Cleveland!" Bibs said excitedly. "Did you know the Davenports?"

"No," he said, shaking his head and smiling.

"The Davenports are from St. Louis," Douglas said.

"You're wrong, wrong, *wrong*, they're from Cleveland!"

"And what did your father do?" Douglas asked.

"My father wasn't in the picture," Dr. Brown said. "My mother was a teacher. We lived in a small town, a few hours from Cleveland."

"That's fascinating!" Bibs said, slapping the table in excitement. "Don't you think so, Douglas?"

Her husband nodded.

"To grow up the child of a single mother in rural America!" Bibs slapped the table again.

"Do you have any brothers or sisters?" Laura asked.

"A twin sister," Dr. Brown answered. "Tina."

The subject of Emma's infancy came up. After talking about how big she was, Dr. Brown asked if Laura, too, was a large baby at birth.

"Oh, no, no." Bibs shook her head. "She was a beautiful, delicate little thing."

"Premature," Douglas added.

"I *was?*" Laura asked. She'd never heard this before, but it would explain why she was so much shorter than all the women in her family.

"She was *not* premature," Bibs countered. "She was perfectly healthy, just *small.*"

"How small was I?" Laura asked.

"Small enough that they kept you in the hospital for a bit," Douglas said.

"When she finally came home," Bibs addressed Dr. Brown, "she was so tiny, I thought she might break. I was too scared to hold her, but the baby nurse said I had to. She said it was important. So every morning after breakfast, I'd sit on the floor and she'd bring the baby downstairs and put her in my arms for fifteen minutes." Bibs mimicked rocking a baby.

"Marge?" Laura asked.

"No, this was your baby nurse." Bibs's eyes narrowed in concentration. She snapped her fingers. "What *was* her name?"

"Something Polish," Douglas responded with a shrug.

"Poor thing never had any children of her own and she was very possessive of you," Bibs continued. "It was unhealthy. The two of you became so attached, you started screaming every time I held you, so we had to let her go. Wasn't *that* the ordeal." She looked at Douglas.

"It was an unhealthy bond," he agreed, taking a sip of scotch.

THE PREEMPTIVE FANFARE BEGAN EARLIER each year. For weeks it seemed like anything they did and everywhere they went, they were accosted with reminders: *Father's Day Sale! Happy Father's Day! Looking for a gift for Dad?*

Now the actual day was upon them. Laura and Emma arrived at the park to find the group huddled next to a lamppost. It took Laura a moment to register the conflict: some men of Latino descent were playing soccer in the spot where the T-ball game was supposed to be. Everyone was looking at Trip, the class father, who'd coordinated the event. Trip stood there chewing the inside of his lip, unsure of how to proceed. Seeing her husband wasn't going to rise to the occasion, Margaret, who had no qualms handling these things, intervened.

"If you wouldn't mind taking your game somewhere else," she told the soccer players, "we've scheduled a father–daughter T-ball game."

The men looked confused.

"Anyone know Spanish?" Margaret called back to their group. When no one stepped forward, she tried again.

"*Our* turn," Margaret barked with authority, pointing to the field. "So sorry, but *no juego* here!

"*Mucho gracias!*" she bellowed as they packed up their things.

Nicholas was ten, fifteen, then twenty minutes late.

"I'm sorry," Laura told the group, holding a hand over her eyes as she scanned the premises. "Maybe I should take his place on the team?"

Trip looked down at her feet—she was wearing espadrilles. "Let's just start without him."

Nicholas finally appeared after the first batter, casually strolling through the Ninety-seventh Street entrance.

"Nicholas!" Laura shouted as he sauntered past them. "Over here!

"Get out there!" she directed him, pointing to the field. "They already started."

"Go, Charlotte!" Margaret yelled when it was her daughter's turn at bat. "Knock it out of the park!"

Charlotte made contact on the first swing. The ball soared up and over to where Emma stood staring at the ground looking for four-leaf clovers.

"Emma!" everyone screamed.

Laura winced as the ball came down—had Emma been a few yards to the right, it would've hit her in the head.

It took Emma a moment to snap out of her dreamy stupor and notice the ball. And then another to realize she was supposed to get it. After placing the ball in her mitt, she reached behind to pick a wedgie. Then she took the ball back out of the mitt and threw it with such exertion that she lost her balance and fell forward on her knees.

"Home run!" Margaret whooped as Charlotte rounded the bases.

All too soon came the moment Laura had been dreading: Emma's turn up at bat. Emma swung and missed, swung and missed, swung and missed.

"Three strikes means you're out!" someone hollered as Emma positioned herself for a fourth attempt.

"Is that the case with T-ball?" Laura spoke up. "Only three tries?"

Everyone looked at Trip, the class father, who once again appeared flustered by his authority.

"Laura's right," Margaret announced. "In T-ball, each child gets as many turns as it takes to hit the ball."

When Emma finally made contact with the ball, the ripple of excitement was followed by a silence, which Laura realized she was expected to fill.

"Yay, Emma!" she called out. "Good job hitting the ball!

"Don't forget to run!" she added a moment later as Emma stood by home plate wearing a sour expression and staring at her thumb. "Quick, darling! Run to first base!"

As Emma continued to stand there, others joined in. "Run! Run! Run!" they yelled.

Now Emma looked irritated. "When I hit the ball, the ball hit my thumb!" she shouted back.

There were no visible indications of a thumb injury, but Emma insisted the pain was too much to continue playing and joined Laura on the island of blankets with the other mothers.

"You were supposed to cheer for me," Emma said bitterly, taking a seat on Laura's lap.

"I *was* cheering," Laura whispered back. "Did you not hear me? I was saying, *Yay, Emma, good job, run!*"

"You weren't cheering, Mom." Emma's body stiffened. "You were talking to me in a *normal voice*."

"I agree, Emma," Margaret chimed in from a few feet away. "Your mom could work on her projection. Do you know about projecting?"

Emma shook her head glumly.

"Projection is . . ." Margaret got on her knees to demonstrate. "It's when you take a deep breath and really belt out your words, like you're shouting from the rooftops, to make sure everyone CAN HEAR YOU!"

Margaret had a shrill voice to begin with; Laura winced, Emma smiled with amusement.

The inning ended but Emma refused to join her teammates in the field.

"My thumb," she whimpered. "It really hurts."

Nicholas came over, tapped Laura on the shoulder, and mouthed, "If she's out for the game, should I stay?"

"I think it's over soon," Laura whispered. "Do you need to be somewhere?"

"It's a difficult day for Stephanie," he whispered back. "Having lost her father . . ."

Laura was confused. As far as she knew, Stephanie's father was very much alive and well.

"Mike?"

Nicholas shook his head sadly. "Mike's just her stepfather. Her *real* dad died when she was just a baby."

Laura knew she should drop the matter, but she couldn't help herself. "How old was Stephanie when Mike arrived on the scene?"

"A kid," was Nicholas's answer.

"What age?"

"Two."

So Stephanie's biological father was dead, but she wasn't exactly fatherless. For all intents and purposes, Mike was her father. She even called him "Dad." To make a fuss about Father's Day seemed a little emotionally immature.

"You should leave," Laura told Nicholas. "Go be with her."

"I'll stay a little longer."

"No, really, it's okay. Leave. I insist."

"I'll stay for another inning," he said with conviction.

The inning ended, but Nicholas did not leave. He stayed for the remainder of the game, and then stuck around after, to participate in the father–daughter group photo.

*   *   *

SUMMER AGAIN.

Their first morning in Ashaunt, Emma disappeared after breakfast, declaring beforehand that she was allowed to explore on her own now that she was six. Laura consented so long as she didn't set foot in the ocean.

An hour passed and Laura was still reading the paper when she came back in.

"Mom, when you're done with the newspaper, you better come outside. There's a mystery I have to show you."

"A *mys*tery," Laura repeated with halfhearted inflection.

"Not the good kind," Emma said cryptically.

Laura followed Emma down a path that led to a little inlet by the shore.

"You're not gonna believe it," Emma said as they arrived at the end of the path. Hands on hips, she shook her head and surveyed the premises. It took Laura a moment to realize what she was supposed to be reacting to: the absence of a small body of water that used to be there.

"Your pond," Laura said. "Emma's Pond is gone."

"Is it because of acid rain?" Emma wanted to know.

"No, it's a natural thing," Laura reassured her. "Some years it's here, some years it isn't."

"But what happened to it?"

"The shoreline shifted and now it's an inlet."

"What's an inlet?" Emma asked.

"It's what it is now. A private spot where you can go to read a book or watch the sunset. I know you're sad about the pond, but to tell you the truth, I think this is even better—Emma's Inlet, you can call it."

"But why did it happen?" Emma looked skeptical, mildly suspicious.

"The word for it is *erosion*," Laura explained as they walked back to the house. "That means very small changes over time. It has to do with the tides and currents. Storms and winds and waves. You'll learn about it in science class." But Emma wasn't listening.

"Emma's Inlet," she was saying. "Emma's Inlet."

EMMA AND CHARLOTTE HAD BEEN playmates since they were little, and as first graders at Winthrop they announced they were best friends.

The elevation of their self-declared friendship status was something in which Emma took great pride: "Teachers are always trying to break us apart, other girls are always trying to join in, but it doesn't work—we're best friends."

The friendship had its volatile moments. There were fights, which led to accusations, which became character-assassination campaigns in which their classmates took sides. Though the two girls were thrilled to see each other upon arriving at school each morning, it was not uncommon that Laura and Margaret would arrive at pickup to find the union bitterly dissolved.

Laura and Margaret refused to get involved, but this didn't stop the girls from trying to solicit their support.

"I *wish* Charlotte would stop lying and bragging," Emma said when Laura picked her up from school one day. A few feet away, Charlotte greeted Margaret: "The thing about *Emma* is that she has to be the center of everything and she's a liar!"

As the girls carried on the mutual recriminations, their classmates rallied around them and chimed in, echoing the sentiments of whichever girl they'd decided to ally themselves with.

It was painfully obvious to Laura that these girls wanted to be Emma and Charlotte's friends, but that the duo had no interest in them except as pawns in situations like this. Tomorrow morning Emma and Charlotte would be exclusive again, the classmates cast aside until the next conflict arose.

How Emma and Charlotte had come to occupy the top rung on the social ladder of their first-grade class was a mystery to Laura. Was it a fluke, or an indication of some kind of innate social fitness that would ultimately prove to be a Darwinian asset? In either case, Laura was not proud. Far from it. She didn't like how Emma and Charlotte conducted themselves; it wasn't a good way to treat people or operate in the world.

That evening she called Margaret to discuss the matter. Growing up, the two of them had not been part of the in-crowd, and she was sure Margaret would share her concerns.

She did not. "Girls will be girls. You can't play God in these situations."

The next morning—as was always the case—all ill feelings were forgotten when the girls encountered each other outside the entrance to school.

"Charlotte!"

"Emma!"

An urgent, hysterical embrace morphed into a do-si-do. Giddy laughter ensued.

Laura and Margaret stood off to the side, watching the dramatic reunion.

"It's like they hadn't expected to see each other," Laura remarked with amusement. "As though this were some kind of miraculous coincidence."

Margaret started to say something in response to this, then fell silent. Her chin dimpled and rose. A single tear fell down her left cheek.

"Mags," Laura said, resting a hand on her arm. "Is something wrong?"

Margaret shook her head and smiled. "I'm fine." She wiped her eyes and blinked. Composed, she waved goodbye to Charlotte and headed down the block.

Laura walked after her. "Please tell me what's upsetting you," she said when they'd turned the corner. "You know you can tell me anything."

"What you said about the girls, how it's like they hadn't expected to see each other, as though it were a coincidence . . ." Margaret's eyes welled up with fresh tears. She pulled a Kleenex from her purse. "It reminded me of this feeling I get when I go check on Charlotte in the middle of the night. I sit on the edge of her bed, watching her sleeping, just thinking how random it is, of all the babies up for adoption in America . . . that I got *her*."

"And she got you," Laura added.

"To think," Margaret continued, "we could have been strangers living in the same city. Even if Staten Island is a world apart."

Laura tried to imagine this other version of Charlotte. There were certain fundamental characteristics one was born with, Charlotte would still be Charlotte, but she would dress and speak differently. Her favorite food wouldn't be smoked salmon. She would grow up with different expectations of life.

But here she was now, perfectly at home. An Upper East Sider to the bone.

EMMA'S CLASS WAS INSTRUCTED TO bring a paper bag lunch to school that day, as they would be going on a field trip over the lunch hour. Their destination was a short walk down Fifth Avenue: St. Christopher's School for Boys. After filing into the lobby, Miss Russell led the girls down a flight of stairs and into a gymnasium. Dressed in khakis, blazers, and ties, the boys stood in a single-file line on the other side of the room.

Normally, when they spotted each other in the park or crossed paths on the street, there were whispers and snickers and maybe a taunt. Today was a new and different kind of occasion, and the dread and embarrassment it generated was palpable. As the two groups of first-graders shuffled across the rubber floor to meet in the middle, the buzz of the fluorescent lights grew louder.

Each Winthrop girl was to be paired with a St. Christopher's boy. Students were called up one at a time, and after being assigned to each other, they had to shake hands and introduce themselves. Miss Russell and the boys' teacher demonstrated how this was done.

Emma's lunch date introduced himself as Teddy. He came up to her chin.

"Where do you wanna sit?" Teddy asked, eyes darting around the room.

"You can pick," Emma told him.

After a moment of puffing his cheeks out and tapping a finger on his upper lip in theatrical deliberation, Teddy swaggered off. Emma followed as he lapped the room, his hair swinging behind him like a bowl that was about to fall off his head. Eventually everyone was sitting but them.

"Teddy!" his teacher called as he continued to walk around the room. "Is there a problem?"

"Looking for a place to sit," he shouted.

"What's wrong with where you are?"

Teddy shrugged and plopped on the floor. As Emma took a seat across from him, he made a face and covered his eyes.

"Your underpants are showing," he said.

"That's *not* my underwear," Emma clarified. "That's my *bloomers*—it's part of our uniform." She wanted to smooth the skirt of her tunic down so that it covered her crotch, but feared doing so might counter the impression of what she'd just told him.

"What the *heck*." Teddy's shoulders drooped in disappointment as he pulled a sandwich out of his bag. "She *knows* I hate brown bread."

Miss Russell and the other teacher circulated around the gym. Sensing his teacher's proximity, Teddy reached into the pocket of his blazer and removed a flash card, which he proceeded to read from as he chewed: "If you could be an animal, any animal, what kind of animal would you be?"

"A person," Emma said, and before Teddy could reject this answer she added, "A person *is* an animal."

Teddy didn't say anything, but his face turned pink and he started blinking a lot. When this continued, Emma got nervous and raised her hand to summon a teacher's attention.

"I think he's choking," she told Miss Russell.

Teddy shook his head no and held up a finger.

"A little bit of spit went down the wrong pipe," he explained in a slow, whispery gasp, wiping away tears.

Having fully recovered, Teddy answered his own question. "I'd be a *Vampyroteuthis infernalis*. You probably don't even know what that is. It's a vampire squid. It can make itself invisible. It can turn its body into a light that confuses its enemy."

Done with their sandwiches, it was time to exchange desserts. Emma pushed a Saran-wrapped brownie across the floor toward Teddy, who tossed a small red box in her direction. It landed near her foot with a rattle. On the front of the box was a drawing of a woman in a bonnet holding a basketful of grapes. Emma took pride in being a child who would try anything and eat everything, but there was one exception: raisins, which had the leathery skin of a cockroach and were also the same color. As she pondered her predicament, there was a piercing scream at the other end of the gym. Charlotte lay on her back, kicking her legs up in the air like she was riding an upside-down bicycle.

"Yes! Yes! Oh, my God, *yeeeeessss!*"

As the screaming and scissor kicking continued, Miss Russell walked very fast in her direction. Before she could get to her, Charlotte popped back up into sitting position and thrust her hand in the air to show everyone the reason for her excitement: sour straws that her lunch date had brought. Charlotte loved sour straws; they all did. Standing up to get a better look over the other children who were now standing, too, Emma saw that it was the big kind of bag—the one that cost two dollars at Million Dollar Deli.

The disparity of their desserts was beyond anything Emma could have imagined. Blinking back tears, she put a raisin in her mouth, chewed, and swallowed—repeating the process until the gross, sticky box was empty, her disgust rendered bearable by the feeling that struck in situations of unfairness: a feeling that her life was a movie and the audience was God, and a faith in knowing her grace and fortitude in this moment would not go unnoticed.

AT WINTHROP, PARENTS—SPECIFICALLY MOTHERS—WERE expected to volunteer at various school functions, something that never would have happened during Laura's era. She signed up for the book fair. The day of the event Emma woke up with a fever, and Laura wondered if this meant she could get out of it. As a single parent it seemed like a valid excuse—but would it mean she'd be reassigned to the Strawberry Shortcake Festival, in which volunteers were expected to wear festive hats and aprons? It wasn't worth the risk. She bundled Emma up and delivered her to 136 so Sandra could watch her and then headed back uptown to report for her shift.

Stepping into the gymnasium, Laura was relieved the event fell on a day Emma was absent. She was appalled to discover that, in addition to books, the fair included tables full of the kind of junk that was marketed to young children: Disney coloring books, Care Bear placemats, stickers featuring meaninglessly extravagant positive affirmations: SPECIAL KID, A NUMBER ONE, THE SKY IS THE LIMIT, YOU ARE THE BEST. Most upsetting were the dolls and stuffed animals whose cartoonish likenesses to various beloved characters from children's literature— Curious George, Winnie-the-Pooh, dear old Eloise—struck Laura as sacrilegious.

She had promised to buy Emma a new book at the fair, but she couldn't bring herself to support this kind of shameless marketing event. On her way to 136 to retrieve Emma, she stopped at the Corner Bookstore, where she'd been a loyal customer for years and was friendly with the staff. As Laura opened the front door, she looked forward to telling whoever was on duty about the table full of junk at the book fair (they would surely share her opinion), but the man who greeted her wasn't a face she knew.

"Welcome," he said from behind the counter. "Can I help you find something?"

"Oh, no," Laura told him. "I know where everything is, I've been coming here for years."

The attendant clearly hadn't been trained in the ways of the Corner Bookstore, which was to leave customers alone.

"Are you looking for anything particular today?" he asked, hovering by Laura in the kids' section.

"Just a book for my six-year-old."

"These are very popular." He gestured to a display table featuring a collection of books about professionally talented children, with real photographs: *A Very Young Rider*, *A Very Young Dancer*, *A Very Young Gymnast*, *A Very Young Circus Flyer*, and *A Very Young Actress*.

After picking one of the books up, Laura promptly put it back down. Emma needed no help when it came to nursing grandiose visions of her future, which already included the Olympics and *The Nutcracker*.

Laura continued to survey her options, but the man's solicitous, shadowy presence made it impossible for her to concentrate on finding something for Emma. Eventually she gave up and bought *The Little House*. They already owned a copy, but she would give it to Stephanie, who'd just announced she was pregnant.

*   *   *

LAURA HADN'T KNOWN HER GREAT-UNCLE Bert in a personal way. His service was dry and impersonal, and when she'd asked her parents about him as they drove to the cemetery, Bibs had summed him up as "a jerk and an anti-Semite," and Douglas had affirmed this with his silence.

The cemetery was adjacent to a golf course in the Connecticut suburb where Bert had moved with his third and final wife, who'd ended up leaving him for a local politician.

About two dozen relatives had now been gathered for nearly forty minutes around the plot of earth where Bert was to be buried. It was only one o'clock, but the late October light cast a brassy glaze over everything, and this made it seem more like three or four. They were cold and hungry, restless and bored, but there was no going anywhere until the hearse arrived. That it was late made no sense—it had been the first vehicle to pull out of the church parking lot, then raced ahead to make a yellow light, losing the rest of the procession. Where it was now was anyone's guess.

Emma kept herself entertained by crawling around digging in the dirt. Her dress would have permanent grass stains, but that was a small price to pay for the miracle of her not complaining or creating a scene.

When a full hour had passed Douglas tapped Laura on the shoulder. "We're going to quietly take off," he whispered. "Your mother is feeling faint with hunger and fatigue."

"I think that would be a little selfish of us," Laura whispered back, "considering no one wants to be here."

Douglas didn't dispute this, but discreetly gestured toward Bibs, who was walking with strident conviction toward the car.

"I'll try to reason with her," Laura said.

By the time she caught up to her mother, Bibs was opening the passenger-side door.

"We're leaving," she said, climbing in. "That's that, end of story, and don't try to talk him out of it."

"I think it's a little rude for the four of us to bow out now," Laura said, holding the door ajar.

Bibs rubbed her pearls between her fingers. "That's why we decided you and Emma will stay on," she said, putting on her dark glasses. "You can take the train home."

"I see," Laura said.

"Dickie will drop you off at the station," Douglas said as he approached. "The train comes twenty-four minutes after the hour, every hour. Let me give you some cash for the tickets."

"I have cash," Laura said meekly as Douglas pulled out his wallet. She did, enough for two train tickets, though not enough—she realized—to stop for dinner at Jackson Hole on the way home, as she'd promised Emma as part of a deal they'd struck the night before in exchange for her coming to Connecticut.

Douglas held out a hundred-dollar bill. When Laura looked reluctant to take it, he licked his finger and procured another.

"Oh, don't be such a Puritan," Bibs said when Laura shook her head and slid her hands into her pockets.

"I insist you take this," Douglas said, looking genuinely cross when Laura continued to hold her ground.

"*Darling.*" Bibs tried softening her tone. "It's not fair to make us abandon you up here with no money."

Laura's instinct to defuse, appease, indulge, and absolve did not kick in. Her resolve only hardened. To refuse the money was to withhold what her parents expected in exchange—something Laura so readily and routinely provided that she was unaware it had any currency. But in this moment it felt like the most valuable thing she had. The only thing she had.

"I have plenty of cash to get us home," Laura told her parents. "You should get going. Don't worry about us. We'll be fine."

She turned around and strolled back to resume her spot in the faithful vigil around the gaping hole.

"Mom?" Emma shuffled over on her knees, cupping something in her hands. "Do you have a jar?"

"A jar," Laura repeated. "Why yes, I have lots of jars in my pocket. What size would you like?"

"Doesn't matter," Emma said. "Long as it has a lid."

"I was kidding," Laura told Emma as she waited expectantly. "What do you think I am, a kitchen cupboard?"

Laura was rarely sarcastic with Emma and immediately felt guilty. But Emma looked more concerned than hurt. "What am I supposed to do with these worms?" she said with a labored sigh.

At long last the hearse was spotted in the distance. The driveway was long and winding, and as the vehicle snaked its way toward them, Emma tugged Laura's sleeve and whispered, "Guess what their names are?"

Laura drew a finger to her lips. *You can tell me later*, she mouthed.

"Pee and poo!" Emma whispered.

Laura ignored her.

"Mom, did you hear me?" Emma asked, a little more loudly. "I said their names are *pee* and *poo*."

Laura leaned down. "That's *very* amusing," she whispered in Emma's ear. "But we need to be *quiet* now like you were in church."

Emma's face brightened. *"Mom*, you think it's inappropriate, but it's *P* as in *the letter P*, and *Pooh* as in *Winnie-the-Pooh!"* She giggled, pleased with her cleverness.

The hearse parked and the casket was brought out and gently lowered into the cavity of earth. To everyone's distress it would not go down; the hole wasn't big enough. The casket was placed on the grass and there was a hushed conference among the pallbearers, who were joined by a graveyard employee, who pulled out his walkie-talkie. Moments later a bulldozer appeared at the top of the hill and barreled down at a speed Laura didn't know bulldozers were capable of (certainly not one that was legal), weaving between the stones and monuments with the implausible grace of a figure skater.

The group took a wary step back as the bulldozer advanced in their direction. It stopped with a violent jerk and its claw snapped into action, frantically digging to make the hole bigger and scattering dirt in the process. After a few minutes the bulldozer backed up and the casket was lowered once again. There was a collective sigh of relief as it went in, followed by a sucking in of breath. The box was in but it was not going down—not all the way. The pallbearers attempted to lift it back up so that the bulldozer could expand the hole more, but it was now too tightly lodged in the hole.

"It's a cork-in-the-bottle situation," someone muttered. Ceremonious pretense suspended while they awaited resolution of the logistical dilemma, the funeral-goers began chatting.

The driver of the bulldozer stepped out, conferred with the pallbearers, and made an authoritative hand gesture signaling everyone should take a step back. The group fell silent and did as instructed, and the bulldozer roared back to life. This time the driver angled the claw so that it was like the back of a hand, palm side up, and made it come down upon the casket. At first gingerly, and then not so gingerly, the claw pushed the casket down into the hole. It was not the visual one thought of in conjunction with the phrase *laid to rest*.

Tugging the hem of Laura's coat, Emma articulated what everyone was thinking. "He's gonna break it," she squealed. "*Mama*, he's gonna *break* it."

"No, he's not," Laura whispered, holding a finger over her mouth.

Miraculously, he didn't. When, at last, the coffin was in the ground, there was a tentative smattering of applause, followed by an even more inappropriate *hurray*, the echo of which rang louder in everyone's ears as it was immediately followed by chagrined silence.

Laura's thoughts drifted to a PBS special she'd once seen about how Eskimos handled the whole business of death. Rather than tending to the comfort of their dying elders, they put them on a chunk of ice and watched as they drifted out to sea.

Where and when had she seen this? She couldn't remember now. Perhaps it wasn't a documentary after all, but an article in *National Geographic* she'd conjured up in such vivid detail that she recalled it now as footage in a film. Or maybe it was a tall tale she'd heard as a child. Either way, it had made an impression on her. She'd thought it was the strangest thing.

But what about the scene that was unfolding right now? She was very much one of them, but this didn't stop Laura from recognizing that her people, they were weird.

*   *   *

LAURA'S MOTHER WANTED TO INVITE Dr. Brown to join them for Thanksgiving.

"Let me think about it," Laura said.

"I'm not asking for your permission," Bibs told her. "I'm asking for his phone number."

Laura sighed. "Dinner is one thing, a family holiday is another. I just don't know if it's appropriate."

"If you won't give me his number, the operator will," Bibs said and hung up.

Fifteen minutes later she called back. "Guess who's coming to Thanksgiving!" her triumphant voice chimed through the receiver. "He's very excited! He asked what he should bring and I told him nothing, and he said he didn't like the idea of me in the kitchen doing everything, and I said I didn't either—that's why we get it catered."

An hour later the phone rang again, and this time it was Dr. Brown.

"Your mother invited me to Thanksgiving," he said.

"I know. I'm sorry. She can be very persistent. I hope she didn't bully you into saying yes."

Dr. Brown laughed. "You're making it sound like she asked me to donate a kidney!"

"It's not too late to back out."

"*Laura*, will you relax? I wouldn't have said yes if I didn't want to."

Laura was silent. The way he'd said her name, the demand to relax, made her smile. He'd completely shed the veneer of their professional relationship. This had been happening in degrees for some time, but now it was really gone. He was very fond of her, and she of him, and here they were on the phone together talking about Thanksgiving. Catching a glimpse of herself in the mirror, Laura noticed she was blushing and twirling the phone cord in her finger, and she blushed even harder imagining him watching her do this right now.

"I want to come and I'm coming," Dr. Brown said. "My question for you is, do you think it would be okay if I brought my partner?"

"Dr. Wendell?" Laura was confused.

"No," Dr. Brown said. "Not that partner."

BIBS, WHO APPRECIATED ALL-MALE COMPANY, especially the tall and handsome kind, couldn't have looked more excited when Dr. Brown introduced her to Chris. Sherry was served, ginger ale for Emma, and they all took a seat in the living room. Douglas began to ask Chris about his work, but before their conversation could go anywhere, Bibs interrupted to ask the guests if they believed in ghosts. Neither had a chance to answer; Bibs launched into a story about a friend of hers whose first husband, long dead, had visited her in a dream to tell her the new husband was a philanderer, and the *very next day* the cleaning lady found a brassiere tucked beneath the cushions of his study—could they believe it? Wasn't that the most absolutely bizarre thing they'd ever heard? Chris made an effort to match Bibs's animated incredulity, indulging her with questions.

He was not what Laura had expected. His Hollywood good looks surprised her, as did the fact that he worked on Wall Street. She would have thought Dr. Brown would have chosen someone in a more ethical profession, someone more soft-spoken and bashfully reserved like himself. Emma, too, seemed taken aback by this man. Uncharacteristically quiet, she retreated to a corner of the room with her coloring book, periodically looking up to cast an appraising glance in his direction.

Soon it was time to eat and they filed into the dining room. As Sandra circulated the table with platters of food, Bibs regaled her guests with one colorful anecdote after the next, all grossly exaggerated for comic effect. Laura winced each time Chris's baritone laughter shook the room, wishing her father would speak up, as he sometimes did in these situations, warning guests that this was like putting a quarter in her, she'd keep going—they better have another fifteen minutes.

"I adore homosexuals and they adore me," Bibs said with a smug grin after the couple left.

"What's a homosexual?" Emma asked on their way home.

Laura considered her answer before deciding Emma was too young. "I don't know," she said. "Must be one of Bibs's made-up words."

THE FOLLOWING WEEK LAURA WAS on the phone with her mother when Bibs casually mentioned having made plans with Dr. Brown to go see a play that night. Laura was surprised her mother hadn't thought to include her.

"But, darling, you hate the theater. Last time I took you, you fell asleep."

"I was eight months pregnant," Laura reminded her.

"Well, I'm sorry, I only got three tickets. Next time I'll get four."

"Three tickets? But Daddy's the one who really hates the theater."

"Don't be a dummy." Her mother laughed. "Of course I'm not bringing that old philistine boor! The third ticket is for Bruno."

"*Bruno?* Who's Bruno?" Laura asked.

"Dr. Brown's lover."

"The term is partner, not lover. And that's not even his name—it's Chris."

"I know, but he's such a *Bruno*, isn't he?" Bibs said.

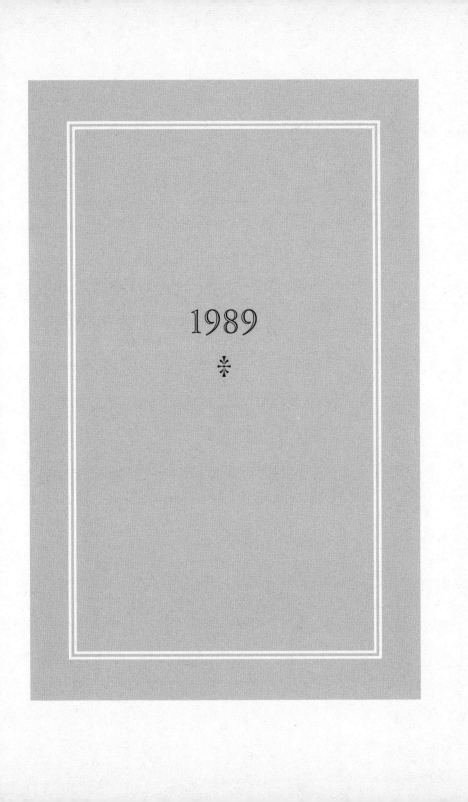

1989

❊

Laura wasn't able to take off work for Stephanie's baby shower, but she and Emma paid her a visit the following weekend to hand-deliver their present.

"Hopefully no one got this for you already," Laura said, presenting Stephanie with the book. "It's called *The Little House*. Have you heard of it?"

Stephanie shook her head and smiled.

"It's a classic, been around since my childhood," Laura said. "Do you remember Marge used to read it to us, Nicholas?"

Stephanie held the book up for him to see. Nicholas looked up, squinted, shook his head, and returned to his *Wall Street Journal*.

"Anyway," Laura continued, "it's about this little house in the country that gets sad when the beautiful meadows that surround it are gradually destroyed by developers who erect high-rises and turn the countryside into a city."

"Never too early for kids to learn about urban sprawl," Nicholas said dryly.

"Don't worry," Laura told Stephanie. "Eventually the house gets bought and the new owners have it lifted off its foundation and relocated to the country."

Stephanie nodded but looked puzzled.

"So the book has a happy ending," Laura clarified.

"Oh," Stephanie said. "Well, I see it won an award," she added, fingering a gold sticker on the cover.

* * *

IT WASN'T A CUSTOM IN their family to name sons after their fathers, but Stephanie was adamant, and in March she gave birth to Nicholas Jr.

Emma was so excited she convinced Laura to let her take the morning off from school so they could visit the baby in the hospital.

"I hope we aren't bothering you," Laura said, holding Emma's hand as they peered into Stephanie's room. "We'll only stay for a few minutes."

Infant asleep in her arms, Stephanie looked up, a dazed smile on her face. Emma tugged Laura forward to get a closer look.

"Baby Nicholas," Laura said, taking a seat in the chair beside Stephanie's bed.

"We can't tell who he looks like yet," Stephanie said, tucking a lock of hair behind her ear.

Stray wisps had come loose, and as these caught the light they formed an ethereal halo around her face, which Laura had never seen without makeup. She had the porcelain complexion of a redhead— though she was more strawberry blonde—and her cheeks bore a youthful dusting of freckles. Stephanie's eyelashes were also strawberry blond, Laura observed for the first time, as they were typically caked with mascara.

As sisters-in-law, it was inevitable they would get closer over the years. Laura looked forward to the day she could tell Stephanie what a mistake she'd been making, that to wear makeup was to mar her natural, delicate beauty and she looked a hundred times better without it. Then she would bring Stephanie to Sufrina to get her lashes done.

Stephanie asked if Laura wanted to hold the baby and Laura said she would, but not now, as he looked so peaceful and she didn't want to disturb him.

"Don't worry," Stephanie said, passing the swaddled bundle of him over.

It had been a while since she'd held an infant; Laura adjusted her position so that the baby's head rested in the crook of her arm. At one point his face scrunched up in an expression of discomfort, but this quickly passed, and once he'd settled back into a tranquil slumber, Laura's guilt and anxiety for having taken him away from his mother subsided. She allowed herself to enjoy the cozy tingling where the warmth of his little body rested against hers.

"Look at him," Laura said in a whisper.

Emma leaned over the arm of the chair, scrutinizing his face. "He looks Chinese," she remarked.

"Those lashes," Laura said, almost wistfully.

"He hardly has any hair," Emma observed.

"Actually, he has quite a bit of hair for a newborn," Laura said.

"As much as I did?"

"You had a little more," Laura conceded.

"How much more?"

Laura held up her free hand and created a modest space between pointer finger and thumb.

"That smell," Laura said, inhaling his scalp.

"I know." Stephanie smiled. "Isn't it the best?"

"There's nothing like it," Laura agreed.

Emma leaned in for a sniff. "Smells like yogurt," she said, plugging her nose.

The baby yawned, and Laura's heart did a little cartwheel. Her previous trips to the maternity ward to visit friends had not been like this; she'd had to pretend to have the reaction she was having right now.

"Yo-Yo Ma." Emma poked Laura's shoulder. "Would you please take me to school before I get in trouble for missing gymnastics?"

"Okay," Laura said. "But give me a few more minutes with this baby."

"What the heck is that for?" Emma asked, pointing to a medical contraption on the wall.

Laura looked up with a frown and shook her head; Stephanie put on a pair of tortoiseshell glasses and shrugged. Emma let out a dispirited sigh and wandered over to the window. Pressing her face against the glass she took a deep breath, wrote her initials in the cloud of condensation, and drew a heart around them.

On their way out they bumped into Nicholas, who'd been on a Zabar's run, and Laura felt moved to convey her feelings about his baby—how the affection she had felt was much deeper than anything she'd felt for her friends' infants, that it was particular to this one.

She'd expected his face to light up with paternal pride, but instead he looked mildly annoyed.

"Well, he's *not* a friend's baby," he said, pressing the elevator button. "He's your *nephew*."

Nicholas and Stephanie's apartment was only a few blocks from the Library, and recalling how isolating that first year of motherhood could be, Laura made a habit of dropping by when Stephanie was alone there during the day. With the hope of cultivating a more casual, more familial relationship with her sister-in-law, Laura wouldn't call beforehand; she'd just show up. Occasionally she brought food, but most of the time she arrived empty-handed. Due to the frequency of these impromptu visits, the doormen came to recognize Laura and would send her straight up without buzzing to let Stephanie know she had a guest.

Stephanie, however, clung to a certain sense of protocol and was often flustered when she opened the door, apologizing for her appearance, for not having anything for Laura to eat, for the state of the apartment.

Laura was never hungry and would insist that the apartment, and Stephanie, looked fine. In the beginning Stephanie appeared sweetly disheveled, and the apartment, once so immaculately kempt it felt sterile, now had an air of homey disarray. But as the weeks went by Laura began to notice things that left her troubled. Dirty dishes haphazardly perched in odd places, mounds of unfolded laundry tucked behind oversize couch cushions, a stack of starchy Christmas cocktail napkins on the back of the toilet in lieu of toilet paper. They'd received a lot of flowers after arriving home from the hospital, and as they began to expire they released a vaguely fecal odor.

More than anything, Laura wanted to go through the apartment and restore order, but she suspected that even offering to do so would stoke Stephanie's shame over the condition of things, and so she resisted the urge. The visits usually only lasted about fifteen minutes, and Laura did most of the talking.

One afternoon she was waiting in the checkout line of Associated Value when she noticed Princess Diana on the cover of a tabloid newspaper; the headline suggested the royal couple was headed for a divorce. She was shocked and wondered if Stephanie knew. It would be fertile conversational fodder and she studied the questions beneath the headline so that she could put them to Stephanie: *What would happen to Charles? Could he still be king? Would he ever marry again? What would Di do? Where would she live? Would she ever be allowed to see her kids?*

Later that evening, in the middle of putting Emma to bed, the phone rang; it was Nicholas calling to say Stephanie was feeling overwhelmed.

"Of course she is," Laura said, touched that he was confiding in her. She told Nicholas that she had a meeting scheduled the next morning and an appointment in the afternoon but she would be more than happy to cancel one or both of them to come over and help out. She could bring groceries, run errands, watch the baby so Stephanie could go out and get a haircut—whatever she could do to make life easier for Stephanie.

Nicholas told her not to cancel the appointments, that it would be better, actually, if she didn't come by tomorrow, or quite so often, as Stephanie found it difficult to entertain while taking care of a newborn—especially when guests dropped by announced.

"I see," Laura said after a pause.

"I know you're just trying to help," he said. "I hope this doesn't hurt your feelings."

"Not at all," Laura told her brother.

She knew better than to allow it to upset her. The problem was Stephanie's: she needed to let down her guard—to figure out how to relax and be comfortable around people. It would be childish for Laura to take it personally.

* * *

DEPRESSION WAS AN ILLNESS, AND Laura felt for anyone who suffered from it, but there was something about the modifier, *postpartum*, that she wrestled with. The concept seemed vaguely Victorian, and she wondered about its scientific credibility. In any case, Laura felt terrible for Stephanie, but also vindicated. This explained Stephanie's reaction to her visits. There was no need to feel foolish or guilty about having come over so often.

It was Bibs who called to let Laura know Stephanie had been admitted to the hospital. Laura didn't want to bother Nicholas, so she called 136 for updates.

Laura had never heard of such a thing as a private psychiatric facility that had a specific program catering to mothers suffering from "PPD," but apparently one existed, in northern Westchester, and after a few nights at Columbia Presbyterian, Stephanie went there.

"It's the best," Bibs said, the way she spoke about restaurants and hotels. They were completely booked, but Bibs's longtime therapist, Dr. Clarke, had made some calls and gotten Stephanie a room.

Every Friday after work, Nicholas, who'd never learned to drive, took the train up to visit his wife and child. This went on for five weeks, and Laura was starting to worry. Finally Bibs called to say that Stephanie was doing much better and scheduled to be discharged that coming Friday. Laura dialed Nicholas at the office and offered to drive him up to get her so that they wouldn't have to take the train back.

IN KEEPING WITH THE TREND of the last decade, it had been a prematurely warm spring. It was not yet June and the punitive humidity of summer was already upon them. The newspaper predicted today's high would be ninety-four degrees—a new record for this date. By nine a.m. a fuzzy yellow haze had already descended upon the city, obscuring the horizon and enshrouding the tops of skyscrapers like tufts of steel wool. Stepping outside felt like entering the tropical bird section of the zoo. Rarely a day went by where Laura didn't think about the greenhouse effect, and on days like this, rarely an hour.

The parking garage on One-hundred-and-third Street was only a few minutes from Laura's apartment, but walking there in the heat, with Nicholas, it felt much longer. He didn't say anything, but she could sense his disapproval that she would keep her car in Harlem. People didn't believe Laura when she told them how little she spent on parking: one hundred dollars a month. She wanted to share this figure with Nicholas, but being ignorant of the cost of keeping a car in the city, he wouldn't be impressed.

As they waited to cross One-hundred-and-first, something transpired that made Laura question whether the saved money was worth it. For the last block or so she'd been aware of the encroaching presence of what sounded like a group of teenage boys behind them. Apart from the occasional profanity, their rowdy, slangy banter was beyond Laura's comprehension, though it put her on edge. As she and Nicholas waited for the light to turn, the group caught up to them, and Laura felt a hand on her bottom. The thin cotton fabric of her skirt was a flimsy barrier between the sweaty compress of the groper's palm and her own skin, which hadn't completely dried after getting out of the bath that morning.

Nicholas was either oblivious or shared Laura's instinct that the best thing to do was avoid creating a scene. Too scared to turn and see who was touching her, Laura stood perfectly still and pretended nothing was happening. When the light turned and the hand let go, a trio of adolescent boys on bicycles rolled off the curb. They couldn't have been more than twelve or thirteen years old. Their bikes were much too small for them. Laura felt a mix of fury and sorrow as she watched them pedal on, knees bent out at awkward angles.

Turning the car's AC on was like opening the door of an oven. "It takes a few minutes for it to get cool," Laura explained, adjusting the vents to direct the air away from them. "While we wait for that to happen, we can drive with the windows down."

"AC *and* open windows," Nicholas said with phony excitement. "How *frivolous*."

"I admire people who never learned how to drive," she told him. "Given the impact of automobiles on the planet, it must feel nice to know that you're not contributing to that problem."

It made her feel better to say this, knowing how much it would irritate him since he refused to believe in global warming.

"I can drive," Nicholas said. "I simply prefer not to."

Neither of them spoke for a while after that. Laura worried she'd gone too far; perhaps he felt emasculated that he wasn't able to retrieve his wife and infant on his own. Her thoughts drifted to an afternoon more than three decades ago.

Bibs had been away at Seven Oaks—"summer camp for grownups," as it was explained to Laura and Nicholas. It was her first of what would be several stints there and the only time that Douglas had taken the two of them to go see her. The four of them had had a picnic outside and gone for a walk to a pond. When it was time to say goodbye to their mother, Nicholas, who was just five years old, didn't want to leave. Douglas had to carry him kicking and screaming to the car, and as they drove back to the city his howling continued. "That'll be enough, Nicholas," Douglas kept saying. "You're giving me a headache."

At a certain point their father couldn't take it anymore and pulled over with a violent jerk on the shoulder of the highway.

"Enough!" he barked. "Enough! Enough! *Enough!*"

To see their father, who was normally so composed, like this was very upsetting. Someone at Seven Oaks had given them a balloon in the shape of an animal; Nicholas had been clutching it in his lap and now he squeezed it with such force it popped—first the head, then the tail, then the torso. He started crying even harder.

Douglas glanced at Laura. "You *must* calm him down," he pleaded, an angry, desperate look on his face. "I simply can*not* drive like this."

Laura was at a loss for how to handle the situation. She felt like someone had taken a spoon and scooped out the inside of her chest, as one does a pumpkin to make a jack-o'-lantern. As they continued to sit there on the side of the Bronx River Parkway, their station wagon rattling in the turbulence of cars whizzing by, it started to rain—a sharp, prickly, slanted rain that landed on the windows in jarring splats. It was as though a curtain had been pulled back and something terribly ugly had been revealed and nothing would ever feel the same. They could never go back to how it was, to how life was supposed to be, because it had never really been that way. Everything up to that point had been a game of make-believe.

When they reached the Saw Mill River Parkway, Nicholas asked if she had a nail clipper. Laura said she might have one in her purse; she'd check at the next light.

"Never mind," he said, picking one of Emma's barrettes off the floor, which he used to extract the dirt from beneath his nails.

Laura asked if he'd made any special plans for Stephanie's home-coming.

Indeed he had: tea at the Plaza, a horse-and-carriage ride through Central Park, dinner at the Boathouse—all of her favorite New York things to do.

"Assuming she's up for it, of course," Nicholas added.

"I'm sure it will make her very happy," Laura said.

When they got off the exit, she asked, "Right or left?"

"Right," Nicholas said. Laura put on her blinker, but as they approached the end of the ramp, he changed his answer.

"Left?" she repeated.

"Right!" he said with conviction.

"You mean *correct*, go left, or take a right?"

Nicholas, who'd inherited their mother's geographic dyslexia, held up both hands to make L's with his thumb and pointer fingers, a trick to discern left from right which Laura had recently tried to teach Emma, who was already demonstrating signs of being similarly challenged.

"Go this w-w-way," he said, tapping the passenger-side window.

After she made the turn, Nicholas casually mentioned that he didn't know the directions from the highway. "Just drive to the village where the train station is," he instructed. "I'll know where to go from there."

A mile later, no sign of a village, Laura pulled into a gas station that was also a general store to ask for directions. Stepping out of the car, Laura's simmering frustration with Nicholas abated. The air smelled like warm gravel and honeysuckle; the country heat felt less apoca-lyptic, more recreational. The husky pulse of insects and the mindless twitter of birds had a pacifying effect. *We could move here*, she thought, walking toward the store's entrance.

She envisioned a modest house with a front porch and a wood stove. They would buy a rake and a snow shovel, learn how to grow a vegetable garden and compost their leftovers. Each morning Laura would stand in the driveway and wave goodbye as a yellow school bus shuttled Emma to the public school, where her classmates would be the children of the local shopkeepers, plumbers, and policemen. Growing up, the children would spend time in one another's house, which in a town like this people called a "home." And the two of them wouldn't be known by their family name, but simply as *Laura and Emma*.

A lifelong problem Laura had when receiving directions from strangers: so much energy went into smiling and nodding to convey her appreciation for their assistance that she struggled to retain what they told her. The man behind the counter had made it sound very easy, however, and Laura did exactly what she'd been told, but Nicholas objected to the final turn, claiming he did not remember the driveway being so rustic.

Laura thought it made sense for a psychiatric institution to have a driveway like this, long, unpaved, woodsy, and narrow; it created a sense of remove, discouraged the casual flow of traffic, generated the impression of being safely sequestered from the cold curiosity of those for whom places like this existed only in movies or as the punch line of jokes.

"Nope, doesn't look right," Nicholas kept saying.

"It has to be," Laura insisted, though she, too, was starting to have doubts.

The farther up this driveway they drove, the unrulier it got. Sticks cracked and popped beneath their tires and bushes brushed against the windows like curtains of a car wash.

"I will say this driveway is awfully narrow," Laura said, coming to a stop. She put the car in park, unbuckled her seat belt, turned the ignition off, and opened her door. Stepping outside, she noticed that the only tire treads on the ground were behind them; what lay ahead of the path they were on appeared to be unblemished. A sylvan green light filtered down through the canopy of leaves, creating the sense of a room.

"I think we may have made a wrong turn," Laura conceded, getting back in. "It looks like this isn't technically a road, but some sort of hiking trail, or a private path that cuts through someone's property."

Laura explained that there wasn't enough room to do a three-point turn, which meant they'd have to reverse all the way out. Nicholas nodded, chewing the inside of his lip. She sensed that he was very frustrated, that he wished he'd just taken the train. But Laura refused to feel guilty. She had volunteered to do a nice thing; Nicholas should have thought ahead and come prepared with directions from the highway.

"Backing up has never been my forte," Laura warned as she put her seat belt back on, "but I'll do my best."

Putting the car in reverse, she twisted around and gingerly lifted her foot off the brake. When the car didn't move she gently pressed down on the accelerator. It was difficult to manipulate the rear wheels to make the car's progression adhere to the trail, which was not straight. They'd gone a few yards before they came up against a tree.

"Whoops-a-daisy," Laura said, adjusting the wheels and putting the car back in drive. She proceeded to give the accelerator a series of tentative taps. They were on an incline, so each tap of the accelerator would take them a few inches forward, and then they'd roll a couple of inches back.

"At this rate, we should be back on the road by tomorrow," Nicholas remarked.

"Do *you* want to give it a try?" she asked, craning her neck around to see out the back. "You know, I never thought about it before, but of all the New Yorkers I know who never got around to learning how to drive — or *simply prefer not to* — they're almost all men.

"It's interesting, and I don't think it's a coincidence," she continued. "Learning to drive requires a certain humility, and then there's the additional humiliation of being late to the game."

When it became obvious that reversing their way back out was hopeless, Laura pursued their only other option, which was to go forward and hope for the best.

The woods eventually ended, but the path continued onto a field of tall grass, which brought them to the foot of a freshly mown lawn, at the other end of which sat a house. Laura slowly nosed the car out of the field and onto this lawn. She paused before proceeding. There was a car parked in the driveway next to the house.

"I wonder what the people who live in that house are going to think when they see a car driving through their backyard," she said.

"I imagine they'll be a bit surprised," Nicholas said. "And not so happy."

"Well, how else do I get us out of here? Call a crane service? Pull a *Chitty Chitty Bang Bang*?"

Laura rolled her seat forward as far as it would go and sat extremely erect. White-knuckled, her elbows gripping the wheel like it was the helm of a ship that was about to get carried out to sea, she set out across the lawn. So as not to frighten the residents of this house, or come across as a fugitive or a drunk, she wore a friendly smile and drove very slowly, prepared to stop at any moment and explain herself.

If anyone was home, they stayed inside, and if the police were called, Laura successfully vacated the premises before they arrived. The house's driveway was wide and newly paved, and it delivered them back to the road they'd been on. Giddy with adrenaline, Laura made a right, and shortly after doing so, Nicholas spotted the correct turn.

"Well, that was an adventure!" Laura said, pulling up to the facility's main entrance. She felt victorious—the hero of the day. Now that the ordeal was behind them, it was a funny story she couldn't wait to tell.

Laura waited in the car as Nicholas went inside to collect Stephanie and the baby. She wanted the car to be cool for them, so she kept the ignition on and the AC running, though it made her wince. When fifteen minutes passed, she turned the car off and opened all the windows. After another fifteen minutes, Nicholas came back out on his own.

"Stephanie's not in a great place right now," he said, leaning in the passenger-side window. "It was decided she and the baby are going to spend a little more time here."

Laura was confused. "They're not letting her come home today?"

Nicholas shook his head. "I spoke to her this morning and she sounded great; I told her I'd be here by one, and apparently when we were late she thought I wasn't coming and she got quite worked up."

"Did you explain what happened? How you didn't know where we were going and we got lost?"

Nicholas looked annoyed by the question. "Of course I did. But the point is she didn't know that at the time, she felt abandoned, and she got quite worked up, and as I said, she's not in a great place right now."

"Oh, dear." Laura bit her lip. "I'm so sorry, Nick. I feel responsible."

Laura knew she was not responsible for what happened. Any rational person could see this. She waited for him to reject her apology as unfounded, to thank her for taking the day off from work to drive up here, to commend her courage and competence in getting them out of the woods—and in doing so acknowledge that the detour had been his own fault, as he should have come prepared with directions from the highway. But Nicholas expressed none of the above. Instead he reached into his back pocket and took out his wallet.

"What's this for?" Laura asked as he passed her two fifties.

"Gas money," he said. "I'm going to stick around for the afternoon. I'll take the train home. You should get back to Emma."

"She's having a playdate with Charlotte. Margaret's got her for the day."

"Well, I'm sure you have things to do," Nicholas said. Jaw clenched, he put his hands in his pockets.

"Nick," Laura said, feeling her mouth go dry. "This isn't my fault. You can't be mad at me."

"I appreciate your taking the day off from work and trying to help," were his parting words.

But he didn't appreciate it. He thought this was her fault and he was mad at her. Even before they'd gotten lost, his demeanor had been far from gracious. Laura had never experienced road rage, but it didn't seem like a good idea to drive this angry. She sat in the parking lot, ignition running, AC blasting, trying to calm down. She tried to put things in perspective by thinking about today's record-high temperature and how the earth was doomed. Normally the sobering reality of the trajectory they were on eclipsed whatever trivial thought or anxiety she'd been grappling with, or at least dulled its edge, but today it had the opposite effect.

There were steps leading to the building's entrance. A righteous momentum carried her up these two at a time, then a pair of magnetically operated glass doors swooshed open in cowering deference to her clipped advance.

"I can't let you in if your name isn't on our visitors' list," the receptionist coolly informed her.

"Understood," Laura said, "but as I just explained, I'm not here as a visitor, I'm the *driver* of a visitor. My brother is visiting his wife and their baby—my nephew. I need to speak with him."

The exchange caught the attention of a passing doctor, who said he would get Nicholas and invited Laura to take a seat in the waiting area.

Enough time passed so that her outrage subsided and she began to feel silly, but then Nicholas appeared, looking confused and a little cranky to see her, and it riled back to life. As Laura stood up, the seat of her chair made a flatulent squeaking sound. Her skirt was still damp from sitting in the clammy heat of the car and now it clung to her thighs like cellophane. She peeled it off but it immediately reestablished contact.

"I feel like you hate me," were the first words that came tumbling out. "And I don't know why."

Nicholas looked more weary and annoyed than concerned or defensive. "I don't hate you, Laura," he said, his eyes half-shut.

"Then why do you treat me with such contempt?"

Lids fluttering half-mast: "I don't know what you're talking about."

"This." Laura's voice quivered. "What you're doing right now: closing your eyes when I talk to you, making me feel small and ridiculous—like I'm some irrational, emotional woman."

Nicholas sighed, looked down, and cupped the back of his neck. "I'm not sure what's going on, or what you want from me right now, but whatever it is, it's going to have to wait." Standing up straight, he crossed his arms and looked her in the eye. "Visiting hours are over soon and I would like to see my family."

"Your *fam-ily*." Laura's voice rose and cracked over the word, which came out in a regrettable high pitch. "You say that like *I'm . . . like I'm . . .*"

Nicholas appeared to exchange a look with someone over her shoulder, and Laura turned and saw that they had a small audience. Staff, judging from their clinical stares and white coats.

"Go be with your family," she said curtly, and walked out to her car.

As she drove home Laura's anger cooled. By the time she reached the Henry Hudson tollbooth she was deeply ashamed. All those people watching her erupt like that, and now Nicholas had to deal with the embarrassment of it, too, as if he didn't already have enough on his plate. She called him as soon as she got back to the apartment and left a message on his answering machine to apologize and let him know that there was no need to continue their discussion—in fact, she'd love it if they never spoke of the episode again.

"I don't know what came over me," she reiterated before hanging up. "It must have been the heat."

*   *   *

EMMA WASN'T THE ONLY ONE with the stomach flu; Dr. Brown's waiting room was full.

"Ally Hutchinson," the receptionist called, "Dr. Brown is ready to see you."

"Our appointment is with Dr. Wendell," Ally's mother spoke up.

"Yes," the receptionist said, "but he's running behind, so Dr. Brown is taking some of his patients."

"We will wait to see our doctor," Ally's mother said briskly and disappeared behind a copy of *The New Yorker*.

The receptionist read the next name on the list. "Thomas Du-Pont!"

"Is this for Dr. Wendell?" the boy's mother asked. "If not, we'll wait as well."

Laura was baffled by Dr. Wendell's sudden popularity. In the beginning, Dr. Brown had been the more sought-after of the two partners, but recently things had reversed. It made no sense. Dr. Brown was everything anyone could hope for in a pediatrician, while Dr. Wendell, old and gruff to begin with, was only getting older and gruffer. It was amazing more children weren't scared of him. When she was very young, Emma had once asked Laura if he was Mr. McGregor—the evil farmer who tried to kill Peter Rabbit. That was the kind of energy he projected.

Laura wondered what Dr. Brown made of his overnight demotion to second fiddle of Carnegie Hill Pediatrics. She hoped it hadn't hurt his self-esteem. He was a wonderful doctor, competent, wise, patient, and compassionate. She wanted to convey these sentiments to Dr. Brown, but couldn't imagine doing it in person; he was too modest and would start to laugh or tell her to stop. She would have to write them in a letter. But when and how would she give him the letter? One day Emma would be too old to see a pediatrician—perhaps that would be the appropriate occasion. Thinking of that day, their final appointment with Dr. Brown, Laura's throat swelled, and she had to blink back tears.

"You know what the best part of diarrhea is?" Emma greeted Dr. Brown as he entered the examination room.

"Getting to see Dr. Brown!" Laura answered.

"No." Emma shook her head. "You're allowed to drink Coke."

"I would switch to ginger ale," Dr. Brown told Laura in a no-nonsense tone. Putting on a pair of rubber gloves he added, "Caffeine is never great, especially when a child is dehydrated."

Laura nodded. Dr. Brown must have been having a bad day; his curt tone was out of character. Everyone was allowed to have bad moods, she told herself.

UNLIKE ACTORS IN FILMS WHOSE performances at least tried to feel true-to-life, stage actors seemed determined to remind you that they were in show business. Between their affected gestures, exaggerated facial expressions, and hammy delivery of their lines, Laura found it difficult to believe whatever story it was they were trying to tell. Not to mention that plays invariably contained at least one major, implausible revelation about a family secret or some such, after which the cast fell silent and the audience was supposed to gasp with shock.

However, like church, it was something she knew it was important to do every so often, and when Margaret called to say she had two tickets to *Miss Bennett* that night, Laura pretended she'd heard of the show and said she'd love to go.

"I'm not exactly looking forward to it," Margaret confessed before getting off the phone, "but as the secretary of the alumni association, I feel I ought to see what all the fuss is about."

And then Laura realized she *had* heard of *Miss Bennett*, an off-Broadway musical about Winthrop, written by a girl who'd been in the class below theirs. It was a satire and, according to the *New York Times* critic, "a scabrous, gender-bending send-up of female prep-school culture." The gender-bending part was that it featured an all-male cast.

Margaret believed in dressing up for the theater, and Laura felt obligated to change out of her turtleneck, skirt, and cowboy boots. She was on her way out the door—pumps, blouse, blue satin skirt—when she remembered this wasn't Lincoln Center they were going to. The theater was on Broome Street. The turtleneck, skirt, and cowboy boots went back on. Her instincts were right; Laura felt a smug sense of victory upon arriving at the theater in her uniform, where she fit right in among a downtown crowd of blue jeans and leather jackets. For once in their lives it was Margaret—in her pearls and pink tweed skirt and blazer—who looked out of place.

They sat in the front row. The actors were dressed in the school uniform as it had been in the sixties, which, in addition to the tunic, included hats and blazers. Laura had mixed feelings about her alma mater, but watching it ridiculed in a small black box theater stirred up tender affection for the institution.

The second scene depicted Prayers. As the cast recited Bible verses, they got really into their roles, and their enunciation of certain words released a spray of saliva, the heavier, dewier fragments of which occasionally made contact with Laura's face. Margaret, who'd always been deathly terrified of germs, slunk back in her seat, but this did little to protect her from the mist, and after a minute of looking very uncomfortable and unhappy and taking deep nervous breaths, she incrementally leaned forward until she was no longer on her seat, but on all fours and crawling down the narrow space between the stage and the knees of everyone in the front row. After reaching the end of the row she stood up and disappeared through the swinging doors that led to the cocktail lounge. Laura waited until intermission to join her.

"I didn't feel safe with all that spitting," she whispered, pulling Laura into the ladies' room. After fishing around in her purse she held up a little bottle of Listerine.

"Here, drink this," she said, handing it to Laura.

Laura took a swig and spat it out in the sink.

"No, you need to *drink* it," she said. "One capful, don't spit it out."

"You're not supposed to swallow Listerine," Laura protested.

"It's nothing," Margaret said dismissively. "It's like taking a shot of vodka.

"*Do* it," she said, when Laura hesitated to take the bottle back from her. "Please, Laura, don't be stubborn. I took you here tonight and I couldn't live with myself if . . . if you caught . . ."

Laura laughed. "If I caught a cold?"

"I'm not talking about a cold, Laura," she whispered sternly. "I'm talking about . . ." She looked around the ladies' room to make sure no one was listening and whispered the letters: "*A-I-D-S*."

They did not return to their seats for the second half of the show. Margaret buckled her seat belt in the taxi home and shook her head.

"I don't know what I was thinking, getting front-row seats. We're already so vulnerable living in New York City, the homosexual capital of the world. So much is already out of our control. God forbid you get hit by a bus and need a blood transfusion!"

"What made you think any of them were homosexual?" Laura asked.

"Oh, Laura," she said. "Most theater actors are. And these ones *certainly* were."

"They were?"

"You really are slow to pick up on things," Margaret said, looking at her fondly. "It's kind of sweet."

Within seconds, however, Margaret's face turned serious.

"I've been meaning to talk to you about your pediatrician," she said.

IT WAS THEIR FOURTH DAY in Ashaunt and they'd yet to see the sun. The rain had been intermittent but today it was steady. According to the thermometer it was sixty-two, though the damp draft made it feel much colder. Laura tried to light a fire but ran out of newspaper before it got going. Poking around the attic, she found a copy of the *New York Times*. She was about to take it before she saw it was from August 10, 1974, and the front page announced Nixon's resignation. She couldn't bear to burn that. Instead she used a 1964 edition of the *Summer Social Register*.

"You're *burning* a *book*," Emma said, sounding vaguely impressed. "Isn't that bad?"

"Normally, yes," Laura acknowledged, ripping out another page. "But this is an idiotic book." She got on her knees and stuffed the balled-up paper beneath the logs. Palms on the floor, she leaned in close and blew until the flame caught.

Emma laughed. "Mom, you're sticking your butt in the air."

The weather became more volatile as the afternoon progressed, with thunder and sudden gusts of wind that shrieked like a teakettle.

They ate an early dinner of leftover lasagna. After doing the dishes, Laura went back to the living room, revived the fire with a fresh log, and returned to her book. She'd read *Anna Karenina* in high school, and then again in her twenties, but it was just as engrossing a third time. Laura didn't even notice it had stopped raining until Emma came scampering downstairs.

"Gotta go save the worms before they get run over!" she announced.

The front door was swollen with moisture, making it difficult to open. As Laura wrestled with it, Emma lost patience, opened a window, jostled the screen loose, and climbed through.

"*Wait*," Laura called, crawling out after her.

The front had passed, leaving the sky in fluorescent shambles. The light was shrill and cast everything in bewitchingly crisp resolution. A beautiful, bruised sunset was in the works.

The lawn was like a soggy sponge beneath their bare feet, and by the time they reached the road, their toes were threaded with loose strands of grass. There was only one worm on the stretch of road in front of their house, and after Emma relocated it to a bank of moss beside the driveway, Laura suggested they take a walk to look for more.

On their way up the point they crossed paths with Uncle Frank and Aunt Alice, their perky gaggle of corgis faithfully trundling behind them. As was their custom to do in the evening, the couple was dressed up: Alice in pearls and pink lipstick; Uncle Frank in his faded red pants and brass-buttoned jacket. What was left of his hair wasn't much, but he'd parted it to the side and matted it down.

Laura admired Alice and Frank, but not for the reasons everyone else did. Among their extended family, Alice and Frank's childlessness was alluded to as a tragic circumstance, their upbeat, cheerful demeanor hailed as "brave." Laura found this patronizing because Alice and Frank struck her as genuinely happy—the rare husband and wife who truly enjoyed each other's company. Certainly more so than any other couple she could think of.

"We were just talking about the new millennium," Alice said with a mischievous smile. "We're in the eighties now, soon it'll be the nineties, and I asked Frank, 'What will we call the decade after that?' And Frank said—"

"And I said," Frank cut in, " 'We won't call it ana-thing, dear, we'll be up *there*.' " He wagged a finger at the sky and the two laughed merrily.

"Didn't you call it the *aughts*?" Laura asked, realizing they would've been children in the first decade of the nineteen hundreds.

"Yes." Alice nodded. "I think that's right."

"I *ought* to agree," Frank said, and Alice made a raspberry sound of playful disapproval.

A butterfly came along and landed on a nearby stone wall. Emma slowly approached to admire it. Alice and Frank continued on their way; as Laura turned to watch them go, a frisky breeze snaked out of the bushes and inflated the skirt of Alice's dress like an umbrella. At the same time it gently lifted Uncle Frank's comb-over, revealing the primitive contours of his skull, which was the delicate pink of the inside of a conch shell. If either of them noticed, they didn't seem to care. Unfazed, arm in arm, on they strode, each step just barely grazing the cusp of their shadows, which, being longer and more limber, loped valiantly ahead into the evening.

IT WAS COMPLETELY IRRATIONAL. THERE was no reason to believe Dr. Brown had AIDS. Furthermore, in the event he did have the virus, the possibility of his infecting Emma involved ridiculous scenarios of a highly unlikely nature. Still, this didn't stop Laura from conjuring them in the middle of the night.

Margaret had succeeded in planting a seed of anxiety, and Laura couldn't deny that her immediate reaction was relief when, in August of that summer, a letter was forwarded to her at Ashaunt announcing that, after thirty-seven years of serving the community, Carnegie Hill Pediatrics would be closing its doors in November. Dr. Wendell was retiring and Dr. Brown would be joining a new practice: Downtown Pediatrics.

Given his new office's location near the Bowery, it wouldn't make sense for them to see him anymore. Laura knew Dr. Brown would understand this, but the thought of picking up the phone and telling him put a lump in her throat.

"I'm afraid the location is a little inconvenient," she wrote. "You have been an important part of our lives and it's hard to imagine someone filling your shoes. You have gone above and beyond. We wish you the very best of luck."

After reading the letter over, Laura decided it wasn't enough. She would pick up the phone and call him. Not this afternoon, but tomorrow or the next day, by the end of the week, she promised herself.

In the meantime, she canceled Emma's back-to-school checkup.

It didn't make sense to have her see two different doctors in the same school year. She called Margaret to ask for the number of Charlotte's pediatrician.

NOW THAT EMMA WAS IN second grade, Laura allowed herself the luxury of sleeping in until eight on weekends. This meant that Emma, who rarely slept later than seven, was in charge of making her own cereal.

"Get back in bed!" Emma demanded one Sunday as Laura walked into the kitchen. She was standing in front of something she clearly didn't want Laura to see.

"Get back in bed?" Laura laughed. "But it's eight o'clock!"

"Get back in bed!" Emma barked again.

Laura got back in bed.

A moment later her door was flung open. "Breakfast in bed!" Emma announced, bearing a tray with a bowl of oat bran.

"Breakfast in bed?" Laura affected a gasp of surprise. "What a treat!"

Emma proceeded across the rug in ceremoniously staggered steps, moving her right foot forward, dragging her left foot up to meet it, and so on.

"Happy birthday!" Emma said, passing her the tray.

"How sweet of you to remember," Laura said. "Thank you."

She had just picked up the spoon when Emma whisked the bowl away. "Forgot the milk," she said, running out and returning a minute or two later.

"*Mmm*," Laura said after the first bite.

"Why are you sad?" Emma asked, scrutinizing her face.

"I'm not sad." Laura smiled, but Emma looked unconvinced, and her probing stare did not relent. Laura became aware of her breaths. She felt brittle and hollow. She wasn't sure why. She had always felt this way on birthdays, starting in her childhood.

"I made you a present." Emma unzipped her fanny pack and procured a piece of clay in the shape of a ball. "It's a paperweight. It's so your papers don't blow away."

"How *useful*," Laura said, cradling it in her palm. It was still moist; she must have made it that morning. "How thoughtful of you."

"It's supposed to look like a rock," Emma explained. "Sorry it's not very good."

"It's beautiful. And that's *exactly* what it looks like. A rock."

The intensity of Emma's gaze was too much.

"Okay, maybe I'm a little sad." Laura smiled through her tears. "It's the happy kind, though."

"You're not supposed to cry when someone gives you a present." Emma grabbed the ball of clay from Laura's hand and threw it against the wall, where it stuck.

Upon retrieving it, Laura discovered it had left a mark. After scrubbing the residue off there was a faint discoloration. A subtle brown smudge. It was too low to hang a picture over it, but too high to hide behind her bureau. Like the liver spot on her left temple, she would have to get used to it. Then a solution came to her.

"That's it, dear?" Bibs asked. "Are you sure that's all you want for your birthday? Wallpaper?"

* * *

EMMA ADMIRED THE ELEGANTLY DRESSED women of the Upper East Side—if only her mother would also wear lipstick, perfume, and high heels. She could at least carry a proper patent leather purse.

That fall a suit appeared in a store window they passed by on the way to and from school. In keeping with the fashion of the times, it consisted of a short skirt and matching blazer. If the mothers of Emma's classmates had a uniform, this was it.

The first morning Emma pointed it out to her, Laura said, "We're late," and tugged Emma along, but when they passed by it on the way home that afternoon, Laura paused to have a closer look. After a suspenseful silence, she frowned and shook her head. On they walked.

The suit remained in the window for several weeks, and each time they passed it, Emma's hope would be rekindled as Laura slowed down and registered the suit with a glance. On more than one occasion, Emma would grab her mother's hand and attempt to coerce her into buying.

It was so pretty! Please, please, *pretty-pretty-please*, would she at least try it on?

They were in the middle of one of these exchanges when Emma noticed someone inside the store, waving at them through the window. It was her mom's friend, Janet. They stepped in to say hello.

"Look at what Emma wants me to buy," Laura laughed, pointing at the suit in the window.

Janet did not laugh.

"Emma's right," she said, "you could use some grown-up clothes."

Emma pushed Laura into the dressing stall and asked the shopkeeper to bring over the suit in her mother's size. In a few minutes Laura emerged from the stall, zipped and buttoned up.

Emma held her breath as Janet and the shopkeeper gushed their approval. Watching Laura take out her credit card, Emma had the feeling that this was all a dream and she was about to wake up.

And that's what it was like when they got home.

"I don't know what I was thinking," Laura said, reevaluating her purchase as she stood before the full-length mirror in their front hall closet. "I'm too small for short skirts and blazers—they made me look ridiculous. And the pattern reminds me of a carpet in a movie theater."

Emma was crushed.

And so the suit went directly from a Madison Avenue mannequin to one of the women at the homeless shelter.

WHEN LAURA RETURNED HOME FROM the shelter that Sunday, the babysitter was not doing her homework at the kitchen table as she usually did after putting Emma to bed. She wasn't in the living room either. Seeing the light was on in Emma's bedroom, Laura assumed they were still reading, but stepping inside she saw the bed was still made—no sign of Emma or Daisy. Her own bedroom was dark, both bathrooms were empty. Daisy always left her backpack and boots by the front door. The backpack was there, but the boots were not. A dizzying panic set in. Laura picked up the phone to dial Frank, in case he had seen them go out. Frank answered the phone after four rings; yes, he had been in the lobby that evening; no, he had not seen Emma or a teenage girl leave the building.

Laura retraced her steps through the apartment. What the hell had she been thinking, leaving Emma in the care of a teenager? Emma. She was the only thing in the world that mattered—to keep her safe, that was it. Without Emma there would be no point to anything.

She went back to the kitchen and dialed Margaret. Trip answered. Margaret couldn't speak right now—she was tucking Charlotte in.

There was a tap on the window. Laura was so startled she dropped the phone.

It was Emma—she and Daisy were out on the terrace. They were trying to tell her something.

"Hold on, I can't hear you," Laura said, tugging on the door that led outside; it frequently got stuck. Daisy helped push it open.

"There was an *eclipse*!" Emma's voice chimed with excitement. "It was so cool, Mom, the moon completely disappeared."

ALL ACROSS THE CITY, HOLIDAY lights were going up. The flamboyant fire escapes of Harlem abruptly halted at Ninety-sixth Street, where the demure twinkling of Carnegie Hill took over, eventually surrendering to the manic flash of midtown.

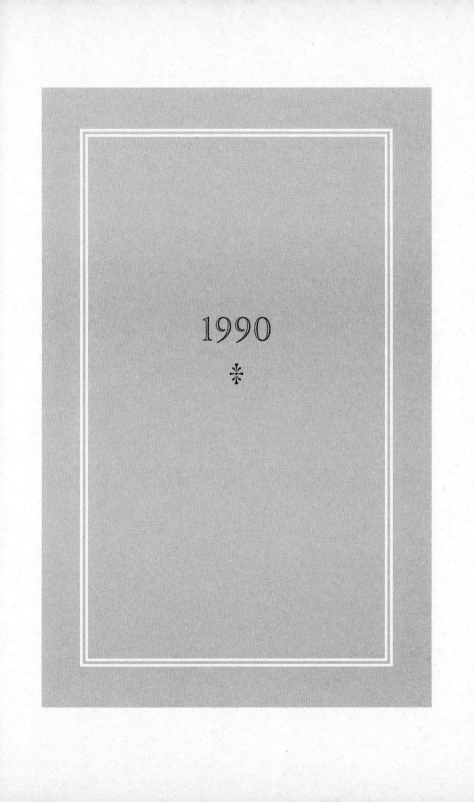

1990

THEN IT WAS JANUARY, WITH ITS SOBERING RETURN TO ROUTINE and tree corpses on the curb. Laura still hadn't called Dr. Brown; the New Year was a good excuse.

But it didn't happen.

Now it was February. Discovering Dr. Brown's home number had been disconnected, Laura phoned Downtown Pediatrics.

"Dr. Brown is no longer affiliated with this practice," she was told. "Would you like to schedule an appointment with one of our other doctors?"

"Where did he go?"

There was a silence.

"Would you like to schedule an appointment with one of our other doctors?"

"No, we already have someone. I'm calling because I'm looking for Dr. Brown."

"Dr. Brown is no longer affiliated with this practice. I'm sorry, ma'am, that's all I can tell you."

Swallowing her pride, Laura called her mother to see if the two had been in touch recently.

"No, and to tell you the truth, I'm a little irritated. I sent him a Williams Sonoma gingerbread house for Christmas and he didn't call to say thank you, which is very unlike him."

"You've known him for barely a year. You don't know what he's like."

"It's very unlike him," Bibs repeated.

*   *   *

THERE WAS A MAN WHO lived on the fourth floor of Margaret's building who hosted a supposedly famous daytime television show. Laura had never heard of the show, which bore his name, but after an encounter in the elevator with him she was curious to watch it.

It was like nothing she had ever seen. It featured emotionally unstable people confronting estranged family members or former lovers before a live audience. High-octane, profanity-riddled shouting matches ensued, with sordid revelations, accusations, and threats. Just as things felt on the verge of erupting into violence, a burly security person would lumber out onto the stage and there would be a commercial break.

When the show resumed the guests would be subdued, and the host would summarize the conflict before inviting members of the audience to offer their take on the situation. The audience had no shortage of opinions of these people and their problems, and the crueler these were, the rowdier the applause they generated.

This was the part Laura could hardly bear to watch. Fortunately, most of the guests seemed incapable of seeing themselves for who they really were and were thus indifferent to the audience's impression of them.

It appeared the host of the show was blessed with the same deficit of self-awareness, Laura concluded, as she recalled the man she'd shared the elevator with—who'd been delighted to confirm his identity to a third passenger, one of the building's nannies, whose excitement bordered on hysteria.

"I am he," he'd said, the corners of his mustache rising in an un-abashedly self-satisfied grin.

"Look, that's our apartment, right up there!" Emma pointed as they waited to cross the light at Ninety-sixth Street.

Emma's classmate Tiffany squinted as she looked up. "I don't think my mom would like me to be in a neighborhood like this," she said.

"Why not?" Laura asked.

The light turned; Laura took the girls' hands as they crossed. As they passed by James's corner, Emma waved and called his name but James did not wave back. This had been the case recently; Laura was a little worried about him.

"Why do you know that guy?" Tiffany asked.

"James is our homeless man," Emma answered. "He calls me Goldi-locks. Most of the time he's the friendliest person, but sometimes he's a little out to lunch."

As he often did, Frank had set up his easel in the lobby, and was painting a picture of an angel. On the table where he'd put his supplies was an ashtray. It was so full that the cigarette butts protruded like the needles of a porcupine. The door to his apartment was ajar so the cats could wander in and out.

"Who was that man?" Tiffany asked when they were in the elevator.

"That's our doorman," Emma said.

"Why wasn't he wearing a uniform?"

"Frank is not a normal doorman."

"Actually, Frank isn't a doorman," Laura spoke up. "He's the super."

"Then where was your doorman?" Tiffany addressed this question to Laura.

"Not every building has a doorman," Laura said.

"Hungry!" Emma announced, kicking off her shoes as they entered the apartment. Laura went into the kitchen and put some Oreos on a plate.

"Not allowed to have those," Tiffany said when Laura called them in.

"I am," Emma said, reaching across the table and stacking all four of them in her hand.

"How about some Wheat Thins?" Laura said, opening up the cupboard. Tiffany nodded glumly. Laura arranged some crackers on a plate and set it down in front of Tiffany. She went over to the fruit bowl and cut up an apple.

"I don't care for apples," Tiffany said when Laura set the plate on the table.

"Me neither," Emma said, licking the inside of her Oreo. "Hate 'em, get 'em away from me before I barf." Tiffany laughed as Emma pushed the plate toward Laura, who sat at the head of the table, which also functioned as her desk. It was not her job, but she'd agreed to stuff envelopes for the Library's annual upcoming fundraiser.

She mostly tuned out the girls' conversation until she heard Emma inform Tiffany, in a certain nah-nah-nah tone, that her mother was thirty-nine years old.

Tiffany looked at Laura, expectantly, as though waiting for her to dispute this fact.

"I'm coming up on forty," Laura told her.

"That's *so* much older than her mom." Emma beamed with triumph. "Guess how old her mom is?"

"I have no idea," Laura said, trying to affect indifference, though she was a little curious.

"*Twenty-five*," Emma declared.

"Really?" Laura had to fight a smile as she looked at Tiffany, who confirmed the number with a defeated nod.

"So she was . . . quite young when she had you."

Tiffany shrugged.

"You have an older sister," Laura said to Tiffany. "How old is she?"

"Eleven," Tiffany answered.

"Soon she'll be in Upper School and she'll have to wear a bra!" Emma snickered. Done with her Oreos, she got on her knees and reached across the table for a Wheat Thin.

"You're supposed to ask first," Tiffany said, jealously pulling the plate toward her.

"My house, my crackers!"

"*Emma.*" Laura shook her head.

"Fine!" Emma said. Clasping her hands together in a prayer pose and batting her eyelashes, she said, in a mock English accent, "Pardon, Madam, can I have a crack-ah."

"*May* I," Tiffany corrected her, passing her the plate.

Done with their snack, the girls disappeared into Emma's bedroom. Laura continued licking and stuffing. An hour passed.

"Pardon?" said a little voice from behind her.

She turned to find Tiffany standing in the doorway to the kitchen.

"Emma is not being very nice, and I would like to go home please."

Laura tried to play diplomat, but neither party was interested in an apology or compromise. What each girl wanted was for Laura to vindicate her position and disavow the other. The conflict had arisen from the earlier exchange in the kitchen regarding the discrepancy in their mother's ages. Was it better to have an older mom or a younger mom was the crux of it. Emma insisted that Laura's seniority in years translated to superiority; Tiffany pointed out that having an older mom meant Laura would die sooner.

That Laura found the whole thing quite amusing infuriated Emma. "Why are you *laughing?*" she demanded. "You think this is *funny?*"

Unable to mend things, Laura proposed the girls play a game. Do an arts and crafts project. Get started on their homework. "Could we watch *Hey Dude?*" Emma asked.

"I love that show!" Tiffany squealed with excitement.

At five o'clock Tiffany's mother arrived to take her home. Mrs. Vavra was one of the tall, tall, rakishly thin specimens. Her face, Laura had to admit, was smooth as a teenager's, but she no doubt wore more makeup than an Olympic figure skater and her hands had the telltale pronounced blue veins.

Laura opened the door but Mrs. Vavra did not step in; she lingered in the doorway, waiting for her daughter to get ready to leave.

"Is that real fur?" Emma asked, pointing to Mrs. Vavra's coat.

"Yes," she answered.

"But the animal died of old age," Tiffany added.

"Oh." Emma nodded approvingly. "Well, then it's okay."

As Tiffany struggled with the many brass buttons that secured her coat, Laura bent down to assist.

"Emma's allowed to have Oreos after school," Tiffany announced as Laura crouched further to tie her shoes.

"*Is* she," Mrs. Vavra responded.

"Guilty as charged." Laura looked up and smiled at Mrs. Vavra, who did not smile back.

"Also," Tiffany continued, "Emma gets to watch TV on school nights."

"Different households have different rules," Mrs. Vavra said. "Where's your headband?"

Tiffany reached up and patted her head.

"I think it's in my room," Emma said.

"Go help her find it," Laura told her.

"Usually I don't allow TV during playdates," Laura explained as the girls ran off. "But they had a little argument and it seemed like the best way to . . ." Laura now struggled to convey the logic of it. "To get them to drop it."

"I'm sorry to hear that," Mrs. Vavra said.

"It was actually quite funny," Laura told her. "It was about our ages."

Mrs. Vavra looked puzzled.

"I'm thirty-nine, and Tiffany told Emma you were twenty-five . . ." Laura paused, waiting for Mrs. Vavra to acknowledge the lie. Her refusal to do so emboldened Laura.

"Emma was confused by the math," she continued, "and to be perfectly honest, I wasn't sure how to explain it to her."

Mrs. Vavra raised her eyebrows. She looked like she wasn't planning to say anything.

The girls returned. Laura held out Tiffany's backpack, but rather than take it, Tiffany turned around for Laura to mount it on her back. After slipping her arms through the straps she nodded at her mom. "Ready."

"What do you say?" Mrs. Vavra said, ringing for the elevator.

"Thank you," said Tiffany.

"Thanks for coming over, Tiffany, see you tomorrow," Laura said, shutting the door.

When they were safely out of earshot, Emma asked, "It *is* better to be thirty-nine than twenty-five, right?"

"Twenty-five minus eleven," Laura responded.

Emma looked confused.

"It's a math problem," Laura said. "You can do it. *Twenty-five* minus *eleven*."

"Fourteen, no *duh*," Emma answered after a lengthy pause. "Is it better to be thirty-nine or twenty-five?"

"There's a certain kind of woman who is terrified of getting older," Laura said. "I am not one of them."

Emma looked unimpressed and frustrated by this answer. "You never take my side," she said, and stomped off to her room.

"It's a like a cocktail party, at eight a.m., without the cocktails," Trip commented dismally.

Margaret shot him a look, but Laura agreed—class parent breakfasts were tedious. As Margaret strolled off to circulate among the other, more social parents, Laura and Trip were left on their own.

Above the mantel hung a life-size oil portrait of the Vavra family standing in front of the very same mantel, above which hung a slightly smaller oil portrait of the Vavra family standing in front of the mantel, and so on, until they were tiny dots. Laura discreetly called it to Trip's attention.

"That's crap," he said.

What most struck Laura about the Vavra's lavish Park Avenue duplex was that there was just one shelf of books, a line of leather-bound and gold-leaf British and Russian classics. Upon closer inspection, they'd clearly never been opened, but were part of a set intended for décor. Laura brought this up when she spoke to Margaret on the phone that evening.

"Are you surprised?" Margaret said with some irritation. "They're not exactly intellectuals, Laura."

When Laura got off the phone, Emma looked up from her homework. "Who were you talking about? Who cares they got no books?"

"No one," Laura told her. "And remember what I told you about listening to my private grown-up conversations."

"But I don't *get* it," Emma persisted. "Why does it matter they got no books?"

Ignoring the question, Laura turned on the stove to get dinner started.

"Who cares about books," Emma said, furiously erasing something in her workbook. Satisfied, she blew the paper clean and wiped the remaining eraser debris with the sleeve of her turtleneck.

"Some people don't care about books," Laura reflected. "Which is too bad, because books are a wonderful thing—" Noticing she had Emma's attention, Laura struggled to articulate the sentiment of what she was trying to say. "It's *important* to read."

"I know," Emma said. "Already read three books this week."

"You're getting to be a much better reader," Laura told her.

After dinner, as Laura got started on the dishes, Emma reappeared in the kitchen to announce that she hadn't yet watched her allotted hour of TV and wasn't planning to.

"That's fine," Laura said absently.

"You know why, Mom?" Emma lingered in the doorway. Hands folded across her chest, she waited until she had her mother's full concentration. "I want to read instead. Because I like books more than TV."

Emma's tongue explored the interior of her cheek. She looked down, dragging her toe along a groove between the kitchen tiles.

The declaration caught Laura by surprise, and something in her went slack with tenderness. A dish slipped from the rubbery grip of her yellow gloves, sliding back into the soapy water of the sink.

MARGARET AND LAURA WERE INVITED to a private salon held at the apartment of Winthrop parents.

"He's even more handsome in person," Catherine Poe, a fellow Winthrop alum and the host of the event, whispered as she took their coats.

The featured guest was an author who had recently published a bestselling novel, the kind of book everyone they knew was reading. Laura didn't need to read it to know it was trash. She could tell from the cover: two pairs of feet and rumpled bedsheets. The author himself looked like he'd just emerged from an afternoon in a hotel room, with his tousled hair, slap-happy grin, and dress shirt unbuttoned one louche button too many. Laura guessed he was forty-five or fifty.

As he read the first chapter—a handsome high school English teacher, trapped in a stale marriage, receives an anonymous love letter—Laura was reminded of someone, but she couldn't think of who until Margaret leaned over to whisper, "He reminds me of Mr. Zinsser."

Mr. Zinsser—their tenth-grade English teacher, an anomaly on the Winthrop faculty. He'd had sideburns, wore tight-fitting black turtlenecks, and often ended class by reciting his own poetry. Everyone professed to be in love with Mr. Zinsser, and Laura spent class after class staring at him, trying to nurture the appropriate feelings.

One afternoon she was gathering her books to leave when Mr. Zinsser asked her to stay behind. She assumed he wanted to discuss her marks (English had always been her strongest subject, but she'd been unfocused recently), but this wasn't the case. He wanted to talk about the way Laura looked at him in class.

"It's not the way a student is supposed to look at a teacher," were his exact words.

Laura's panic must have shown, because Mr. Zinsser immediately followed this with a confession: he didn't think of her the way a teacher should think of a student, either. Laura didn't know what to say to this. He proposed they continue their conversation that evening, outside of school, and wrote down an address on a note card.

Laura knew she should be flattered, that this was validation of the highest order, but the prospect of meeting up with Mr. Zinsser, alone and outside of school, gave her a stomachache. She told her mother, in hopes that she might forbid her. But Bibs got very excited and insisted she wear lipstick and carry a comb in her pocketbook, as her hair sometimes looked limp.

The address turned out to be Mr. Zinsser's apartment. After taking Laura's coat, he pointed to a couch and told her to make herself comfortable, then disappeared into the kitchen. The couch was leather and there wasn't any friction between its slick surface and the seat of Laura's skirt, and in the process of trying to make herself comfortable she kept sliding around, like she was in the back of a taxicab. Mr. Zinsser returned with two glasses of white wine. He handed one to Laura and sat down beside her.

After a moment of not saying anything, Mr. Zinsser reached out to tuck a strand of hair behind her ear and said, "Hi." Laura said hi back, and took a long sip of wine. Mr. Zinsser did the same. Then he leaned over and kissed Laura on the lips, and while this had been the thing she was dreading, now that it was happening it was a relief, because she was no longer embarrassed or afraid; she wasn't anything. She felt nothing.

After a few minutes of kissing, Mr. Zinsser pulled back and asked if she wanted to go to his bedroom. Laura apologized and said no, thank you, she had to go home. To her relief, Mr. Zinsser didn't protest, and he never asked her back again.

The author was a teacher himself, a professor at Sarah Lawrence. He brought this up during the Q&A, by way of explaining why it would be a few years before his next book came out.

"Sadly," he said with a roguish smile, "even a bestseller does not preclude one from needing a day job." The room laughed, and a moment later he added, "And of course I love teaching. I learn a lot from my students."

When the questions ended, the waitstaff circulated among the guests with hors d'oeuvres. Catherine corralled Laura and Margaret into a conversation with the author, who was gushing about a novel that would be coming out next month, and which he predicted would be the next big thing, so much so that they might consider selecting it for their next salon.

"The author is very modest," he said, "so I better stop talking about it, as here she comes now."

A woman Laura had not noticed earlier insinuated herself into their circle. She couldn't have been more than twenty-five or -six, tops. Her hair was an artificial shade of red and she wore too much eye makeup. In spite of this, she was strikingly beautiful.

The author was quite taken with himself and emotionally immature. He didn't interest or impress Laura in the slightest. But this woman he was with—there was something unusual and fascinating about her. Her name was Elise and she did not smile when he introduced her to the group, though she did repeat each person's name after it was told to her, with a self-possessed confidence that was vaguely masculine. Laura couldn't tell if she was British, or simply spoke with an affect. Beneath her black, formfitting dress she wore scuffed black boots. Men's boots, the kind a soldier would wear.

When the author excused himself to get a drink, he looped his arm around Elise's lower back, taking her with him.

Laura glanced at Margaret, but she was already exchanging a knowing look with Catherine. Laura's gaze drifted back to the couple as they made their way to the bar, and focused on the author's arm, just below which the shifting contours of the woman's backside strained against its tight, silken container.

IN SECOND GRADE EMMA STILL requested the occasional picture book for bedtime reading, but for the most part they had graduated to chapter books. Laura was on the chapter in *Little Women* in which Jo meets a homely professor when Emma tapped her on the shoulder to deliver the following information: "In the olden days it was against the law to get pregnant unless you got married first."

"Was it," Laura said, and went back to reading.

A page later Emma interrupted again. "Are they going to do it?"

"Do what?" Laura asked.

"*It*." Emma sniggered.

"What is 'it'?"

Emma covered her mouth with her hand as she laughed again. "S-E-X," she whispered.

Laura rested the book on her lap. Dr. Brown's book had highlighted the anatomical function of certain body parts without explicitly spelling out the mechanics. They had yet to have the traditional facts-of-life conversation.

"Do you remember that book we used to read," she asked, "*A Very Special—*"

"I *know* this, Mom," Emma cut her off. "I'm in *second grade*."

"You know what?"

"What you're going to tell me." Emma tugged at a loose thread on her quilt. "A man sticks his ding-dong in a woman's vagina, a seed comes out, and that's how a woman gets pregnant."

"That's the conventional way to get pregnant," Laura said. "How most women do it. But there are some women—"

"No duh, Mom," Emma interrupted. "You would *never* let a man stick his sausage in your vagina."

"Sausage?" Laura repeated. She'd never heard it called that before and hated to think where Emma had picked it up.

"I came from a seed you got from Sweden." Emma spoke these words with casual indifference. "I'm Swedish, that's why I have blond hair, *no duh*."

"Where did you hear that?" Laura asked. She was dumbfounded.

Emma's gaze briefly met Laura's then returned to the loose thread, which she was coiling around the tip of her finger.

"Bibs," Laura said. "Bibs told you that."

Emma shrugged and puffed her cheeks out.

"How old were you when she told you?"

Another shrug.

"I never told anyone," Emma said in a baby voice. "She said it was a secret, that you'd get mad at her if you knew she told me."

"What else did Bibs tell you?" Laura asked, tucking a lock of hair behind Emma's ear.

"That Swedish is the best country in the world to be from." Emma looked at Laura, her forehead lined in worry. "Mama, please don't get mad at her."

"Have you ever seen me get mad at Bibs?" Laura asked.

Emma thought for a moment and shook her head.

"That's because it doesn't do anything. I know you love Bibs very much, and she loves you very much, but she doesn't always think about how her behavior or decisions affect others."

Laura took Emma's hand in her own. "I'm so sorry she told you all this, darling—and then asked you to keep it a secret. How unfair of her. It must have been so confusing."

"Nope." Emma shook her head. "Ever since I got Kirsten . . ."

She got out of bed and picked up one of her American Girl Dolls. Part of the brand's appeal was that each doll represented a different era of American history and came with a unique backstory. Kirsten's family had emigrated from Sweden, hence her brass-button cardigan sweater ($19.95).

"Ever since I got Kirsten," Emma continued, climbing back in, "I always had this feeling I was Swedish."

AFTER A FEW WEEKS OF headaches and dizzy spells, Bibs had gone in to see her doctor. Some tests were run, and the results were not good. She was scheduled to have surgery with the top neurosurgeon at Beth Israel the following morning. Douglas reported all of this to Laura over the phone.

"Where are you now?" Laura asked.

"We just got home," Douglas told her. "She's upstairs resting. Maybe you could stop by after work."

Laura stood up and put on her coat. Then she sat back down and dialed Nicholas.

"I won't be able to leave the office until four," he told her. "But I just talked to Stephanie and she's on her way over."

Stephanie got there first. When Laura arrived, the baby was asleep in his stroller parked beside the umbrella stand. Nicholas Jr., not yet a year, was a large and indolent baby, much like Emma had been. Laura had yet to see him in the same outfit. Today he wore a smocked one-piece with a Peter Pan collar embroidered with sailboats, a matching blue cardigan, white kneesocks, and red sandals with brass buckles.

As Laura gently removed a Cheerio stuck to his cheek, he stirred. Eyes barely open, he drowsily groped between his legs, where there were more Cheerios. After securing one, he brought it up to his mouth. Nostrils flared, he chewed it slowly with his front teeth, the only ones he had. After swallowing he reached for another, but his eyelids shuttered and his head went slack before he managed to retrieve it.

Stephanie was sitting in the armchair beside her mother's bed, sipping a Diet Coke and giggling.

"You think I'm kidding," Bibs was saying. "I'm not. One day I looked in the mirror and I saw the beginnings of a beard, and I thought, *oh no, uh-uh, not this face.* And so I covered my chin in cold cream, and I picked up Douglas's razor, and I"—Bibs mimed the gesture. Spotting Laura, she smiled and patted the mattress.

"I was just telling Stephanie that my biggest fear isn't death, it's what I'll look like should I become a vegetable. I'm entrusting you two with my skin-care routine, which includes something I've never told anyone I do but is part of the reason my skin is so smooth for a woman my age." She took Laura's hand and pressed it to her cheek.

"It's very smooth," Laura said.

"I'll tell you why," Bibs said. "It's because once a week I shave my face with your father's razor. He doesn't know.

"It's on the shelf in the medicine cabinet," she said, pointing to the bathroom. "What do you think? Do you think you'd be able to do that for me?"

Laura nodded.

"It wouldn't be a little weird for you, psychologically?"

Laura smiled. "I think I can handle it."

"Excuse me while I go downstairs and make a phone call," Stephanie said.

"You can use that one," Bibs said, pointing to her bedside table.

Stephanie looked flustered. "I don't want to disturb you. I should also throw this away." She held up the empty can of Diet Coke.

Stephanie left the room. She wanted to let the two of them be alone, Laura realized.

"Look at the man dangling from a tree," Bibs said, pointing to the garden. "What do you think he's doing?"

Laura got up and walked over to the window. In the garden behind their garden, a man was suspended in a harness attached to a tree. He was holding some kind of instrument that looked like a saw.

"Tree maintenance," Laura said.

"What?"

"He's cutting a branch off."

The branch looked fine, though. She wondered if it was for aesthetic reasons.

Laura watched the man saw through the branch until it gave.

"Oh, darling, don't cry," Bibs said tenderly. "I don't know what Daddy told you, but there's nothing to worry about."

Laura continued to stand by the window, facing the other way.

"Nothing, nothing, *nothing*, and I absolutely mean it. I've got the best doctor in all of New York City—he performs this sort of procedure all the time."

Laura nodded.

"You should see his hands—he's got the fingers of a penis!"

"A *what*?" Laura knew her mother had deliberately misspoken, but feigned amused dismay as she turned to look at her.

"A *pian*ist." Bibs smiled her mischievous smile. "What did you *think* I said?"

LAURA COULDN'T REMEMBER HER GREAT-GRANDFATHER Hendon, but she would never forget his funeral. At six, she was old enough to recognize the solemnity of the occasion and was thus understandably embarrassed when, in the middle of the service, something had struck her mother as amusing and she began to giggle. Unable to compose herself, Bibs had gotten on all fours and crawled out of the pew and down the aisle.

"Suffice it to say," Laura told the congregation, "if you feel the urge to laugh at any point during this service, please go ahead—my mother would have loved it."

A polite echo of titters was pierced by a shrill sob in the first pew. It came from Emma, whose periodic fits of audible grief were amplified by the acoustics of the church.

Douglas, on the other hand, seemed to be taking everything in from a lighthearted remove. When Laura and Emma had shown up at 136 that morning to accompany him to the funeral, he'd looked at his watch and said, "I suppose we shouldn't wait any longer for your mother," and laughed to himself. At the conclusion of the service, he turned around to survey the crowd and chuckled, "We should've booked Madison Square Garden." There were indeed a lot of people in attendance. As they processed down the aisle, Laura looked up and saw that the balcony was full, too.

Emma's tears abated when she laid eyes on the vehicle Stephanie had ordered to take them to the Library, where the reception would take place.

"Is this a stretch limo?" she sniffled as they climbed in.

After taking a seat, Emma smoothed the skirt of her black velvet dress, one of several outrageously priced dresses she'd brought home after spending an afternoon with Bibs the previous winter. Laura had told Emma she could keep one, but Emma had bargained her up to two. The rest went in the children's bin of a local donation center. Laura felt a little guilty about this now.

"Are we in a stretch limo?" Emma asked again when the question went ignored.

"I guess it is," Laura said. She reached out to squeeze the plump kneecap of Nicholas Jr., who sat in his father's lap. When he smiled she did it again.

"That was quite the turnout," Stephanie remarked as they cruised down Fifth.

"The minister told me it was the largest one he'd ever seen," Nicholas said.

"I feel bad for baby Nick," Emma said, looking forlornly at her cousin. "When he grows up, he won't even remember Bibs."

As they pulled up to the Library, Stephanie let out a gasp. "We forgot your father!"

"He wanted to walk," Laura and Nicholas said in unison.

"*Walk?*" Stephanie repeated, perplexed. "But that's a *long* walk—the reception might be over by the time he gets here!"

"I think that's the point," Laura told her.

They'd reserved the East Hall, the largest room in the Library, and within minutes of their arrival it was packed. Only a fraction of the guests were people Laura recognized, but they all wanted to talk to her. They hovered about waiting for an opportunity to jump in and introduce themselves, compliment her eulogy, share their Bibs anecdote, and then utter the embarrassing phrase: *So sorry for your loss.* That Bibs had scores of fans was no surprise, but Laura was struck by how many claimed Bibs was their best friend—their primary confidante.

They weren't all Upper East Side socialites, either. A handful of her mother's doctors were in attendance, along with Frank, her florist;

several store clerks; Bill, her favorite London Towncar driver; a pair of waiters from Claude's; and of course, Jean-Paul, who had refused payment for his final, unscheduled bedside visits to touch up her roots. Several nurses she'd only met in her final month were also there — people with hourly wages who had taken off work to attend.

Though her mother had been socially promiscuous, this didn't delegitimize the love others had for her. For the most part Laura was touched and proud. But there was also the occasional spasm of a painful thought: If a life is measured by the affection one earned, where would that leave her?

Over the years, when meeting her mother's friends, Laura was aware that she was not what they expected, perhaps a disappointment, and it made her feel bad about herself. Today, however, her natural reserve and sober disposition suited the occasion, and she didn't feel as though she had anything to prove. She sensed that people were impressed by her quiet dignity, her restraint and composure.

At one point Laura got trapped by a man who was talking much too loudly, standing much too close, his breath smelling of scotch and ham. When she thought she couldn't take it anymore, a female guest came along and rescued her.

She was older than Laura, possibly in her sixties. "It must be exhausting," the woman said, "being the receptacle for everyone's feelings for your mother."

Interpreting this as an apologetic preface to her own monologue about Bibs, Laura smiled and waited for her to begin, but instead the woman continued on this train of thought.

"It doesn't leave much room for you own feelings," she reflected. She wasn't conventionally beautiful, but there was something arresting about her face. It was her eyes, Laura decided, which were as blue as they come. She didn't color her hair or wear any makeup.

"It doesn't," Laura agreed. She hadn't thought of it that way, but it explained the fact that she hadn't cried at the service. She'd told herself she'd held it in for Emma's sake, but the truth was she'd been numb. All week she'd been unable to feel anything.

She was about to thank this woman for her helpful insight, when along came Stephanie. "Excuse me while I borrow Laura for a moment," she said.

"Your father's still not here," Stephanie gravely informed her. She looked annoyed by Laura's unfazed shrug. "People are asking for him and I don't know what to say."

"Say you last saw him over there," Laura pointed vaguely into the crowd.

Stephanie looked unsatisfied but nodded. "Who were you talking to?" she asked.

Laura glanced over her shoulder, but the woman was gone. She hadn't gotten her name.

The afternoon dragged on.

Emma appeared, sporting a Coca-Cola mustache. "I'm bored and I have a stomachache," she announced. "When can we go home?"

"Not until the end, I'm afraid," Laura told her. "Why don't you go play with Baby Nick."

"Not allowed." Emma crossed her arms and let out a defiant sigh. "Stephanie said I was too hyper."

Laura glanced across the room to where Stephanie was keeping vigil over her son's stroller.

"Nick-Nick-Nick-Nick, Nick-Nick-Nick-*Nick*," Emma sang, "Nickel-*o*-de-*on*."

"Remember, Stephanie doesn't like that song," Laura said.

"It's not a song," Emma said. "Can we go to Jackson Hole for dinner?"

"I suppose so, when it's time to leave."

"*Yesss.*" Emma made a fist and pulled her arm toward her chest before dashing off.

Laura spotted the woman across the room. She was wearing a coat and appeared to be on her way out. Laura felt a twinge of panic—at the very least she wanted to find out her name.

The crowd had started to thin, but this only made it more difficult for Laura to navigate her way across the room because she was more visible. Every step she took there was another person wanting a word with her. One of these people was the minister.

"Laura," he said, and, in the manner of an old friend, clasped both of her hands in his.

Laura nodded respectfully and waited to be released, but the minister was in no rush to move on. Her parents' relationship with the church was based on its convenient location, social affiliation, and their ability to pay its annual suggested dues and then some. This particular minister had officiated a handful of ceremonies Laura had attended over the years, but they'd been formally introduced only that morning. No history or connection existed between the two of them; that he insisted on pretending otherwise stripped him of any spiritual credibility, even integrity, in Laura's opinion. Moreover, a while ago he had left the church to return to his previous occupation as an auctioneer for Christie's, only to come back a year or two later, telling the *Times*, in a write-up about his career switch, that the two professions "aren't really all that different."

"The service was beautiful," Laura told the minister, when he persisted in standing there, pretending they were having a moment. "Thank you."

"It was a privilege," he said. "She was an extraordinary woman."

Laura was eager to extract herself from his holy presence when someone tapped her on the shoulder. Again the woman had rescued her!

Her name was Philomena, but she told Laura to call her Phil.

SATURDAY EVENING FAMILY DINNERS AT 136 had been Laura's idea, but she soon realized they were unnecessary. Douglas was not lacking for company. On the contrary, widowers were constantly invited out, and in return her father routinely hosted weeknight dinner parties for friends and business associates. These were frequent enough that Sandra couldn't be bothered to adjust the wings of the dining room table to accommodate their smaller family meals, and so there was too much space between their chairs, especially tonight, as Emma had been invited to spend the weekend at a classmate's country house. Nick Jr. was at home with Colette, his nineteen-year-old Parisian au pair. It was just the four of them: Laura, Nicholas, Stephanie, and Douglas—with Sandra periodically bursting through the swinging door to survey their progress and see if it was time to start clearing.

Laura saw them through Sandra's eyes, and it was a vaguely tragic image; there was an unnatural formality to the way they addressed one another, and with Bibs gone, it was more obvious than ever that they took no joy or even comfort in each other's company. Stephanie made a valiant effort to fill the silences, but her attempts to generate a group conversation were rarely successful. After all these years of being married to Nicholas she was still an outsider, and her attempts to ingratiate herself to their family more often rendered their differences more pronounced. Laura felt like they were characters in a play about WASPs—a satirical production that yielded no new insights, just desiccated clichés. She imagined an Upper West Side Jewish audience getting bored and leaving before intermission.

At seven-forty-five the brass clock on the mantel chimed, and Stephanie remarked what a nice clock it was—*a one-of-a-kind antique, I've always meant to ask where it came from.* Douglas shrugged absently, and Stephanie smiled stupidly, oblivious to her faux pas. To fawn over a particular object felt like an appeal to Douglas's pride of ownership, his material vanity, and that wasn't the nature of his relationship to possessions. Most of their things had been passively acquired, passed down from the previous generation; their existence felt as arbitrary and predetermined as height and eye color.

As Laura strived to come up with a way to validate Stephanie's comment about the clock, her father stood up and walked over to the mantel, picked up the clock, and carried it back to the table.

"Take it home with you," he said, placing it by Stephanie, who looked thrilled and mortified.

"I *couldn't*," she balked.

"You'll be doing me a favor," Douglas grumbled. "It's always driven me nuts, the sound of that clock."

"Mom, too," Nicholas said. "*Ding-dong*, one hour *older*, one hour closer to *death!*" He smiled at his own impersonation.

"Maybe you would like to have it," Stephanie said, looking at Laura, who was not smiling.

"No, no, you take it," Laura said, and stood up to help Sandra clear the dishes.

For as long as she could remember, that clock had lived on the mantel. It had felt like an organic extension of the marble, its meticulous tick-tock the pulse of the house. From there on, every time she stepped in the front door of 136, she was momentarily unnerved by the silence.

PHIL LIVED WITH HER DOG on a houseboat in the Seventy-ninth Street Boat Basin off the West Side Highway. It was a temporary situation. She'd recently gotten divorced and wasn't ready to commit to a new apartment. Maybe she never would, maybe she would move to San Francisco or Barcelona. She wasn't sure what the future had in store for her. Right now she was enjoying her new life. Her *freedom*.

He hadn't liked to do things, Phil's ex. Wasn't interested in trying new food, didn't appreciate travel or art, wasn't curious about the world. "A creature of routine and habit," she summed him up. "No appetite for life."

Phil volunteered all this as they waited in line to get their buttons at the Metropolitan Museum of Art. Now it was Laura's turn to speak. She asked how Phil had known Bibs.

"From group," Phil said.

"Group?" Laura repeated.

"With Dr. Clarke," she added. "She only joined last January, but before that we had back-to-back individual sessions on Thursday mornings, so I'd been crossing paths with her for years."

"I see," Laura said.

"What's your star sign?" Phil asked, as they headed toward the American Wing.

"I believe I'm a Virgo," Laura said.

"*Believe?*" Phil repeated, incredulous that one wouldn't know for certain.

"I've never paid attention to any of that stuff," Laura admitted.

"You know, I credit your mother for my freedom," Phil told her. "We would talk about our marriages and she would say, 'It's too late for me, Phil, I'm an old lady, but you have a chance of finding the real thing out there.'" Laura was surprised Phil thought it was appropriate to share this with Laura—that it was something she'd want to hear. She cringed to think at what else Bibs might have disclosed to this roomful of strangers.

Phil shook her head and smiled. "Which I always thought ridiculous because she was *only* . . . not that much older than me. Not to mention extremely beautiful."

As she said this last thing Phil looked at Laura in a way that conveyed the compliment extended to her, and Laura smiled and nodded, though the whole thing made her very uncomfortable.

When they'd met at her mother's service, Laura had had the feeling of being in the presence of someone who saw her exactly for who she was, who possessed a certain wisdom and maturity. In the days leading up to this Saturday at the museum, she'd been animated by foolish expectations of a potential friendship. But this woman was not the person Laura had imagined her to be.

"She was quite a woman, your mother," Phil carried on. "Whatever it is that governs our inner child and dictates how we behave as we get older, your mother had a deficit of that, which enabled her to say exactly what was on her mind, eschew social conventions, fully inhabit her emotions, to live a life uncompromised by shame or anxiety or self-doubt. She truly knew how to be present."

Was this how people spoke in group therapy? The words sounded lifted from the pages of a psychology manual, Laura thought.

"To be around her," Phil continued, "just for an hour a week, made it harder and harder to go to this man who did *not* inspire me . . ."

"This has always been one of my favorites," Laura said, pointing to a painting that, in truth, she'd never seen before. It was of Central Park in the nineteenth century, and featured a group of children sledding at dusk. From their various poses you could imagine the sort of adults they would grow up to be. Some of the children went belly-down headfirst; others took a more cautious approach, straddling their toboggans, dragging their feet along the sides to slow their descent. Some slid down in pairs, the one in the back clutching the one in the front.

The painting's inscription didn't specify the exact location, but Laura was almost positive it was Dog Hill, above the Seventy-second Street entrance. She shared this with Phil, and then felt silly when she neither affirmed nor disputed her hunch.

"And what does it *do* for you, this painting?" she asked. "What does it *trigger*, what does it *say*?"

Laura didn't know how to respond. There was the tranquil beauty of Central Park in the snow, the yesteryear simplicity of the activity, but there was more to it than that. On the painting's lower-right quadrant, a toddler held a string attached to a red toboggan. She seemed unsure of what to do with it—as though she were waiting for it to make the first move. Off to the side, her mother leaned against a tree, ankles crossed, lost in contemplation. The contrast of their inert figures amidst this swirl of activity unspooled a series of dark thoughts, at the center of which was a question the painter had surely not meant to inspire: What was the point of it all?

In Laura's childhood, her mother had had dark moods where she'd ask questions like this and Laura wouldn't know what to say. Once Douglas had come into the room and sat beside her on the bed. Taking his wife's hand in his own, he'd recited a fragment of a poem:

> *Comb your hair, comb your hair*
> *Don't you worry about despair*
> *Despair is a strange disease*
> *I think it happens even to trees*

It was one of the more tender moments Laura had witnessed of her parents' marriage, and remembering it now, it brought tears to her eyes.

"Life is meant to be enjoyed," Phil answered for herself. "That's what this painting says to me."

LAURA WAS GOING TO INVOLVE Emma in the disposal of Bibs's ashes, but she'd changed her mind. Emma, being Emma, would become so overwhelmed with emotions that it would be impossible for Laura to feel anything herself. She wondered if it was selfish, but she'd arranged for Emma to spend the afternoon with a classmate, and, after leaving work at the usual time, Laura headed alone to Central Park.

It was November—her favorite month. The sky was low and gray and it was the coldest day of the season so far. There weren't many people out, but there was a sense of habitual activity beneath the surface of things, the plucky endurance of the natural world. Squirrels scuttled about in feverish pursuit of chestnuts and acorns, occasionally pausing in the middle of the path, as if paralyzed by a sudden troubling thought, before abruptly springing back to life, reversing course, and scampering up trees, their cheeks loaded with loot. The air felt clean and decadent with the sweet rot of leaves and the occasional whiff of horse manure. Stripped bare, the arched limbs of the London plane trees that lined the pedestrian walkways appeared in whimsical harmony, like the arms and legs of a procession of ballerinas, choreographed to achieve such an effect.

Laura hadn't had a specific location in mind for the scattering of the ashes, but now an idea came to her, which was to divvy them up among Bibs's favorite spots—to "sprinkle hither and thither," as *The Moosewood Cookbook* would say.

The Boat Pond was deserted. To be outside in Manhattan and not see a single other person! Laura paused by the *Alice in Wonderland* statue to savor the novelty of it. The buildings that were visible along the perimeter of the park were all prewar; from where she stood, it could be any decade. It felt like the right place to begin.

Laura had just procured the canister from her tote bag when she noticed a man in a trench coat walking in her direction. Her irritation was short-lived when she realized who it was.

Laura had seen Woody Allen in the neighborhood before, most

memorably when he'd arrived at a restaurant where she and Bibs had met for lunch. (Bibs had tried to make them switch seats so Laura would be visible to him, insisting she was "his type." When Laura had protested, citing the fact that he was currently involved with Mia Farrow, Bibs had clarified that she'd meant the type of actress he cast in his movies.)

To see him today, however, and of all occasions! Laura didn't believe in such things, but this felt like too much of a coincidence: being alone at the Boat Pond with her mother's ashes, with Woody Allen strolling by at the precise moment she was about to open the lid. Like finding the old-fashioned kind of penny or a four-leaf clover, it was a good omen, an auspicious nod from the universe.

But as he got closer, she saw it wasn't Woody Allen—just a small man with similar glasses. Her disappointment robbed the moment of its spiritual charge, and Laura slipped the canister back into her bag and moved on.

Immobile, the carousel didn't feel like an inspired location, nor did the Bethesda Fountain, which had been shut off. Laura tried a few other beloved spots, but none sparked the feelings she'd hoped they would summon. Perhaps it would make more sense to do this in April—Bibs's favorite month.

And so she left the park, her bag as heavy as when she'd arrived.

BIBS'S PARENTS HAD DIED TOGETHER in a boating mishap in their sixties. In the wake of the accident, ownership of Round Bush, the Long Island estate where Bibs had grown up, had been transferred to her eldest brother, Percy. Bibs thought this was unfair and lawyers had gotten involved, but in the end the court ruled in Percy's favor.

Laura was sad when Bibs forbade them to have any contact with Percy moving forward, not for the loss of her uncle, whom she didn't really know, but that she would never again be able to visit Round Bush.

It was called Round Bush because there was a bush in the middle of the circular driveway, and it was round. Laura had always thought it was an informal, family nickname, so she was surprised to see it was her uncle's address in the *Social Register*: "Round Bush, Locust Valley." Just that, no house number.

She'd looked up his listing a few weeks after Bibs died, but it was several months before she screwed up the nerve to dial it. So as not to get Emma emotionally worked up, Laura told her they were going to see relatives, but didn't mention they lived in what had been Bibs's childhood home.

"It's like a hotel," Emma said as they pulled up to the house, a rambling Tudor covered with ivy. Percy's wife, Emma, had found the house too large, and the east wing had been demolished. Apart from this, it was just how Laura remembered from her visits there as a child. She was amazed to see that her grandmother's parrot, Arthur, was still alive. He had been trained to say two things: "Hello" and "Vote Republican." According to Emma, he'd just gone in for his annual checkup, and at sixty-two had been declared in perfect health.

"He'll outlive us all!" Percy declared with a hearty chuckle.

Laura had told Emma not to make any sort of fuss, that all she'd wanted to do was see the house and go for a quick walk in the woods, but Emma insisted on serving them lunch—or "supper," as it was called at Round Bush.

Food had never been Round Bush's forte, and the meal was also exactly what Laura remembered being served there as a child: meat, potatoes, and a vegetable, all cooked in a way that stripped the food of individual characteristics. Even Emma, who was known to eat everything, looked a bit daunted by the plate of greasy gray food that was set in front of her.

"This is just like ketchup," Laura whispered as she spooned currant jelly onto her meat. "Promise you'll like it."

It was not and she didn't, but, recognizing that things were a certain way at Round Bush, Emma put forth her best effort to finish as much as she could and to hide her disappointment when dessert plates materialized—bearing salad.

After all the dishes had been cleared, a silver box was passed around the table containing a row of black wax-paper envelopes. Inside each envelope was a disc of chocolate, thin and delicate enough that it dissolved like a snowflake on Emma's tongue, leaving behind a sticky mint goo that was so delicious it felt a shame to swallow. When the box of chocolates had made its way around the table once, it did not come around again. It went back to its perch on the side table, and everyone stood up and left the table.

Learning the grown-ups were planning to take a walk, Emma asked if she had to go. When Laura hesitated to respond, she added, "I have a tummy-ache."

"Poor dear," older Emma said. "Would you like to lie down and see if a nap helps?"

Emma had no interest in naps, but she was caught in a lie. She nodded and accepted the hand of older Emma, who led her upstairs.

Laura trotted after them, protesting that Emma would be just fine on a couch in the living room. "Don't be silly," older Emma said.

*   *   *

EMMA STOOD AT THE WINDOW of the bedroom she'd been given and watched as the adults set out across the lawn. She waited until they'd disappeared into the woods before leaving the room.

At the end of the hallway she opened a door that led to a secret spiral staircase, which delivered her to the kitchen. Marie, the woman who had served them lunch, was not there. It occurred to Emma that there was no one else in the house.

Being alone in the house felt like trespassing in a museum that was not open; you had to be careful not to open the wrong door, touch something you weren't supposed to touch—an alarm could go off, the police could come.

She quietly passed the parrot's cage in the living room.

"Vote Republican," Arthur said.

Emma had assumed the dining room door would be locked. It wasn't. The tick-tock of the grandfather clock felt like the collective heartbeat of the ghosts of her ancestors whose oil portraits hung on the wall, their faces bearing down on her in stony disapproval. It was a dark room to begin with, having only one small set of windows, and the curtains were drawn but not all the way. A single beam of light slipped through the crack, illuminating a path across the rug, beginning where she now stood, and continuing all the way across the room to the side table, on top of which sat the box of chocolates.

Opening the box, taking out one of the envelopes, and placing the chocolate disc on her tongue gave Emma a funny feeling. It was like her heart was beating—except you-know-where. It was like she had to pee, but she didn't actually have to pee. It was a feeling she'd had before, but never this powerful. It made her want to press herself up against the hard, sloping angle of the leg of the dining room table.

Chocolate dissolving in her mouth, Emma sidled up to the table and enacted the pose she'd had in mind. The grown-ups would be returning from their walk at any minute, but she couldn't help herself; she kept doing what she was doing. A minute passed, and then another. The grandfather clock chimed deeply to signal a new hour. Another minute ticked off, and then, like a stuttered sigh, like a yawn between her legs, something deep inside her came unsprung.

It was the greatest feeling she'd ever known, but before she knew what was happening, it was over. A sudden drowsiness descended, and she returned upstairs to the bed on which she'd been left.

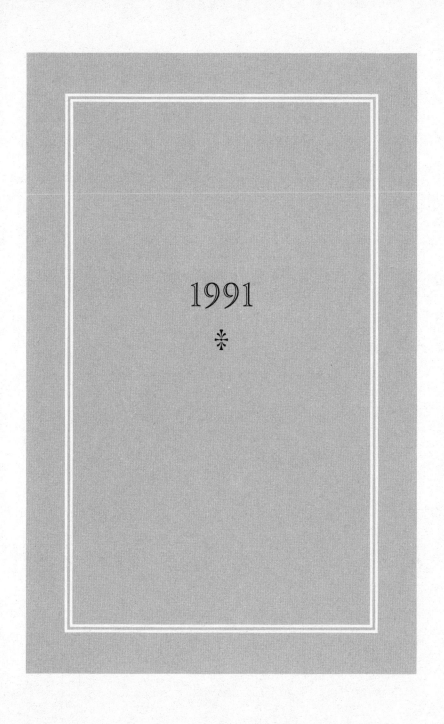

1991

✳

FREE SKY, A NEIGHBORHOOD ASSOCIATION DEVOTED TO FIGHT-
ing the development of new high-rises, to protect the New York City
skyline from turning into Tokyo, was holding its annual benefit at the
Library that year. Laura had helped coordinate some of the logistics
and was named an honorary host.

The East Hall buzzed with the din of hundreds of tipsy people
talking at once. Leaving the apartment in her silk peasant blouse and
the skirt she wore to special events—custom-made from a pair of
old Pierre Deux curtains—her hair swept back in a velvet headband,
Laura had felt confident and pretty. But in this room teeming with
long-legged women in miniskirts, tossing their professionally blow-
dried locks back in laughter as they struck poses like storefront man-
nequins, she felt like a child.

"You're *here!*" Edith shouted in her ear. "Good! There's someone
I'd like you to meet!" She whisked Laura through the crowd. "I know
you think I'm pushy, but I'm telling you, my instincts are right on this
one."

Eventually they reached their destination: a man standing alone
by the bar.

"*James*, this is Laura! *Laura*, this is James! *She's* single, *you're* wid-
owed, you both have daughters named Emma—now *talk!*"

Edith took a few giddy steps back, as if she'd just taken a match to
a firework that was about to detonate.

Laura and the widower shyly shook hands.

"Is your Emma named for anyone?" Laura asked lamely.

The widower seemed to consider the question for a beat longer than necessary before shaking his head.

Laura tried to think of another, better question. "It's a great name—what a shame it's become so popular these days."

The widower nodded, staring into his drink.

"If you'll excuse me," he said, and disappeared into the crowd.

"I guess it was too soon," Edith said, returning to Laura's side.

"When did he lose his wife?" Laura asked.

"Around Thanksgiving," she answered. "Cancer. Didn't know her well, but she seemed lovely. Unpretentious, a little shy, down-to-earth, endearingly clueless when it came to clothes." She shook her head sadly. "Adorably unstylish."

THE PHONE RANG AND A male voice Laura did not recognize spoke her name.

"I hope you don't mind, I looked you up in the phone book," he said. "I'm calling to apologize."

"Sorry, who is this?" Laura asked.

"James. James Ettinger. We met a few months ago at that Free Sky thing. Your friend introduced us."

"Of course," Laura said. "Hello again."

"Anyway, I'm calling to apologize for my abrupt departure. It was my first night out since losing my wife. My first night leaving my daughter at home, and I wasn't prepared to socialize."

"I completely understand," Laura said.

There was a silence.

"Anyway, I'm sorry it's taken me so long to call."

"Don't be ridiculous," Laura said. "An apology is completely unwarranted."

"The other reason I was calling," James said, in a jauntier tone, "is that Emma has since become very fond of her babysitter. Which is nice, as it means I'm able to have the occasional evening out—"

"How nice that she likes her babysitter!" Laura interrupted.

"Yes, she's actually scheduled to arrive here in an hour," James continued. "But my plans for this evening just fell through, and I was wondering—and this is very last-minute and I'm sure the answer is no . . ."

"I'VE HEARD WONDERFUL THINGS ABOUT the Day School," Laura said upon learning this was where James's Emma went.

James nodded slightly as he browsed the menu. Laura pretended to be absorbed in her own menu until James abruptly snapped his shut, clasped his hands on top of it, and smiled at Laura. It was a tired, peaceful smile, the kind one wore in the company of someone so familiar that their physical proximity didn't require small talk, conveying the simple comfort of being reunited at the end of the day. If the feeling behind the smile was genuine, it was not mutual. Laura didn't know this man, but she wanted to, and the pressure to conduct herself in a way that legitimized the smile made her very anxious. She wished he would say something.

"I've heard wonderful things about the Day School," Laura repeated, in case he hadn't heard.

"It's a different kind of school," James responded.

"Yes, it has a reputation for being very . . ." The immediate phrases that came to mind were Janet's rhyming slurs: *hippie-dippy, loosey-goosey, artsy-fartsy*. She smiled at James, hoping he would finish the sentence, but he continued waiting, patiently, for Laura to compose the rest of her thought.

"It has a reputation for encouraging kids to think outside the box," she managed.

James's expression indicated he remained in listening mode.

"To be free-spirited," Laura added. "March to the beat of their own drum."

James cocked his head in consideration.

"Maybe that's not the right way to put it," Laura said. "Anyway, I'm just going on secondhand information. What do I know?"

James smiled. "No, no, the rumors are true. It's very much that kind of place." He stared thoughtfully at his butter plate. An amused expression flickered across this face and he shook his head as though recalling a joke.

"To give you an example," he said, "they just had an election for first-grade class president. The students were never told they had to vote for a peer; it was assumed they'd know this. Turns out they didn't, and their ballots had all sorts of ridiculous candidates: the class rabbit, MC Hammer, Big Bird, the tooth fairy . . ."

The waiter appeared to take their orders. When James said he'd stick to water—flat, not sparkling—Laura said the same.

"How funny," Laura said after he'd left. James looked confused. "The class election. The kids voting for all those outlandish characters!"

"Ah, yes. After announcing a sixteen-way tie, there was a second election, and the kids were told they should vote for a person in the classroom."

"And who won?"

"You're looking at him."

"You? How flattering!"

"Yes, well, I've spent a lot of time in the classroom recently." He raised his eyebrows. "After Emma lost her mother we both took some time off. Eventually it was time to go back, me to work, her to first grade, but she got very worked up when I started to leave her at drop-off, so I ended up staying for a few hours, and it's since become the new routine. We go to school together, I leave around noon and head to the office."

"And what do you do?" Laura asked. She meant for work, but he misinterpreted the question.

"Oh, I do whatever they're doing: music, art, chess, free time—there's a lot of free time at the Day School." A fond look came over his face. "A lot of hanging out on the rug."

"I think that sounds very nice," Laura told him. "Let kids be kids."

"Yes, it couldn't be more different from the atmosphere of where I was sent as a kid. I went to St. Christopher's, which was a little less nurturing, to put it mildly."

"Oh, I know." Laura nodded. "I went to Winthrop. I'm embarrassed to tell you that's where my Emma goes. It wasn't my first choice. Pushy alumnae committee."

Their meals arrived. After setting down their plates, the waiter whisked off their metal tops with theatrical flair. "*Bon appétit!*" he said with a bow. As he started to walk away, James did charades for a pepper grinder. This was unnecessary, as a younger waiter was already advancing in their direction, holding the grinder out before him as though it were a sacred offering. Laura smiled in embarrassment; she hated this aspect of French restaurants.

"You know, I think I will have a glass of wine," James said shortly into the meal.

"On second thought, I will, too," Laura said.

Their wine arrived. To Laura's relief, James did not try to initiate a clinking of glasses—nor had he attempted to hug or cheek-kiss her hello. So many dates began with such gestures, the premature, forced intimacy of which doomed any chance of the real thing's blossoming.

ON THEIR SECOND DATE, LAURA noticed that James had an earring. The restaurant was dim, but occasionally it caught the light and glittered. It appeared to be purple, in the shape of a heart. She wondered why she hadn't noticed it earlier. Could James have been in Vietnam and received a purple heart in the form of an earring—was that even possible? No; he'd never mentioned the military, and besides, it was surely a medal.

Laura knew that earrings on men were considered stylish these days, but her own earlobes weren't pierced and it was difficult to entertain a romantic future with a man whose were. Likewise, it seemed odd that such a man would pursue a woman whose weren't. Laura's progressive politics and tendency to embrace forward-thinking ideas excluded fashion, and she didn't see this changing. Were she and James to become a couple, she imagined others struggling to make sense of their mismatched aesthetics and then drawing the conclusion: *beggars can't be choosers*. Although his late wife, she now recalled, had been "adorably unstylish," so maybe he didn't care about it in women.

As the evening went on, James told her more about his work as a lawyer for the National Resources Defense Council, and Laura was so impressed by this that she forgot all about the earring. Then he turned his head to catch the waiter's attention, and the resulting angle revealed a *second* earring on the other lobe. This one was pink and appeared to be a star.

Earlier in the night, James had proposed a postprandial nightcap at the Carlyle, where some jazz band he liked was playing. Laura's enthusiasm for the plan had been restrained after noticing the first earring, which was perhaps a hallmark of a passing midlife crisis. But a second earring was too much, clear evidence that they weren't meant for each other, and she began brainstorming excuses to go straight home after the meal.

James got up to use the restroom. When he returned to the table, Laura was about to apologize that she'd just remembered she'd promised the babysitter to be home by nine when she noticed the earrings were gone. Perhaps her gaze lingered a little too long on his newly naked lobes.

"You may have noticed that I was wearing earrings." He smiled sheepishly.

"I see you took them off."

"They were stickers," he said. "This morning on the rug Emma and her friends were playing beauty parlor. I was the customer, and they did my hair in all these little pigtails. I looked so ridiculous, the teacher insisted on taking a Polaroid. Anyway, before heading to the office I took the pigtails out, but apparently I missed the earrings.

"This means I went around in them all day," he reflected. "It's not funny," he protested when Laura giggled. "I had an important meeting today!"

"Yes, with the head of the EPA," Laura reminded him. He'd described the meeting earlier, and as Laura imagined it now, she burst out laughing.

James winced. "To think my colleagues didn't say anything. They must think I'm having some kind of midlife crisis!"

Laura laughed even harder. She reached for her water then put it back down, afraid she might choke. People at other tables turned to look at her but she didn't care. It felt wonderful to laugh this hard. The prospect of extending the night at the Carlyle was now much more appealing. She could tell James enjoyed her hysterics, because when it started to subside he reignited it by mentioning other people he'd encountered that day: his doorman, an old acquaintance from boarding school—his father-in-law!

At this final example, Laura's laughter petered out. Laura didn't catch the error, but James quickly corrected himself. "I guess we're no longer technically in-laws."

Laura nodded soberly.

"Next time you see me in *earrings*"—James wagged his finger across the table, trying to resuscitate the levity—"or *pigtails*, or *makeup*, please do me a favor and say something!"

"I will." Laura took a sip of water. The laughter had opened up a space in her, and now that it was over, she felt empty.

The bill came. James took out his wallet, and Laura looked down and examined her hands. They looked older than the rest of her. She'd recently discovered that when she pinched the skin of her knuckle, the fold stayed there for a moment before restoring itself.

When they stepped out into the street, James bit his lip and glanced at his watch.

"Hmm, it's a little late." He frowned. "I should probably get back to Emma and save the Carlyle for another time."

"Yes, me, too," Laura said quickly.

A PIECE OF MAIL ARRIVED that had no return address. Inside was a child's drawing, on a folded piece of construction paper. Laura thought it might be a card, but the corners were glued together so she couldn't open it.

"Did you draw this?" she asked Emma.

Emma scrutinized the picture. "I'm a better artist than that."

The drawing was of three stick figures—man, woman, and child—holding hands and smiling. The man was disproportionately tall; the top of his head abutted the beams of a smiling sun in the upper right-hand corner.

Laura almost threw it out, but then she stuck it under a magnet on the fridge. She'd recently conducted a purge of Emma's early childhood artwork—there was so much of it—and the refrigerator door now looked bare.

THEY CONTINUED TO MEET FOR dinner once a week, sometimes twice. James was kind, made her laugh, and was comfortingly familiar. They had similar values and upbringings. It was premature to call what she felt for him love, but it seemed like a precursor to that.

"How is he in bed?" Margaret wanted to know.

Laura blushed.

"Fine, but is he a good kisser? You have to tell me that much!"

"I'm not sure," Laura confessed. "We're taking it slow."

"He hasn't *kissed* you yet?" Margaret's tone was incredulous.

"I told you, *we're taking it slow.*"

"But you said you were *dating?*"

"Exactly. We're going on dates."

"Laura, meeting for dinner is one thing, but you're not *dating* until there's physical contact."

"Where'd you read that, *Seventeen* magazine?"

"I think it's sweet that you're taking it slow." Margaret reached out and gave Laura's wrist an affectionate squeeze. "I'm sure it'll happen soon. He's probably shy. You might need to make the first move."

Laura decided to wear pumps on their next date. She rarely wore heels, as walking in them made her feel like an amateur transvestite. To get more comfortable, she practiced strolling up and down the hall of their apartment. Emma stood in the doorway of her bedroom watching, a dreamy look in her eyes.

"Oh, Mama." She swooned. "I wish you'd wear those shoes every day. You look so pretty—like a real woman."

The babysitter arrived.

"Tell me the truth," Laura said, opening the door. "Are these shoes a bit much?"

"Love the shoes." Daisy nodded in approval then ran her gaze over the rest of Laura. "The *turtleneck*, not so much, and the skirt's a little music-teacher-spends-the-weekend-in-the-country."

"All her skirts look like that," Emma scoffed. "And she only wears turtlenecks. Every day."

"You got a date?" Daisy asked, chewing gum.

Emma burst out laughing. "Moms don't go on dates!"

"A board meeting," Laura said. She contemplated throwing a wink in Daisy's direction, but decided against it.

Emma grabbed Daisy's hand and began tugging her down the hall toward her bedroom.

"I'll be back by ten," Laura hollered as she headed out.

"Don't forget to kiss me good night!" came Emma's voice through the door.

"I won't! And also, I know what people think of my skirts and turtlenecks, but I don't care, it's my signature look and I'm sticking to it!"

"Go get 'em, girl!" Daisy shouted back.

During dinner, Laura slipped out of her pumps with the intention of grazing her feet against James's legs. Too shy to carry through with it, she ordered a second glass of wine. It wasn't enough. Eventually the check arrived and Laura still hadn't mustered the self-possession to make a move of any kind.

"Thank you, that was delicious," she said as James signed the bill.

After exiting the restaurant, James stepped into the street to hail Laura a cab; he always did and insisted on paying.

"The air feels so nice," Laura called out to him. "I think I'll walk home."

"It is nice out," James said, returning to the sidewalk. "If you don't mind, I think I'll join you."

They cut over to Park Avenue and proceeded north. At one point Laura stepped off the curb before the light had turned, and James jumped out ahead of her and extended his arm like the gate of a toll-booth but, seeing there was no oncoming traffic, retracted it before Laura could initiate a collision.

Before she knew it, they'd arrived at her building. Placing his hands on her elbows, James leaned forward and gave Laura a peck on the cheek.

"You know, you can kiss me," Laura whispered as he withdrew. "On the mouth. The real way."

The kiss was short, quick, and dry, and as she rode the elevator up, Laura was tormented by the lyrics of a song from her youth: *It's in his kiss, that's where it is.*

On her way out, Daisy apologized for her earlier comment about Laura's turtleneck and skirt and the music-teacher reference.

"I think it's awesome that you rock your own style," she added.

"YOU HAVE A VISITOR," SAID Karen.

At her side stood James. His hair was wet, and so were his clothes; Laura could smell the damp fibers of his suit. His shoes made a squeaking sound as he stepped into her cubicle. Laura rolled her chair back to create a distance between the two of them, as if he were a dog who'd emerged from a body of water and was about to shake.

Taking the empty seat by her file cabinet, he flashed her a conspiratorial smile. Laura did not return it.

"What are you doing here?" she whispered. "And why are you *soaking wet?*"

"There was a fire in our office," he explained, still grinning. "Nothing serious, but the sprinklers went off. The building's closed for the rest of the day."

"And what are you doing here?"

"I wanted to see you." He paused and his grin changed somehow without altering shape. "Naked."

Laura fought back a smile of her own. This was unprecedented behavior. She didn't approve of it or want to encourage it, but she couldn't help being amused.

"I have work to do," she told him. "Go home."

James persisted, playfully at first, then less so.

"Come on, Laura." There was an edge to his whisper. "We've been seeing each other for, what, two months?"

A day shy of three months, but Laura said nothing.

"*Two months*," he repeated with emphasis. "And this is our *first* opportunity."

"Go home," she told him. "Dry off. And I'll meet you there in an hour."

THE SILENCE WAS TERRIBLE. LAURA knew this sort of thing was very upsetting for men; she wished she could think of something to say to make him feel better.

"This is a very comfortable mattress," she said.

James smiled dubiously.

"I'm not just making small talk," she said. "I mean it. It's very firm."

He laughed. It was a sharp, abrupt laugh. It seemed to bounce off the wall and land in the space between them.

"What's so funny?" Laura asked.

"Nothing," he said. "And by the way, it's not you. So don't take it personally."

Laura patted his wrist kindly. Then she considered his words.

"If it's not me, then the logical conclusion is that you've tried with others."

"A couple others," he said.

"Two?"

"Three or four. I don't know, it doesn't matter, none of them worked out. This problem got in the way."

"Three or four," Laura repeated. "Simultaneously?"

"At the same time?" James laughed. "No. Maybe in my next life-time."

It took Laura a moment to realize his misinterpretation of the question. It surprised her that he could be so juvenile.

"Have you been seeing them during the same time you've been see-ing me?" she clarified.

"No reason to be jealous, kiddo." He slapped her thigh beneath the covers. "They've all pretty much given up on me. Right now you're pretty much it."

Laura shifted so that their bodies were no longer touching.

"Oh, please, Laura. Don't turn this into something it isn't."

"Turn this into something it isn't?"

James sighed. "They were much too young. There was never a ques-tion that you were the sensible one. The only realistic, viable, long-term option."

Laura recoiled when he put his hand on her.

"Come *on*," he said. "I just want to feel you. Let me hold you."

Laura rolled on her side and allowed him to maneuver her body so that it lay inside his like a peanut in a shell. He wrapped his arms around her. There was an urgency to his grip but it wasn't sexual. She thought of the famous nude photograph of John and Yoko. Any jealousy of Yoko had ended when she'd seen that photograph, imagining John's clammy skin and scrawny body contorted over hers in that desperate, fetal clutch.

"Listen, kiddo," James whispered in her ear. "I was thinking I'd feel more comfortable with you, less pressure to perform, but I guess it'll take more time."

"Me, too," Laura told him. "I need more time also."

"You're just saying that to make me feel better. Why would you need more time?"

"Because I'm out of practice. I've been completely celibate since having Emma."

"You're kidding, right?"

Laura wriggled out of James's grasp and flipped over, facing him.

"No, I haven't sought it out. It's never really been . . . I've never really gotten that much out of it."

"That sounds like a challenge for me to prove otherwise," James said.

"It's not," Laura assured him. And then she thought of the perfect thing to say to make him feel better. "In fact, if it's any consolation, I'm relieved you have this problem. Sex is not important to me. I've lived my whole life without it, and I've been perfectly happy."

"So you want us to live platonically ever after?" He grinned at the ceiling. An angry grin. He looked like Jack Nicholson in one of his unhinged roles. "That's supposed to be a consolation? You're asking me to entertain the notion that this is a permanent condition? Get used to it?"

Laura said nothing.

"Wow, what a life!" James laughed and punched the mattress. "Honestly, Laura, that's maybe the worst thing you could say to a guy in my situation. Jesus Christ, I don't know what I'd do if it never came back."

Laura sat up. Holding the sheet to her neck for modesty, she pointed to her bra, which was on James's side of the bed.

"Thanks," she said as he handed it to her.

"Thank *you*!" James responded, becoming Jack Nicholson again. "Thank you for putting such a positive spin on things. I'll get used to it! There's still food and wine, sleeping and television—that's enough to get me through the remaining four decades."

"Stop," Laura told him, turning to face the other direction to put on her bra. "Please, stop." Her voice shook. "I don't understand why you're being so mean."

"Oh, did I offend you?" he said with sarcastic glee.

"You're suggesting a life without sex is a terrible life," Laura said. "How's that supposed to make me feel?" She stood up and located the rest of her clothes.

"Do you not see how that's hurtful?" she continued, turning to face him as she pulled up her kneesocks.

"No," he said with a righteous smirk. "Because if I heard you correctly, you just said you've lived your whole life without it and are perfectly happy. Well, it's been nearly a year for me, and I'm fucking miserable!"

"I wish you and Emma the best," Laura said.

Tucking her turtleneck into the waist of her Laura Ashley skirt, she headed toward the door.

"Before you leave and we never see each other again," he called from across the room, "can I ask you a question that's also a piece of advice?"

Laura braced herself.

"Let me think of the most delicate way to put this." Propped up against the headboard, James folded his arms across his chest. "You're a beautiful woman, Laura, but you don't dress the part."

"That's not a question, nor is it a piece of advice," Laura responded. "But if you're critiquing my wardrobe, you might be interested to know that Bill Cunningham took a photo of me in a variation of this outfit that appeared in the *New York Times*."

James looked amused by this fact, if a little skeptical. "When was this?" he asked.

"Spring of 1979," Laura told him. "At the beginning of his career."

"It's 1991," he said. "Do yourself a favor, kiddo, go shopping."

"And can I give *you* one piece of advice?" Laura's heart beat wildly as she tried to think of an insult.

"You're a cad," she said. "And my advice is, in the future, if you're dating multiple women, I think it's only fair to let all parties know."

"I agree, but we weren't exactly *dating*, Laura. I mean, we hadn't even slept together."

"Thank goodness for that," Laura said, shutting the door behind her.

Right as she emerged from the building, she thought of a better comeback—how interesting it was that he was so critical of her clothes when she'd heard his ex wasn't exactly Miss Fashion USA. But to go all the way back up to his floor again just to deliver this would look pathetic. If only she'd thought of it at the time.

And, she realized a few blocks later, it wasn't his "ex"—it was his dead wife. The mother of his Emma. She would have felt horrible if she'd said that. Sometimes it paid not to be so quick-witted.

*   *   *

IN FIRST GRADE, EMMA HAD removed the *Kids XXX Large* sticker from a new pair of Gap leggings and stuck it to the base of the wall of their elevator. The experiment was to see how long it stayed there before someone peeled it off. Weeks then months then a whole year passed. And then another year. Followed by another and another, until it was no longer an experiment, but a matter-of-fact reality of her life. It was just there, something Emma saw every day. And then one day it wasn't. Just the spot where it had been—a shade lighter than what surrounded it.

LAURA HAD ALWAYS TAKEN METICULOUS care of her teeth. She flossed and brushed twice a day, and though she was skeptical of the need for biannual dental cleanings, she never missed an appointment. She was shocked, at the age of forty-two, to learn that she had a cavity.

It was her first filling. Dr. Morton, whose office was three doors down from 136 and had been her dentist since childhood, seemed amused when she firmly declined his offer of nitrous oxide.

"Your mother loved it," he said. "Absolutely loved it."

The procedure wasn't as bad as people made it out to be, but the Novocain left Laura's mouth numb, making it difficult to speak afterward. Dr. Morton said the feeling should come back in about an hour. Rather than return to work lisping, Laura decided to wait it out at 136.

It was Tuesday, Sandra's day off, but as Laura let herself in she thought she heard someone moving around upstairs.

"Hewwo?" she called.

"Yes?" a voice called back.

It was Stephanie. A moment later she appeared at the top of the stairs, wearing glasses and pajamas. They were both confused to see each other.

"I can't understand you," Stephanie said as Laura tried to explain about the Novocain. "Are you okay?"

"Dentist," Laura said. "Coming fwom dentist."

"You were just at the dentist." Stephanie grasped her chest and smiled. "Thank God, for a moment I was scared. Your face looks weird—I thought you might've had a stroke or something."

Laura smiled back and shook her head.

Stephanie explained that they were living at 136 while their kitchen was being renovated.

"It was only supposed to be a week but now they're saying two." She rolled her eyes. "You know how it is. Hold on, let me get dressed and come down."

Laura went into the kitchen. The breakfast table was a mess of dishes and newspaper.

"Please don't do that," Stephanie said, stepping in a moment later. "Please don't clean up after us."

After a moment of deliberation, Laura peeled off her rubber gloves and stepped away from the sink.

"It's so nice outside," Stephanie said. "Let's go sit in the garden."

Stephanie opened the fridge and took out a Diet Coke. Then she grabbed a box of Melba toast from the cupboard.

"It's so funny you're here," Stephanie said as they went out to the garden. "Because I've been wanting to call you. I need your advice on something."

Laura nodded encouragingly.

"Maybe it's not the best time, though," Stephanie said. "If it hurts you to talk."

"Doesn't hut," Laura said. "Just hod to enunciate."

They sat down on the two chaise longues.

"Do you think it's selfish to only have one child?" Stephanie asked without turning her head. "When you're in the position to have more?"

Laura shook her head with conviction. "To the contwee. With ovapopwation, the state of the pwanet, and wimited wesauces, it's a conscionable choice."

"I'm sorry," Stephanie said. "I'm having a hard time understanding you. Let me get you something to write on."

She went inside and came out with a pen and yellow legal pad.

Opposite of selfish, Laura wrote. *Good for planet.*

Laura passed the pad to Stephanie, who read it with a worried frown. This didn't appear to be the answer she was looking for. "But what if you're not thinking of the earth—just yourself and what you want?"

It's wise to recognize what you want, Laura wrote. *No one should have a child they don't want.*

"It took me so long to feel like myself again, after having Nick. I don't know if I have it in me to go through that again. But everyone expects you to have two."

Laura responded: *I wouldn't feel pressured to do anything just because it's the conventional thing to do.*

Stephanie stared at the message. "This sun feels good, doesn't it." She adjusted the seat of her chaise so that it was in the reclining position. Then she lay back and shut her eyes.

Laura did the same. They lay there in silence for what felt like fifteen or twenty minutes, but it might have been more. Lulled by the heat of the flagstone, and the fricative hiss of traffic and other city sounds that snaked around them, oblivious—the impermeable serenity of a Manhattan courtyard—Laura was on the verge of sleep when Stephanie spoke again.

"My mother says if I don't give Nick Jr. a brother or sister he'll grow up thinking the sun rises to hear him crow."

Laura was taken aback that Stephanie would say this to her. She felt as though she'd been slapped.

"It's a southern expression," Stephanie explained, sitting up. "It means someone who thinks the world revolves around—"

"I get it," Laura said, her mouth working again. "But I don't think that's the case with Emma. She certainly likes attention, has her theatrical impulses . . ." Laura's cheeks grew hot, recalling her performance at Stephanie's wedding. "But that's a part of who she is, how she's wired. It has nothing to do with being an only child."

"Oh, no. I didn't mean to imply that." Now Stephanie's cheeks were also red. "Emma's a great kid, a spunky gal. You've done a wonderful job with her."

"You don't need to say that," Laura said.

"I *mean* it. I think you're a very good mom."

"Thank you. So are you."

Stephanie brushed Melba toast crumbs off her lap. "I love Nick Jr. to death," she said, "but I'm not good at the day-to-day things. Making sure his lunch is ready, taking him to appointments and playdates, keeping track of everything. I wish I were more like you in that area. You're so in control of everything."

"Well, thank you," Laura repeated, though this time it sounded less complimentary.

"That's why I wanted your advice on this situation we're dealing with." Stephanie looked down and wriggled the tab of her can of Diet Coke until it broke off. "This awful decision we have to make."

"You're pregnant," Laura said, suddenly realizing.

"We just found out," Stephanie answered. "It was an accident."

They were quiet. Now the sounds of the city seemed amplified: the honking of a horn, the trilling of birds, a low-flying helicopter passing overhead.

"It took a long time to get where we are right now, things are good, and when I think about another baby . . ." Stephanie's shoulders collapsed as she covered her face with her hands. "I just can't. I can't go through with it."

"You don't have to." Laura reached out to tap the top of Stephanie's manicured hand, but Stephanie pulled it away.

"I never thought of myself as the type of person who would . . ."

"Lots of women have them," Laura said.

"Not where I come from."

"I'm sure they do," said Laura gently. "They just don't talk about it."

"Have you ever had one?" Stephanie asked, raising her eyebrows in a hopeful way.

Laura shook her head. "How does Nicholas feel about it?"

"He says he wants me to make the decision, but I can tell he doesn't want me to keep it. He's scared of what would happen if we had to go through what we went through the first time." She paused. "Nicholas doesn't like it when I'm upset. He really can't handle it. I've never told anyone this, because I don't want them to think bad of Nicholas, but when I cry"—she lowered her voice to a whisper—"instead of comforting me, he gets mad."

"Oh, dear," Laura said, ashamed of her brother. "I'm sorry about that."

"It's not your fault," Stephanie said. "I figure it's just one of those things. Like how you were saying about Emma being who she is. It's the way he is."

"He wasn't always like that," Laura said. "When he was little, I mean," she added, worried that Stephanie might think she was accusing her of being responsible for the change.

Stephanie delicately pinched two fingers over her nostrils and sneezed twice, a dainty *ptchoo-ptchoo*.

"I can't go through with it," she said.

Laura wasn't sure if she meant the abortion or the pregnancy.

"Does that make me a horrible person?"

"No," Laura said firmly. "Absolutely not."

"This sounds silly," she said. "But I can't bring myself to tell my ob-gyn."

"I can give you the name of mine. He's very good."

"Does he definitely . . . do this?" Stephanie asked.

"Yes." Laura shielded her eyes from the sun. "I believe so."

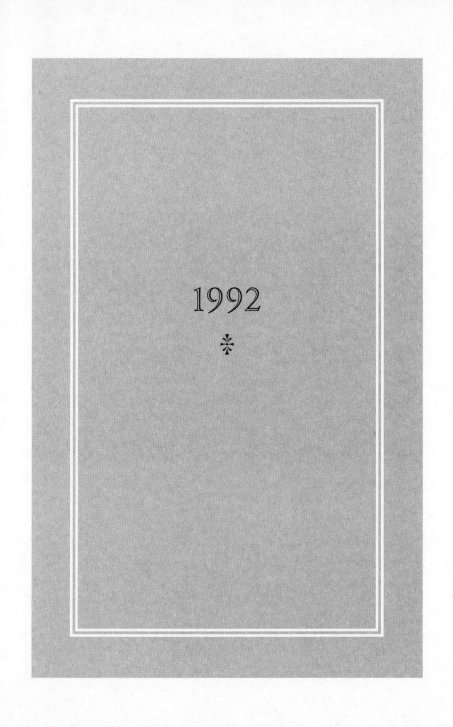

1992

✻

As Laura flipped through the morning paper, she came across some disconcerting news. An asteroid was passing by the earth that day. A collision was not expected, nor had it been ruled out. In the words of one scientist: "As advanced as our technology is, we can never truly predict what will happen. This could be it."

But it wasn't. The asteroid cruised right on by and continued on its merry sweet way through the universe. And so their lives continued, much as they had before, and in what felt like the blink of an eye, Emma was suddenly no longer quite a child, but not yet a teenager. A *preteen adolescent*, Laura supposed it was called.

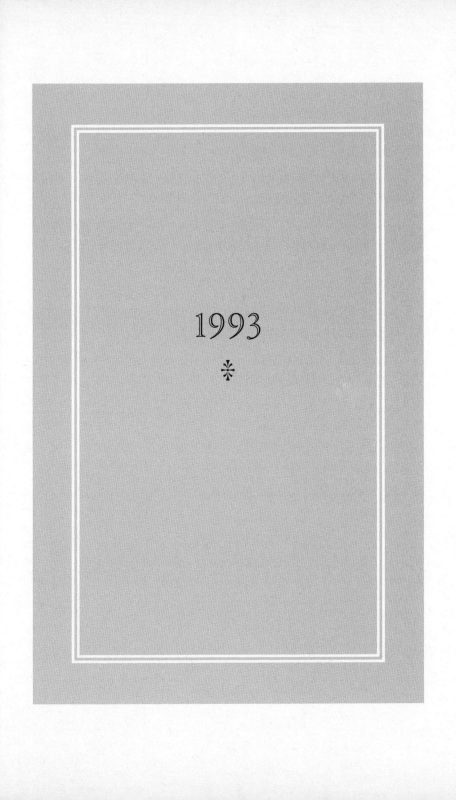

1993

✳

Sixth grade meant graduating from the Winthrop tunic to the Winthrop kilt. Many parents fretted about the attention their daughters' new uniform might trigger from men on the street. Laura wasn't worried; Emma still had a childish roundness about her and her legs were nothing to look at. Changes were imminent, however, and following Margaret's instructions, Laura purchased a copy of a puberty instruction manual called *It's Perfectly Normal* and left it on Emma's desk for her to discover upon coming home from school.

The book quickly vanished from the desk but did not reappear on a shelf or any of the obvious places. A few weeks later she walked in on Emma reading it on the floor of her bedroom. Emma snapped the book shut and sent it sliding across the rug, where it disappeared beneath the curtain of her bed skirt. "What do you want?" she demanded.

"I'm sorry." Laura blushed. "I forgot to knock."

"What do you want?" Emma repeated.

"I was going to ask you something . . . but now I forget. In the meantime, do you have any questions about anything?" Laura pointed beneath Emma's bed.

"No." Emma buried her face in another book, this one for school. "Please get out."

"Okay. But I *did* come in here for a reason. I guess I'll come back when it comes to me."

As Laura returned to her pile of paperwork in the kitchen, Emma's bedroom door creaked open.

"Actually, I do have a question," Emma called from down the hall. "How old were you when you got your period?"

"Oh, don't worry, things happen very late in our family, you've got years!" Laura smiled reassuringly.

"What *age* were you?" Emma barked back.

"Fifteen or sixteen. And I don't think Nicholas started shaving until he was twenty-three or -four."

Satisfied, Emma shut the door.

The exchange reminded Laura of another conversation she was supposed to have with Emma. She could wait until dinner, but the dread of it made her eager to get it over with. This time she knocked on Emma's door first.

"Don't come in yet," Emma shouted. "Wait one second."

When she entered, Emma was sitting at her desk, legs crossed, pen poised above a blank notepad.

"I've been meaning to tell you," Laura began, taking a seat on Emma's bed, "that I tried dope in college one time with Margaret. Do you know what that is?"

"Yes, Mom," Emma said. "No one calls it that anymore. It's called *pot*."

"We were in our dorm room and there was a siren outside and we thought it was the government coming for us, and we were petrified. Then we started feeling silly. We dragged a mattress into the elevator and went up and down. Then I got hungrier than I'd ever been in my life. The only food in our room was a Sara Lee devil's food chocolate cake. I ate the whole thing. By myself."

Emma scratched her elbow. She looked confused and embarrassed.

Laura felt the same. "I never gave you the drug talk," she explained. "Parents are supposed to talk to their kids about drugs."

"But I thought you hate Sara Lee."

"I know. It's disgusting, but when you smoke dope something happens in your brain that makes everything delicious."

"So the lesson is, dope is great," Emma said. "And I should try it."

"Oh, no, that's not what I'm supposed to tell you!"

They both found this very funny and laughed.

"Yeah, that's definitely not what you're supposed to tell me. Also, now I know Margaret is a liar. She told Charlotte she'd never even smoked a cigarette."

This made them laugh again. Laura felt a sudden premonition of Emma as an adult and how their relationship might evolve into more of a friendship. When the laughter stopped she felt shy, like they were two people who'd just met.

"In all seriousness, liquor is what you have to look out for," she told Emma. "The trouble is, it makes you feel great, and you want to keep the feeling going, and so you keep sipping, and the next thing you know, you've crossed a line."

Laura cringed, thinking of all the foolish things she'd almost said and done under the influence of wine—like that time in the restaurant she'd nearly played footsie with that widower who turned out to be a cad.

"Do you have any questions about anything?"

Emma shook her head.

"Okay, well, I guess I'll see you later," Laura said, her hand on the door. "Want me to leave it open?"

"No, that's okay," Emma responded.

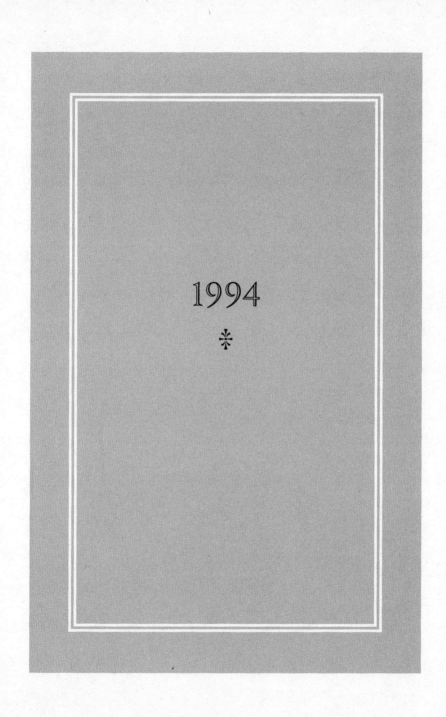

1994

"I THOUGHT YOU WERE GOING TO THE HOMELESS SHELTER," Emma said as Laura swooshed by in a floor-length dress.

"I am. Tonight is their art show. What do you think?" The hem of the skirt grazed the walls of the hallway as she twirled.

"Fancy. You don't even get that dressed up for events at the Library."

Laura considered this. "These women work very hard every year to put this exhibition of their work together, and only a few people show up. Maybe you're right, though, this dress is a little much. I wore it in Suzie's wedding—can you tell it's a bridesmaid's dress?"

"No. You should definitely wear it. You look pretty and the women will like it."

The phone rang. Emma ran to get it. It was mostly for her these days.

"It's Margaret!" she shouted from the kitchen.

"I'll take it in the bedroom!" Laura shouted back.

"Lordy lord, what a day," Margaret responded to Laura's hello. "Trip's going to call Miss Gardner tomorrow. I'm too emotional to handle it. You spend fourteen thousand dollars—"

"Handle what?"

"You mean Emma didn't tell you?"

"I have no clue what you're talking about."

"That awful teacher!" She had to be referring to Mr. Vincent, a new language arts teacher who was unpopular with the girls. "He called her the B-word."

"Brat?"

"No, Laura, *bitch*. At the tender age of twelve—such an ugly, misogynistic slur."

"Out of the blue?"

"Yes! In front of the whole class! He lost his notes or something and he took it out on Charlotte. He called her a *bitch*. Can you believe it? *Fourteen grand* a year sending your daughter to an all-girls school to protect her from this sort of thing, only to have it thrown in her face!"

"Well, it could've been worse." It was the best Laura could think of to say. "At least it wasn't cunt."

"What's a cunt?" Emma asked when Laura got off the phone.

"Did you listen to my phone call with Margaret?"

"I had to, Mom, I needed to hear what she was saying. She's totally overreacting! Why is Trip calling Miss Gardner? It would be *ridiculous* if Mr. Vincent got fired. First of all, he called *everyone* a bitch, not just Charlotte. Second of all—"

"*Everyone* in the whole class?" Laura winced. "Even sweet little Scarlet Wang?"

Emma rolled her eyes. "Mom, don't worry. It wasn't like how Margaret explained it to you. He was stressed because it's the week Miss Gardner randomly comes into classes to grade the teachers. All week he's been especially stuttery, so before class starts he writes out the entire lesson on the chalkboard, so if the problem gets really bad, he can just point to whatever he's trying to teach us. Today he realized he forgot to make us copies of our assignment, so he told Scarlet Wang to be in charge while he went to the teachers' lounge. Ten minutes later he came back, and Charlotte had erased everything he'd written on the board. He didn't say anything but you could tell he was pissed. His face just turned bright red and he wrote everything on the board all over again."

Emma shook her head remorsefully.

"He was still writing everything on the board when Miss Gardner came in. He didn't hear the door open or notice her, he just kept on writing. I felt really bad, because aren't teachers supposed to interact with students?"

Laura put her face in her hands.

"After five or ten minutes he was still writing on the board," Emma continued, "and Miss Gardner got up and left. This time he heard the door and turned around. We told him it was Miss Gardner. That she'd been there and left. He smiled and made a face like *very funny*. Then he looked at Scarlet Wang and she veriated this was true."

"*Validated*," Laura said. "Or *verified*."

"Same difference. Anyway, so after he finds out it was Miss Gardner, he walks over to the board and pretends to bang his head against it. And Charlotte goes, 'Somebody needs to take a chill pill.' And that's when he says it. '*Bitches.*'"

"What's a 'chill pill'?"

"It's an expression. It means you're acting like a spaz."

"And then what?"

"And everyone laughed except me. Because it stopped being funny to me. It was like when Tonya Harding's shoelace broke at the Olympics right before she was about to go on. I felt bad for him, Mom—I really did."

Emma's forehead creased with emotion. She wiggled a loose cuticle on her thumb then ripped it off. "To tell you the truth," she said, sucking the blood off her finger, "I don't blame him for saying the word, because that's what we were acting like."

EMMA WAS TROUBLED TO ARRIVE at school the next day and discover that Mr. Vincent, who was also her homeroom teacher, was absent. Mrs. Greg, the permanent sub, delivered that morning's announcements and escorted her class to Prayers. They filed into the auditorium in the customary two-by-two procession.

Emma hadn't memorized that week's Bible verses, so as the recitation began she mouthed the word *watermelon* over and over again. Next came the Lord's Prayer, which she knew by heart. After this, Miss Gardner walked to the podium and read a story about a flock of geese who all stopped flying when one of the birds was shot by a hunter and fell to the ground. The bird didn't die, and the whole flock waited around for it to recover before resuming their journey north. When she was done, Miss Gardner asked the room what the lesson was, and, as usual, the only hands that went up were in the front, where the younger grades sat.

When Emma heard Miss Gardner call on Isabelle, she thought it must have been another Isabelle—there were a few—but, looking up, Emma saw it was the Isabelle in first grade, who had stopped coming to school after being diagnosed with leukemia earlier that year. She was back! Isabelle wore a headband with a bow on it, as it appeared that she was completely bald. However, as Mrs. Hudson played the opening chords to "Amazing Grace" and Isabelle turned to face the scroll with the words on it, her scalp caught the light, and Emma could see that her hair was growing in. Not a lot, just wisps, like a dandelion gone to seed.

They were still stuck in February but the light that filtered through the windows had a yolky glow. Spring was coming. Soon there would be blossoms on the trees, and Isabelle, who was not going to die after all, would have enough hair to tuck behind her ears. To the tune of "Amazing Grace," Emma contemplated the miracle of these things, and she was overwhelmed with a feeling of goodness, and the blissful serenity that accompanies seeing the world through the simplicity of this lens. As the singing continued, the feeling intensified, and then, like a bolt of lightning, it suddenly occurred to Emma what really mattered in life. It wasn't about cool versus uncool, pretty versus ugly, funny versus boring, or even happy versus sad, but goodness — goodness versus everything else that might not seem bad, but wasn't good, either. To do good things, to be a good person: this was all that really counted.

With a sudden clarity that felt holy, Emma considered her own life through this prism. She had done some things that were not good. She'd known this, and yet she'd done them anyway, because up to this moment she'd wanted to be like naughty Jo in *Little Women*. But now, she realized, she actually wanted to be like Jo's saintly sister, Beth — and maybe she was already more like Beth than she'd thought.

"Are you *crying*?" Charlotte whispered.

Emma let her face speak for itself as she continued to sing. That this was her favorite of all the hymns in the rotating roster they sang in Prayers was no coincidence. "Amazing Grace," Isabelle's hair growing back, her complicity in Mr. Vincent's unexplained absence — all of these things felt predestined, to deliver her right now to this place inside of her. A place within that she'd always known was there, but had never consciously lingered.

"Amazing Grace" ended; Emma's tears dried and the goose bumps subsided. But the feeling of goodness, and the newfound belief that she was, at her core, an exceptionally good person—these sentiments remained. For the rest of the day she carried it around. It felt like a huge secret, like she'd just found out she'd won an award and couldn't tell anyone. But she didn't care, because there was no vanity in goodness.

EMBOLDENED BY HER NEW CONVICTIONS, Emma cut herself off from Charlotte, and in doing so, Claire, Eleanor C., Leslie, and Ashley, who Emma now realized hadn't been her friends, but followers of Charlotte, whom everybody wanted to be around because she made things fun. "The clique" or "the posse," Emma learned they were called by the rest of their classmates, the social proletariat—of which she was now a member.

Sitting for the first time at a different table in the lunchroom, it depressed Emma how preoccupied her new circle was with her old one. It seemed half the conversation was about "the posse." In a transparent attempt to mask their sense of inferiority, they spoke of Charlotte and company in strictly hostile terms. Even more pathetic was that their actual interactions with members of the clique were shamelessly obsequious.

Charlotte was quick to replace Emma with Leslie as her best friend and sat next to her when the class didn't have assigned seating. One day Leslie emerged from the bathroom with the back of her skirt tucked into the waist of her underpants. It was recess, and Emma was one of about a dozen witnesses who'd been sitting in the locker cove—the only one who hadn't leapt up and chased her down the hall in a frantic scramble to heroically alert her before she could embarrass herself. Emma watched Leslie wave them off with a smile and continue on her exposed-pink-butt-cheek way.

"She knows." "She tucked it in on purpose." "It's for a dare." So explained the committee of concerned citizens upon returning to the locker cove.

"They all have to do something," someone testified. "Everyone in the clique wrote a dare on a piece of paper, and whoever picked that slip has to do it."

"Charlotte has to leave a condominium on Monsieur Durand's desk," another added in a whisper.

This elicited a chorus of laughter.

"A condom! A condom!" everyone corrected her.

That was the day Emma decided to disassociate herself from everyone in the whole grade. What did it matter if she didn't have friends?

To do good things, to be a good person, this was what counted.

A NEW HIGH-RISE WAS GOING up one block north of them. A self-proclaimed "luxury" building, it was called the Parkview. The name was ironic as, once upon a time, Laura had been able to look out her bedroom window and see a band of green that was the tops of the trees in Central Park. Now this ugly tower blocked the view. It was so upsetting that she began thinking of it as a temporary thing; one morning she'd wake up and it would be gone, view restored. But no, not only was it here to stay, it was growing taller by the day.

But then something remarkable happened that affirmed Laura's more optimistic feelings about the universe.

A local anti-high-rise activist had been keeping tabs on the building's skyward trajectory and, according to his count, its height exceeded the legal zoning limit by twelve stories. The authorities were notified and justice was served; the building's contractors were forced to take down the additional floors. The *New York Times* wrote an article about it, which Laura cut out and put on the fridge.

"After their cityscape has crept ever closer to the clouds over the decades," it began, "Manhattanites are about to witness something decidedly uncommon: a shrinking skyscraper."

A FEW WEEKS INTO EMMA's new life, a condom was left with an anonymous note on the desk of a controversial middle-school French teacher, and Emma was among those Miss Gardner summoned to her office for an interrogation. To avoid speaking the word, Miss Gardner referred to it as "an object used for adult purposes," and, seeing this wasn't ringing any bells for Emma, had no choice but to show her the item, which she procured from a drawer in her desk and daintily held up in a Ziploc bag.

"The nature of the note left us very concerned," Miss Gardner said, quickly slipping the contraband back into the drawer. "We are in the process of trying to determine who might have left it. Anything you know will remain confidential."

It was then that Emma realized she'd been singled out not as a suspect, but as a tattletale.

"I would guess the sixth-graders," Emma offered.

"It appeared the week they were away at Frost Valley," Miss Gardner said. "If you hear anything, I would appreciate it if you passed it along to me."

Miss Gardner held Emma's gaze for a few seconds then nodded to indicate she was dismissed.

After Emma stepped out of the office, Leslie jumped out from around the corner.

"What did she want to talk to you about?" she demanded.

"Cunt." The word slipped out like a fart. Emma glanced down the hall, terrified a teacher might've heard.

"What did you just say?" Leslie asked.

"I cunt talk about it," Emma said, and walked briskly away.

"Trip snores," Margaret said out of the blue. "Loudly."

Laura nodded sympathetically. They were at Sarabeth's. It was Margaret's birthday and Laura was taking her out for lunch. This used to be a biannual tradition—treating each other to lunch on their birthdays. The ritual slowed down when the girls had arrived. Now neither of them could remember the last time they'd done it.

The waiter approached to take their orders.

"We're going to need a few," Margaret told him. Turning back to Laura, she said, "Anyhoo, it was really bad last night. Which is why I look eighty years old today."

"I think you look great," Laura said, though it was true she looked tired. "Have you tried earplugs?"

"I've tried it all," Margaret said dismally. "Earplugs, Valium, pillow over his face. Doesn't work."

"I've been sleeping very poorly lately, too," Laura told her.

"I was always a great sleeper." Margaret shook her head wistfully. "Until Trip gained thirty pounds and started snoring." Margaret lowered her voice to add: "My shrink says that's the likely cause."

"You have a shrink?" Laura asked.

"I've joined the club," Margaret said. "Sometimes I'll roll over and look at him laying there all slack-jawed"—Margaret did an impression—"snoring, drooling, snoring, his side of the blanket rising and falling, and I'll think to myself, it's a good thing I'm not one of those people who sleeps with a gun in my bedside drawer."

Laura laughed.

"Because if I had a gun," Margaret continued, unsmiling, "I would *shoot* him."

Laura tried to think of a more cheerful topic.

"I would shoot him," Margaret repeated.

"You remember what my mother used to say about marriage," Laura said.

"Yes." Margaret's scowl softened. "But tell me again."

"She'd say, 'It doesn't matter who you marry, one day you'll be sitting across a table from him thinking, *Anything would be better than this.*'"

Margaret smiled. "I miss your mother," she said.

"We should figure out what we're ordering," Laura said, putting on her newly acquired reading glasses so she could see the menu.

*　　*　　*

IN THE HARDBOILED LIGHT OF the day it never seemed urgent—
where and when and how to dispose of them in a ceremonious manner.
But in the middle of the night it struck Laura as unacceptable: it had
been almost four years and her mother's ashes were still sitting on top
of the bedroom bookshelf where she'd put them after her trip to Central Park when she'd hallucinated Woody Allen.

They weren't even in a proper urn, but in the tin container they'd
been delivered in—like a box of cookies from some houseguest,
relegated to the back of the kitchen cupboard, only discovered when
it's time to move, at which point they get discarded.

THE WINTHROP FACULTY ATTRIBUTED EMMA'S sudden status as a
social pariah to her dramatic transformation as a student. Overnight,
it seemed, Emma went from being easily distracted, disorganized, frequently unprepared, and clearly not the slightest bit concerned with
her academic performance to being extremely focused, meticulously
organized, punctual, thorough, and highly invested in her grades. In
classes without assigned seating, she chose to sit in the middle of the
front row, where she became a regular and enthusiastic participant in
class discussions. There was no more silliness in music class, giggle
fits during Prayers, or subversive behavior of any kind. In all her en-
deavors throughout the day, she conducted herself with unwavering
poise, self-respect, and deference for authority. Even her handwriting
was different. Once swollen and sloppy and frequently spilling beyond
the margins of the lines in her loose-leaf notebooks, now it was small,

neat, and contained—as though it had suddenly become aware of itself and was eager to make a good impression.

Miss Gardner called Laura in to relay all this and commend Emma for becoming a model of the Winthrop Way. Laura found herself distracted by the presence of Mrs. Jones, the school social worker. Miss Gardner began by conveying how impressed she was with Emma's newfound maturity and priorities. Then she shifted her gaze to Mrs. Jones, who asked Laura if she had noticed any changes in Emma's behavior at home.

Yes, she had. Each night before bed Emma laid out her outfit for the next day on the armchair in the corner of her bedroom: kilt, turtleneck, socks, and shoes. Then she wrote a little to-do list for the next morning: *Make bed. Brush teeth. Check forecast.* Her once-messy bedroom was now immaculate, and she'd begun chiding Laura for her habit of allowing miscellaneous clutter to accumulate on the front hall table. She no longer had to be pestered to do her homework; she completed this first thing upon arriving home. Once finished, rather than turning on the TV, she took out a book. She'd gotten very into reading, in particular books about children with fatal illnesses. There was a section devoted to such books in the local Barnes & Noble. Right now she was reading *Ryan White: My Own Story*, the autobiography of a boy who contracted HIV through a blood transfusion. For Christmas she wanted to adopt a starving child from Ethiopia.

"Oh, my," Miss Gardner said in response to this detail.

"Not literally," Laura explained. "Just sponsor."

"Adolescence is a difficult time for girls," Mrs. Jones spoke up.

"We are a little concerned," Miss Gardner said, "that Emma may feel alienated from her classmates."

"The phone doesn't ring for her anymore," Laura reflected. "There are fewer playdates and invitations to birthday parties."

Laura wished she hadn't said this out loud. She resented the portrait Miss Gardner was painting. It spoke to Emma's integrity and character that she had chosen to set herself apart from her spoiled, cliquish cohorts to the detriment of her popularity. To be socially successful at Winthrop was at odds with her and Emma's values.

Laura couldn't say this to Miss Gardner, of course, and the meeting concluded on an unresolved note.

LAURA WAS ENCOURAGED WHEN, A few weeks later, Emma announced she would be joining the middle school track team. Though she'd never been particularly athletic or drawn to physical activity, Emma's interest in running quickly blossomed into a passion. *Runner's World* magazine began arriving in the mail. In addition to attending afternoon practice, Emma started setting her alarm an hour early to run up and down the stairs in their building. Concerned with the nutritional value of their meals, she refused to eat certain things, including butter, to which she had developed a sudden aversion. "When you were a baby it was your favorite food," Laura told her. "It was one of your first words. You called it *cheese*."

"You let me eat pure butter?" Emma asked, horrified.

One issue of *Runner's World* featured an advertisement for running camp. Laura found the concept of a four-week sleep-away camp whose sole activity was jogging utterly bizarre, but Emma really wanted to go, and perhaps it would be an opportunity to make new friends.

*　　*　　*

As a little girl Emma's blond locks had received much attention, from relatives and acquaintances to strangers in elevators and supermarkets. Afterward she would often ask Laura to repeat the compliment. It reminded Laura of how Bibs, when praised for something, would frequently respond, "And what do you like about it?" Her mother's ego had been like a hole that got bigger as you filled it.

Laura's instinct had always been not to comment on Emma's physical appearance unless her opinion was solicited, but when she arrived to pick Emma up from running camp, it was hard not to say something. She didn't look good. Her eyes were too big, the contour of her jaw too sharp. When she turned to pick up her suitcase, the wings of her shoulder blades emerged from her back like a piece of mechanical machinery. Her legs, while slimmer, still lacked definition, but everything else was jarringly pronounced.

Laura thought of how she'd used to marvel at having given birth to this plump, excitable, self-possessed little girl, who subscribed to her own romantic notions of how the world worked. Whatever it was that had fueled her unruly ways, her tempestuous appetites for life, it was as if someone had inserted a straw into her veins and sucked it out.

In the past whenever Emma had been sick, Laura's heart had percolated with a love so fierce it had hurt. It disturbed her that she was unable to access such maternal feelings now.

It was so noticeable, so upsetting, that Laura thought she should call Stephanie ahead of time and let her know that she would be shocked to see Emma.

And she was—but not in the way Laura had expected. When they arrived for dinner at Nicholas's apartment, upon opening the front door, Stephanie gasped.

"It's skinny-mini Emma!" she trilled, throwing her arms around her bony shoulders. "You look beautiful!"

LAURA HAD NEVER MANAGED TO develop a rapport with Dr. Marks — Emma's new pediatrician — the way she had with Dr. Brown. This was fine. Laura had no interest in a friendship with this woman, whose reputation as one of the city's top pediatricians was clearly not earned for her bedside manner. Dr. Marks's lovely South African accent did little to mitigate her strictly business, clinically brusque demeanor.

It was known that Dr. Marks had no patience for neurotic parents — which her practice was full of — and so, eager to establish herself as an exception, Laura made a conscious effort not to bring Emma in too often or ask too many questions. Her restraint had earned her credibility, which meant that when she called the office asking if she could speak to the doctor before Emma's annual back-to-school physical, Dr. Marks returned her call right away.

Laura explained that her concern about Emma's weight loss was exacerbated by the positive reception it received from others. In addition to Stephanie, several acquaintances they'd bumped into on the street also commented on Emma's appearance in the affirmative.

"I've been holding my tongue—these days anything I say is the wrong thing," Laura said. "But if *you* could say something to her..."

The days of accompanying Emma into the exam room were over. After her examination, Laura was called in to speak with the doctor privately.

"Her BMI is in the thirty-seventh percentile," Dr. Marks said. "It's on the leaner side, but still within the normal range."

"But she used to be on the rounder side," Laura pointed out. "It just feels like out of the blue she stopped being interested in dessert and starting jogging. When we go to Jackson Hole, she never orders her favorite things—onion rings, milkshakes, grilled cheese. She gets the French onion soup, minus the cheese on top."

"It's normal for adolescents to slim down as they get older and make healthier decisions," Dr. Marks said. "I wouldn't worry about it."

"Why did she want to talk to you?" Emma asked as they walked home.

"She just wanted to go over your booster shots," Laura said.

"But I didn't get any shots."

"Right," said Laura. "She was explaining why you didn't need any."

On their way back, Laura bought a box of Entenmann's chocolate donuts, which Emma used to beg her to buy.

Emma ate a few bites of one for dessert and threw the rest away.

YESTERDAY'S SCIENCE LAB HAD INVOLVED looking at plant cells (onion) under a microscope; today's sample would be animal (human). The cells would come from their mouths. That's what the toothpicks were for. Emma opened her mouth and scraped the toothpick along the inside of her cheek, but when she pulled it out, nothing was on it. Applying more pressure, she tried a second time, and again no luck. She began poking and prodding and eventually punctured the surface of the skin. A little nodule came loose. Since it was too small to spear and tear, she bit and spat. Voila! There it was in the cradle of her palm, raw and pink and glistening, the size of a frozen pea.

A moment ago it had been a part of her body; now it was a separate thing. Emma's tongue probed the spot where it had been. There must have been a little bit of blood because her mouth tasted like a dime.

"What's that?" Mrs. Mullen asked, frowning at Emma's sample.

Mrs. Mullen's ingratiating floral perfume did not match her disgusted and irritated countenance. It took Emma a moment to realize her error: what she held in her hand was much too big. Cells were so small they were invisible — that's what the microscope was for. *Duh.*

Mrs. Mullen continued to hover, waiting for an answer, her eyelids coming halfway down so that all you saw were the whites of her eyes — something that happened when she lost patience or had to explain something twice.

"That's my cells," Emma told her.

"Those are your *what?*"

"My cells," Emma repeated, a drop of bloody drool landing on her lab report. "From my cheek."

"That's a lot more cells than necessary," Mrs. Mullen said with a look of repugnance. Emma's anxiety was laced with shame. She would be more careful moving forward. As Laura often said, *less is more.*

When Emma woke up the next morning, her tongue explored the perforation, and it was just as prominent as it had been the night before.

The cells would not grow back. The landscape of Emma's mouth was permanently altered. For the rest of her life it would be there, this little crater, and when she was at a loss for words it was where her tongue would go. People who knew her well would come to notice it.

You're making that face, they'd say. *You're hiding something.*

*   *   *

ALL HOMEWORK, NO PLAYDATES, EMMA'S funk continued in seventh grade. Beneath the melancholy was an anger, but apparently it only came out at home—according to her teachers, she was "a pleasure to have in class." Her language arts teacher, an uppity young thing who was a new addition to the faculty, was particularly impressed.

During their parent–teacher meeting she showed Laura a copy of a story Emma had written. Precociously titled "A Tree Grows on the Upper East Side," it depicted the life of an emotionally neglected only child whose high-powered, aggressive businesswoman mother didn't have a maternal bone in her body. In one scene the daughter tried to hug her mother, who coldly rejected her: "Oh, please! I'm your mother, not your lover!"

"But I never said that," Laura told the teacher.

"Of course you didn't!" she said with a laugh. "This is fiction! We won't be studying memoir until the spring.

"How wonderful to have such a creative daughter!" she added when Laura didn't respond.

Emma was clearly unhappy, there was no doubt about that. Laura thought it would be nice for her to have someone to talk to, an adult who wasn't a teacher or her mother. Those were her exact words, and they were the wrong ones.

Emma flew into a rage. "Basically you're saying *you* don't want to listen to me, so you'll pay someone else to do it!"

Laura tried to defend and explain herself, but it only made it worse, and that was the end of that conversation.

It was ironic, when Laura thought about it. No sooner had Emma started walking than people began telling Laura what she was in for. *Good luck with that one! You think she's a handful now, just wait till she's a teenager!* Now here she was and, from an outsider's perspective, an exception to the trend—the rare docile adolescent, respectful and polite, pleasant to be around.

"She's like that cliché about March," Margaret observed. "Started out like a lion, is now a lamb."

Laura bit her tongue. Often she would propose doing something such as a picnic in the park, and Emma would affect an enthusiastic smile. "I have a better idea," she'd reply, briefly raising Laura's hopes before the sarcastic kicker: "Let's *not* and say we did."

Emma would ridicule things Laura said by repeating them in a high-pitched English accent. She grew increasingly intolerant of certain habits Laura had—singing to herself in the kitchen, saying *okey-doke* upon concluding a task, clearing her throat. "You don't do that at work, do you?" she'd ask.

Then there was the outrageous accusation that Laura, who, when communicating with immigrants, made an effort to speak slowly, enunciate clearly, and use simple, direct language, was *mocking* these people, insulting their intelligence and dignity.

"How would *you* feel if someone spoke to YOU . . . LIKE . . . THIS."

Laura was racist, too, of course. Only a racist would lock her doors when approaching a red light at One-hundred-and-twenty-fifth Street in Harlem.

In restaurants, when Laura ordered a "Coca-Cola *Classic*" (you had to say *classic*, otherwise waiters assumed diet, given that's what everyone ordered these days), Emma covered her face in her hands.

"It's normal to find your mother irritating," Laura told her.

"Yeah, well, news flash, Mom, I'm not the *only* one who finds you irritating," was Emma's cruelly cryptic response.

IT WAS TRADITION THAT THE seventh-graders put on a Christmas talent show. Laura remembered it from her days; she had worn white gloves and played the C and D bells in a handbell performance of "God Rest Ye Merry Gentlemen." In addition to the younger grades, parents were invited to be part of the audience. To Laura's surprise, both of her parents had shown up. Each time it was Laura's turn to ring a note, Bibs had giggled.

All the seventh-graders were expected to be part of the production, though this year, one had declined to appear onstage, electing instead to be the solitary technical crew member. Dressed in black, Emma stood on the balcony behind the spotlight, shining it on whoever's moment it was.

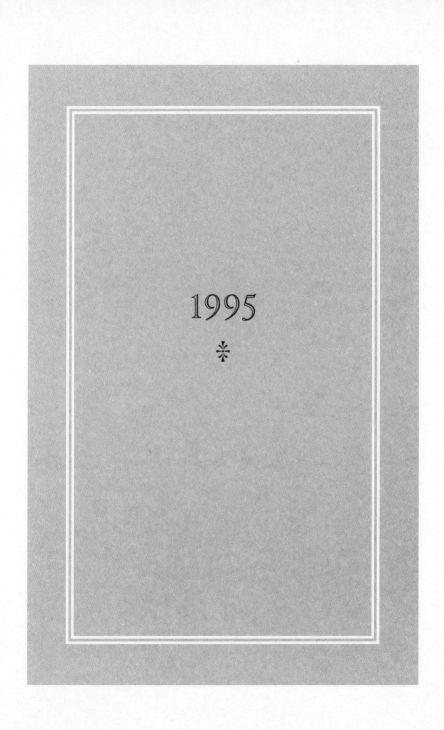

1995

✳

LIFE HADN'T REQUIRED LAURA TO NAVIGATE UNKNOWN TERRI-
tory on her own, and the few occasions over the years where she had
taken the initiative to do so had all been very empowering. Associated
Value, for instance. To think of all the money she'd saved shopping
there. She took a similar pride in discovering the School for the Ethical Individual, a progressive boarding school in Vermont that no one
she knew had ever heard of.

Unable to sleep, she'd been reading *The New Yorker* in bed, and,
bored by the article about O. J. Simpson's upcoming trial; her eyes
drifted first to a cartoon of a fox being interviewed for an office job
by a goose, then to the margins of the page, where a column of boxes
advertised the usual assortment of eclectic frivolities: sailing vacations,
commemorative plates, specialty hats. At the bottom of the page was
a small ad she'd nearly overlooked, with the words *Instead of answers,
school should teach students how to ask questions.*

Laura was intrigued, and the next morning she called the School for
the Ethical Individual and requested a brochure. It arrived a week later.

"What's this?" Emma asked, picking through the mail after school.

"It's a school in Vermont," Laura said. "I thought it sounded like
something you might be interested in."

"A *boarding* school?"

"Not the usual kind," Laura said.

Emma looked dumbfounded. "You want me to go to *boarding
school?*"

"Of course not," Laura answered. "The idea of you leaving makes me very sad. I just happened across an ad for it in *The New Yorker*, and it sounded like the sort of place . . . I don't know, you're only in seventh grade, but I was thinking, down the road . . . you might want to explore other options for high school."

Emma took the brochure into her bedroom. After two hours she found Laura in the living room.

"They have an eighth-grade class," she announced. "I could start next year."

"*Eighth grade*," Laura repeated. "Are you sure? That seems much too young."

Emma nodded and pointed to a page in the brochure. "The deadline to apply is next Monday," she said.

"Four days from now?"

"Eleven days," Emma said. "Not this Monday, the *next* Monday."

"Well, unfortunately, that's much too soon," Laura said. "These things take time. We'd have to ask them to mail us an actual application, then there are forms you fill out, then we'd have to let Winthrop know, then I imagine there's an essay you'd have to write . . ."

"I know," Emma said. "I started writing it."

"What?"

"I already called the office to ask for an application, and the woman on the phone told me the essay question.

"She was really nice," Emma added softly. She twirled a strand of hair around her finger. "The essay's really easy. Just why do I want to go there."

That weekend they drove up for a tour and spent the night in the school's guest cottage, which was tucked between its admissions office and its chicken coop. In addition to chickens, the campus was home to llamas, sheep, ducks, and goats, which students were responsible for caring for. Faculty and staff went by first names and dressed in blue jeans and hiking boots. The students struck Laura as refreshingly earnest and kind, going out of their way to say hi and make Emma feel welcome. They almost didn't seem like teenagers, with their unabashed enthusiasm for their school.

Laura couldn't have been more charmed and impressed on every front.

"I think you should apply for ninth grade," she told Emma as they drove home. "You'll be more emotionally prepared to go away then."

"I'm ready now," Emma said.

LAURA'S HEART SANK WHEN EMMA finally emerged from her room, clutching the letter that had arrived that afternoon, eyes glassy with tears.

"They're idiots," Laura said, shaking her head, though a small part of her was selfishly relieved. "Fools! They'd be so lucky to have you."

"No, Mama," she said, blinking. "They want me. I got in."

IN THE PAST, DOUGLAS HAD met with his children individually to go over their personal finances, but this year he decided to bring them together for a group conversation, which also included Stephanie. The four of them convened for a weekday lunch at Serafina.

"We're going to have to tighten the belt a bit this year," he announced after they'd been seated.

"I know, Dad," Nicholas said grimly. "We'll be canceling our membership to Lawrence Beach Club."

"Dad's been paying for that?" Laura reached for the breadbasket. "That's news to me."

"Like you don't accept the occasional handout," Nicholas said.

"For necessities, of course. Not for frivolous expenses," she said, chewing. "For example, on the way in I handed the maître d' a deposit for Emma's surprise going-away party . . ." Laura paused to swallow—and to allow Douglas a chance to offer to reimburse her. When he didn't, she continued.

"Not sure if you've received the invitations yet, but it'll be taking place in the private room upstairs. Anyway, boy, did that check make a dent. This is the last meal I expect to be eating out for a while, that's for sure."

No one spoke as their iced teas arrived.

"Anyway, I don't doubt your annual dues to LBC aren't extravagantly expensive, but I would've assumed your Wall Street salary would cover them," Laura said after the waitress left. "How much are you making these days, anyway?"

"A lot less than two years ago," Nicholas answered. "Not sure if you've read the paper recently, but my sector was stagnant last year. Some people are calling it another recession."

"And whose fault is that?" Laura muttered, helping herself to a second piece of bread. This time she went with rosemary brioche. She reached for the salt and shook it onto the dish of olive oil before dipping in it.

"Not bond traders'." Douglas defended his son. "It's the Fed."

"Yes, and those who work in bonds are suffering the impact." Stephanie stroked her husband's arm. "His firm took a huge hit."

"You see, Laura, the *economy*"—Nicholas coughed into his hand, and then draped his arm around Stephanie as he leaned back into the booth—"is some vague abstract thing to you that you hear about on NPR, but not all of us are so lucky. Take your annual income, and imagine it was cut in half, and try supporting a family of three."

"I'd be twenty-five thousand poorer." Laura shrugged. "Not enough money to cry about. So yes, it's sort of hard for me to relate, as I imagine in your case that figure is still well into the six digits."

"My salary is none of your business," Nicholas said. "But that's very interesting that you've been able to send Emma to Winthrop all these years on a fifty-thousand-dollar income, and now this socialist boarding school she's going to. That ghetto supermarket you're always gloating about must really be cheap for you to have that much left over."

"Laura doesn't pay for Emma's tuition," Douglas said. "I do, and this is why I called you all here together."

Their waitress reappeared, poised to take their orders; Douglas held up a finger and she went away.

"You see, *my* father . . ." Douglas paused to make sure he had everyone's attention. ". . . was very discreet about the degree to which he financed which children's lives. Some received more assistance than others, and this caused much suspicion and hostility among the siblings. A similar thing happened to your mother's family. I don't want that to happen to you, so I'd like to lay it all out on the table.

"Literally," he said, opening his briefcase and pulling out four copies of a spreadsheet that he passed around the table.

"Daddy pays a quarter of your mortgage?" Laura asked incredulously.

"Yup!" Nicholas responded. "And *one hundred* percent of yours."

"If you look at the next column, you'll see the total amount, and that they're nearly the same figure," Douglas explained.

"And yours is almost paid off, too," Nicholas said, investigating the numbers more closely. "No housing expenses except maintenance. That must be nice."

Laura smiled back. "And it must be nice living on Park Avenue."

"I guess my financial advisor was right." Douglas chuckled. "I was just at his office this morning, and when I told him about this lunch he suggested I invite a family therapist along."

Seeing his comment failed to lighten the mood, Douglas cleared his throat.

"In addition to Nicholas's salary, the recession has affected the family trust, and to ensure that I can continue to help the two of you down the road, there will need to be cutbacks," he said. "Nicholas, if you are prepared to sacrifice your club membership, that will do it. Your mortgage and the other expenses can stay."

"You mean *quarter* of my mortgage." Nicholas's cheeks reddened. "Vastly different from *mortgage*, which implies the whole thing."

Douglas nodded. "Thank you for the clarification, Nick."

"Wait." Stephanie shook her head. "I'm confused. Doesn't this mean that the . . . distribution will be different amounts?"

Douglas nodded. "That is correct. There will be a discrepancy in the numbers and, with your blessing, it will be in Laura's favor. Given her status as the sole provider of a single-parent household, who works in the nonprofit sector, and that it's for Emma's education rather than a club membership, I think it's justified. But if you object, by all means speak up."

"No, of course it makes sense," Stephanie said.

"This isn't an objection," Nicholas said, "just another clarification. But when you said *we* need to tighten our belts, what you really meant is *my* belt."

The sisterly pride Laura felt over Nicholas's progress, in boldly challenging their father without a trace of a stutter, was complicated by his anger toward her—and furthermore by a wistful pang for the vulnerable little brother he no longer was. He'd been an adult for years, of course, he had an important job and a wife and a child and an apartment, but for the first time, she saw him as a man: resolute, rational, and mostly remote, any transparent feelings fenced in by barbed wire.

"I apologize for using the wrong pronoun," Douglas conceded.

Nicholas wasn't done clarifying. "And Laura's belt will be loosening, as I assume the tuition for the School for the Ethical Individual is more than Winthrop, given that it includes room and board. Not to mention llamas."

"Yes, you could call it taking one for the team, Nicholas. So what do you think? Are we all good?"

"Matter resolved!" Nicholas declared with hostile enthusiasm. "I'll call the club as soon as I get back to the office."

"I appreciate this, Nicholas," Laura said, trying to make eye contact with her brother. "It's very generous of you."

"Well, then!" Douglas picked up his menu. "Now that we've got that whole business out of the way, let's order."

No one felt like talking after that; a tense quiet descended upon the table. The waitress returned, took their orders, and left. Their food arrived. They began eating. Their waitress stopped by to see how everything was. Douglas, only a few bites into his steak, asked if he could take the rest to go. As his plate was removed, he smiled sheepishly. "This is a new thing I do now that your mother's gone. It would've mortified her."

"I think it's a great idea, Dad," Laura said warmly.

"You have to be somewhere?" Nicholas asked.

"No, but I have a feeling my optimism that things were resolved was premature." Douglas took out his wallet and put two hundred-dollar bills on the table.

"Stephanie, I'm putting you in charge. See to it they work this thing out."

Stephanie, clearly flattered to have been designated the reasonable one, offered her father-in-law a placid smile. "Thank you for lunch," she told him.

"Yes, thanks, Daddy," Laura added.

Nicholas echoed the sentiment with something between a grunt and a nod.

"Pay to play," Douglas said with a jovial wink, and then he was off.

"Should I drop this off at one-three-six?" Stephanie asked when the waiter returned with a doggy bag.

"Don't bother," Nicholas said. "Sandra's making him dinner anyway. Maybe give it to that guy who's always on the corner."

"James," Laura said. "His name is James."

"Well . . ." Nicholas sighed. "I guess we should return those swim trunks we bought Nicky, now that he won't be needing them for his swim lessons."

He glanced at Stephanie, who looked at her plate.

"The Y has a great pool," Laura offered.

"Yes, I hear they also have a great rec room. A space you rent out for children's parties."

"Emma's surprise party isn't a children's party, as there weren't many children to invite. Nearly all the guests will be adults," Laura said. "The last few years have been very difficult and lonely for her. I want her to feel supported and loved before she heads off to Vermont."

"We're sad to see her go," Stephanie said. "But her new school sounds like a great fit."

"Yes." Nicholas smirked. "She'll learn all about radical feminism, and then she can graduate and start a llama farm."

"Oh, Nick, stop teasing," Stephanie said, smiling.

"No, he's right," Laura cut in. "The great thing about the School for the Ethical Individual is that it encourages kids to pursue all sorts of careers. To do things that don't perpetuate the cycle of inequality that makes it impossible for people who weren't born into circumstances like ours to achieve the American dream."

"Speaking of social justice," Nicholas said, "I attended my first meeting as a member of the board of the Library, and the new director, Karen, raised an issue of concern. Turns out there's an employee, has worked there for years, happens to be a member of the museum's founding family."

"As you are," Laura interjected. "Which is why you're on the board."

"Of course, though being a member of the board is quite different from being a salaried employee, who apparently has taken certain liberties over the years, such as adjusting the hours of her position to suit her schedule, which is perfectly understandable given her home life situation, but has struck some of her colleagues as a little unfair, as they're not granted such flexibility, nor do they enjoy an eight-week paid summer vacation, not that they have seashore summer houses to go to. The reason this all came up—"

"*Nick,*" Stephanie said.

"It's okay, Stephanie," Laura said. "I want to hear the rest."

"It was discovered that eliminating said employee's position to outsource the work to a professional wedding planning service would more than double the museum's annual profits."

"Because they could do it so much better than me?"

"Because they could handle one wedding a weekend as opposed to two a month, plus summers."

"Are you trying to tell me I'm about to lose my job?"

"No, to the contrary, your job's not going anywhere and it never will—don't worry about that," Nicholas said with a sarcastic grin. "The proposal was shot down by the trustees, who acknowledged the director's concerns about unfair advantages enjoyed by that particular employee, and said they were aware of more profitable alternatives, but that it was not within her jurisdiction to do anything about it." He folded his napkin neatly, placed it on the table, and patted it. "That particular employee's job security was a priority."

LAURA WAS ADMIRING THE CAKE for Emma's surprise party when she heard the front door open and, in her frenzied panic, put the cake in the freezer and slammed the door with such force that a few of the magnets slipped off and a flurry of papers fluttered to the floor. Among these was the mysterious stick-figure picture that had arrived in the mail years earlier. When it fell, it unfolded; it wasn't glued together after all, but must have gotten stuck to itself in transit.

It was a handmade card, and the interior featured a shakily scrawled heart containing Emma's initials. A Post-it note read:

I thought you might want to have this sweet drawing by your daughter. Tim spoke very fondly of you.

—*Tina Brown Fuchs*

There was a newspaper clipping tucked inside the fold.

As Laura saw what it was, the sounds of traffic continued, but everything else seemed to stop.

She waited until Emma had sequestered herself in her bedroom before picking up the phone.

"I'm looking for a number for Tina Brown Fuchs," she told the operator. "I'm not sure what state, but you might start with Ohio."

TIMOTHY BROWN, M.D., 1950–1991.

DR. BROWN HAD NOT GOTTEN infected with AIDS, his sister, Tina, told Laura over the phone, but fear of the disease had prevented any of his patients from following him to Downtown Pediatrics. He had similar troubles in San Francisco, where he had moved with Chris, who had gotten infected though apparently he was still living. The two had split up, and Dr. Brown had returned to Ohio to take care of their mother, who was suffering from dementia. Following her death, he had taken his own life.

*　　*　　*

LAURA HADN'T FELT RIGHT TELLING Emma all the details she'd just learned, but Emma, who remembered Dr. Brown well, had coaxed them out of her.

"That's all I know, darling," she said when Emma wanted more information. "That's all the information his sister volunteered, and I didn't want to pry."

"Do you think he had depression?" Emma asked. "Like a chemical thing in his brain?"

"I don't know," Laura said, still too stunned to feel anything. "Life is complicated. You never really know what it's like to be someone else."

The two of them sat at the kitchen table in silence. From the street below came the jingle of an ice cream truck. Soon it would be time to leave for Emma's surprise goodbye party, Laura realized.

"I thought we'd go out for dinner tonight," she told Emma. "I made us a reservation at Serafina."

"I can't even think about food right now," Emma said with a sigh.

"Me neither," Laura agreed. "But it's important to eat."

THE PARTY WAS IN A small private room in the back of the restaurant. Seated around the table were Emma's grandfather, Charlotte and Margaret and Trip, her mother's friends Edith and Janet, Nicholas and Stephanie and Nick Jr., Emma's second cousin Holly, and Holly's mom, Ginny.

"Surprise!" they said in unison as Emma entered.

Her cheeks were chapped from dried tears, she was sure her eyes were still red, her face still felt puffy and swollen, but if any of the guests noticed she'd been crying, their smiles didn't betray it.

"Thank you!" Emma said, doing her best to affect excitement and gratitude.

The grief that had gripped her on the walk over abruptly subsided. A cold, quiet anger took its place as Emma realized she'd been duped. *It's important to eat.* How typical of her mother, to insist on carrying through with a party in the wake of what they'd just learned.

Emma pulled out a chair next to Nick Jr., but Laura pointed to an empty place at the other end of the table.

"I put you over there," she said. "Between Charlotte and Holly."

Emma saw that Laura had made place cards with everyone's name handwritten.

She was relieved to discover that Holly and Charlotte had already seemed to strike up a rapport with each other, as she had very little to say to either of them. She and Holly didn't have much in common outside of Ashaunt, and Emma and Charlotte had barely been on speaking terms for over a year now.

"Were you surprised?" Holly asked as Emma sat down.

"You looked really surprised," Charlotte said.

"I was," Emma admitted. "I had no idea. It's not the kind of thing my mom does — throw surprise parties."

"We were just talking about how cute your mom is," said Charlotte.

"We love her cowboy boots," Holly added. "So retro."

Emma reached for her water as she tried to think of something to say. Making small talk with anyone was taxing, but it was less painful with a stranger. With both Charlotte and Holly there was the unspoken intimacy of having grown up together, in knowing each other first and foremost as children. To carry on as they were now felt like a betrayal of their most authentic, primal selves, further degrading the integrity of their childhood bond.

"I'm so happy it's finally warm out," Charlotte said.

"Me, too," Holly agreed. "I'm so excited for it to be, like, *hot.*"

Emma recalled an interesting fact she had once learned: "The murder rate rises when it's hot."

"*Okaaay,*" Holly responded, raising her eyebrows.

Charlotte mirrored her expression. "*That's* random."

At the other end of the table, Stephanie scolded Nick Jr. for blowing bubbles into his chocolate milk. "One more time and I take the straw away from you," she warned him.

"Emma!" Janet hollered from a few seats away. "Your new school sounds absolutely fantastic!"

"Thank you," Emma responded.

"Are you *so* excited?"

Emma mustered a smile and nodded, but Janet's face remained fixed on hers, as if she weren't convinced, and so Emma smiled harder and added, "I'm really, *really* excited."

She was, though being asked to exuberantly express this—to match the caliber of Janet's enthusiasm—felt perfunctory and made the sentiment ring false. One of the more exhausting aspects of getting older was having to act like an adult. Pretending to like people you couldn't stand, speaking for the sake of filling a silence, smiling when you felt like crying.

"I can't wait to hear all about it!" Janet grinned, and turned her attention to the waiter, who was taking orders.

Throughout the meal, Emma found her mother pursuing eye contact with her from across the table. Once their gazes met, Laura would smile, forcing Emma to smile back. It was as though she were willing her to suppress any feelings about Dr. Brown. Just as it was *important to eat*, it was important to maintain composure in the company of others. Buck up. Fake it till you feel it. The show must go on.

This was the way they did things—these people in the world she'd grown up in.

Emma looked around the table at everyone laughing and chatting as if they didn't have a care in the world. She knew this wasn't the case, but it seemed to be the impression they strived to make. *I'm great. Isn't life fabulous?! How wonderful!*

Deep down, they all knew this was a lie, which was why it was so important that everyone make an effort to pretend everything was hunky-dory—to keep up the collective charade. Which was why individuals who refused to do this were labeled depressed or mentally ill, when really they were just honest—the brave ones who refused to be fake.

She thought of her grandmother.

Douglas had another party to go to and left before dessert. A polite hush fell over the table as he apologized for his early departure, and then announced he had a present for Emma. He reached into the pocket of his blazer and pulled out a book.

"Years ago someone broke into the house and stole a handful of items that we eventually got back, and this was one of them, so either the thief had good literary taste, or this is quite valuable." He held up a book.

"A signed first edition of *Catcher in the Rye*," Douglas said, prompting a chorus of *oohs* and "That's my favorite book!"—a claim that baffled Emma, who felt the book had been written specifically for her, at the expense of present company.

"Thank you, Doug-Doug," Emma said.

"Remember to have fun at school, kiddo," he added before taking off.

After dinner there was a cake from the fancy bakery where her mother ordered wedding cakes. It was decorated with edible flowers and the top was inscribed with the words *Good luck, Emma!* written in icing, next to the image of a bird taking flight.

"Why is there a pigeon on the cake?" asked Nick Jr.

"It's a sparrow," Laura corrected.

"How sweet," Stephanie said. To Nick Jr. she added, "It's like Emma is a bird who's flying off to a new nest."

"When Emma was little, she used to get overstimulated before bed," Laura explained. "Sometimes the only way to get her to settle down was to let her wear herself out. So we played this game where she was a sparrow, and I'd chase her as she flew around the apartment. I'd say, 'I'm going to catch that little sparrow and eat her for dinner!' "

"How fun!" Edith squealed.

Laura looked across the table and smiled. It was a different kind of smile from what she'd been doing all night. A private, fragile smile, fondly wistful, gently probing.

Emma nodded. Of course she remembered.

Her mother in a rare display of silliness, pretending to be a bird catcher, dashing through the rooms, periodically pausing to catch her breath and give Emma a chance to reverse course. Emma, the sparrow, mere inches from her mother's clutch; the heart-thumping, hilarity-inducing suspense of wondering when she'd make her final, swooping move, of not knowing whether you were going to escape once more, or if that was it.

THE SCHOOL FOR THE ETHICAL Individual was a five-hour drive from Manhattan and, as Laura had predicted, there was no traffic, and thus it had been unnecessary to set their alarms for six a.m. on Sunday—as Emma had insisted they do.

"Mom, you're driving between the lanes."

"I know," Laura said. "There were no other cars on the highway and I always wanted to see what it's like." She put on her blinker and coasted back into the right lane.

"You didn't have to stop," Emma said. "I was just wondering if you knew you were doing it."

"I did, I was doing it on purpose."

"I know. You said that already."

"Do it again," Emma requested a moment later. "It was sort of fun."

Laura glanced in the rearview and drifted back toward the middle—then changed her mind and got back in the right. "I oughtn't," she said, shaking her head.

"*Oughtn't*," Emma repeated with disdain; then, in the silly English accent she adopted when ridiculing Laura: "I *oughtn't* break the law."

"Is oughtn't even a word?" Emma asked a minute later.

"It's a conjunction," Laura said. "*Ought not.*"

"I *know* that, Mom. I mean is a *word* still a *word* if nobody uses it anymore?"

"I don't know what you're talking about. I use it all the time."

"Well, nobody else does."

"Nor do they use most of the words in the dictionary," Laura reflected.

"Nor!" Emma scoffed. She put her seat back and rested her feet on the dashboard.

Laura glanced at Emma's legs. At her most recent checkup, Dr. Marks had expressed concern that her BMI percentile had gone down from the previous year, and it would be hard to monitor her eating and exercise habits now that she would be away.

"I wish you'd just say *shouldn't*," Emma continued. "Every time you say *oughtn't*, I don't know why, but it makes me think of that Beatles song 'Eleanor Rigby'—it makes me sad for you."

"'Eleanor Rigby'?" Laura laughed. "That song is about a tragic old woman who lives in a delusional world, and a priest . . . I don't know what it has to do with my vocabulary choices."

They passed a billboard for a personal injury lawyer named Gary (GARY'S YOUR GUY). A mile later one for Vince (HE'S IN-VINCE-IBLE IN COURT!), then for Wayne (IN PAIN? CALL WAYNE!).

"That wasn't very nice," Laura said.

"What wasn't?" Emma asked.

"The 'Eleanor Rigby' comment. I don't know what you meant by it, but it wasn't a very nice thing to say."

"Sorry," Emma said. "I didn't mean it.

"I really didn't," she reiterated a moment later. "I just had that song stuck in my head for some reason."

"Thank you," Laura said. She glanced at the odometer and realized she was going well below the speed limit. "I want to apologize to you for something, too," she said, speeding up. "Something that's been weighing on me recently. Something I didn't tell the truth about."

Emma retracted her feet and hugged her knees to her chest.

Laura checked her mirrors, thinking she'd heard a police siren, but it was nothing.

"I didn't tell the truth about how I had you," she said. "I didn't think it was anyone's business how I came to be pregnant and I had no qualms giving them a different story, but you . . . I never felt right about it."

Emma opened the window a crack. This created an air-pressure situation that hurt Laura's ears. To stabilize the current she opened her own window an inch.

"You weren't conceived with a sperm donor," she continued. "It was a one-night stand."

Laura took a deep breath. The air felt like helium in her lungs. If she didn't have her seat belt on she'd float up out of her seat, get sucked out the window, and slither up into the atmosphere.

"Well." Laura's eyes briefly left the road to glance over at Emma. "I imagine you have questions."

Emma was silent.

"It's not an easy conversation," Laura proceeded, "but I guess we should just get the whole thing over with. It was August. The part of the summer when everyone's out of town—"

Now Emma spoke. Her voice was muffled but it sounded like *Stop*. When Laura turned to look at her she'd pushed her seat as far back as it would go and had draped her sweatshirt over her face.

Laura's sense of gravity returned; she felt very much rooted in the car. "Maybe now wasn't the right time to tell you." She reached out to pat Emma's knee but Emma brushed her fingers away.

"Please, Mom," she said, putting her seat back up. "Just take me to school. That's all I ask of you."

"Of course, darling. I'm sorry. I completely understand." She felt bad for having burdened Emma with this now, but also relieved. The information had been delivered; the conversation she'd been dreading wasn't one Emma was interested in having. The matter was over and dealt with.

Twenty minutes passed.

"What color hair did he have?" Emma asked.

"To be honest," Laura said after a pause, "I can't remember. I would say it was brown. I mean it definitely wasn't red, and I don't think it was black, and I think I would remember it if it was blond. There aren't that many adult men with blond hair out there.

"Do you want to hear the story?" Laura asked a minute later.

"*No*," Emma said emphatically.

Ten minutes later: "I just have a couple other questions."

"You can ask me anything."

Emma paused. "What did he look like?"

"To be honest, I don't really remember," Laura said.

"Was he tall?"

"Yes, I think so. He must have been, since you're so much taller than I am."

"Was he skinny or fat?"

"He was neither," Laura answered. "He was healthy."

"What was his personality?" Emma asked next. "Was he serious, was he funny?"

Laura thought about this for a moment. "He was quite amusing," she answered. "Spirited."

"Spirited?" Emma repeated.

"He had a fun, silly side."

They were quiet. The road made a recurring bumping sound beneath the car.

"No more," Emma said.

"No more what?"

"I don't want to know anything more."

"I understand," Laura told her.

"Ever," Emma said.

"I won't bring it up again," Laura promised.

"I DON'T LIKE THIS." LAURA frowned.

"Your tea?" Emma asked.

"No—I don't like saying goodbye to you in a coffee shop."

"It was *your* idea," Emma reminded her, taking a sip of her water.

Laura looked out the window. Emma's school was through the trees down the road. They'd already been there, checked in, met the roommate, and unpacked. Laura had been about to leave when she'd had a thought: it would be easier to say goodbye in a public place, to keep herself in check in case she got emotional. Now the two of them were seated at a rickety iron table in a coffee shop, their emotions very much in check, and it was terrible.

"Well, I guess this is it," Laura said as they stepped outside. Emma crossed her arms and looked at the ground. Laura realized she was doing the same.

"Can I please drive you back to campus?"

"*Mom.*" Emma groaned. "I *told* you, I want to walk."

"Are you sure?"

Emma nodded and kicked a pinecone. "I'll walk you to your car, though."

It was a small parking lot; they were there in thirty seconds. Laura stood on her tiptoes to give Emma a kiss on the cheek goodbye. "You're so much taller than me!"

"You *always* say that," Emma said wearily.

"Well, it always takes me by surprise."

Emma rolled her eyes.

"You know, you're lucky to be so tall," Laura said. "It's tough being a little shrimp like me—people don't take you seriously."

Laura unlocked the door but paused before opening it. "Parents' Weekend will be here before we know it!" she said with cheerful conviction.

Emma made a face that was a cross between sarcasm and agreement.

"I'm not kidding. Six weeks may seem like a long time, but it'll go by lickety-split." Laura snapped her fingers to convey how quickly it would go by.

Emma waved a hand in the air to indicate she was about to be on her way. This was it, the last time she'd see her for a while—in a parking lot.

"No!" Laura shouted. "You're *not* walking! *I'm* the parent, and *I* make the rules, and you're getting in the car and I'm driving you, and *that's that.*"

To Laura's surprise, Emma surrendered and climbed in the passenger seat. Laura commented on the beauty of the surrounding trees for the two-minute drive, but Emma only grunted in response—until they pulled into the driveway of her school.

"Was he Swe-dish?" Emma's voice cracked. "That's why you told people that story?"

Laura's heart sank, anticipating Emma's disappointment.

"It's possible his ancestors were from Sweden," she said.

LAURA DIDN'T HAVE MUCH OF an appetite and decided to have a bowl of bran for dinner. When she was done, she carried the bowl to the sink and gave it a quick rinse. She was about to put it in the dishwasher when she realized there would be fewer dishes from now on. Dishwashers used a lot of energy and she did not like to run theirs until it was completely full; with Emma gone, it would take a while for this to happen. She turned the faucet back on and gave the bowl a thorough scrub, dried it off with a dishtowel, and left it out on the counter. There was no point in returning it to the shelf with the others; she would use the same one for breakfast.

THAT FIRST MORNING, RIDING THE 6 train to work, Laura felt as though she'd tapped into a sadness that was larger than her own—the collective loneliness, disappointment, and despair of all the people who'd ever ridden through the bowels of the New York City subway system.

If the other passengers noticed that she was crying, they pretended not to, which Laura appreciated. People who thought New Yorkers were cold and uncaring didn't understand that in a city like this, one's physical proximity to strangers necessitated a respect of their psychological privacy.

By the time Laura reached her station she had recovered. The sadness had had to do with saying goodbye to Emma, and she was glad she'd gotten it out of her system. As she ascended the steps, a cathartic levity set in as she considered the possibilities that lay before her.

"It will be a new chapter of your life," people told her.

GRIEF IS LIKE A WATER balloon, someone had told Laura after Bibs had died. You have a certain amount of it in you, and it drips out, until one day all that's left is a shriveled-up balloon with nothing inside it.

Laura thought that balloon had emptied years ago, but in the wake of Emma's departure it seemed to bubble back to life. Thoughts of Emma were interspersed with those of her mother. Long-forgotten scenes of Bibs, which, in contrast to the memories that had precipitated after her death, featured happy times that left her full of tender fondness. Some of them were so strange, so whimsical, she was sure she must have dreamed them or made them up. For instance, the time Bibs had taken a string and strung it around the leg of a dragonfly she'd found in the garden and they'd taken turns holding the end of the string as it circled above their heads like a kite—how was that even possible? And yet Nicholas claimed to remember it, too.

It would take some getting used to, having Emma gone. In the meantime, Laura decided it would be good to switch up her routines a bit, to try new things.

FOUR NIGHTS PASSED BEFORE LAURA heard from Emma. The first few phone calls were brief and perfunctory. *Hello? Hi. How was your day? Good. Good. Just calling to say good night. Okay.*

But then, one night, Emma confessed she was having trouble sleeping. She missed the sounds of the city; it was so quiet up there at night—too quiet to sleep. The urge to sleep wouldn't hit till the day, when she'd walk around in a delirious stupor. Traveling through campus you were expected to smile and say hi to each person you passed. This was exhausting and made her feel phony. She wished she were a llama.

"Why a llama?" Laura asked.

After a prolonged silence came a muffled sob.

"Because they never have to make friends with new llamas," Emma said. "Or if they do, they don't get upset about it."

"I know what you mean," Laura said. "I remember I sometimes used to get jealous of our dog Mr. Baggins. He was always fed and taken care of. People loved him. He didn't know he was going to die someday. And he never really got sad, or at least not sad the way people do."

"*He didn't know he was going to die someday?*" Emma said. "I thought you were trying to cheer me up. Now I'm thinking about how we're all going to die."

"Sorry, you're right." To distract Emma from dark thoughts, Laura started talking about her day. As she rambled on, the receiver grew moist and warm against her skin, which came to feel like Emma's silent presence—the sticky heat of her sadness. When Laura ran out of things to talk about, she proposed she read a book out loud over the phone. She walked over to the bookshelf and pulled out one of Emma's childhood favorites, Roald Dahl's *The BFG*, which—and Laura hadn't even remembered this—began with a description of a girl in a dormitory who couldn't sleep.

"Do you want me to stop?" Laura asked after the first chapter, not having heard any encouraging signals from Emma.

"No," Emma said. "Keep going."

FOR THE PAST FEW YEARS, Margaret had been badgering Laura to get her hair colored. The grays were proliferating, there was no denying it.

Laura arrived early to her hair appointment. She forgot to bring her book, and there was no newspaper in the reception area, just glossy magazines. The cover of one featured a topless woman, presumably promoting some movie, holding her hands over her breasts like a bra. Out of boredom Laura picked it up and flipped to the page promising to share this woman's beauty secrets. According to the article, the woman was forty and she had spent her entire life avoiding the sun—hence her beautiful, unblemished complexion. Laura felt depressed thinking of her own skin. All her life, she had been under the impression the sun's damage was limited to cancer and liver spots, but her dermatologist had recently told her it also wore down the skin's elasticity, which is how wrinkles developed.

Marco, the renowned colorist Margaret had sent her to, shook Laura's hand and led her to his station. As she took a seat he complimented Laura's gray; he said it was a particular variety, more like silver, and that he thought it was becoming.

"Once you start coloring, you can't go back," he warned her.

Coming from a professional, Laura took this to heart. She did not end up coloring her hair that day—but she did stop at a newsstand to purchase a copy of the *Village Voice*.

That evening, as she combed the classifieds, her eyes drifted over the personals, where one of the ads called for *someone who cares about the fate of the planet and believes there's a special place in hell for Newt Gingrich.*

Laura chuckled at this final criterion—and was surprised that the poster, a "46-year-old atheist public defender," described his body as "petite." Then she saw it was listed under the "F seeking F" category.

THE PARKVIEW WAS JUST ONE of many high-rises that had sprung up around them in recent years. While the buildings were still under construction, giant billboards would announce their name, followed by a list of their amenities. Across the street, occupying the lot where the tenements used to be, was the Monterey, which boasted a swimming pool, roof deck, and twenty-four-hour concierge.

As the property values of the apartments in Laura's building increased, some of the old-timers cashed out. The shifting demographic of the residents of the building—younger, more entitled—was reflected in the lobby, where the co-op board had voted to replace the super's religious-themed paintings with floor-to-ceiling wall-to-wall mirrors.

Laura passed by one of these mirrors on her way home one night, and her face looked particularly weathered. She peered closer before going upstairs to investigate—maybe the lighting was just unflattering.

She undressed before the full-length mirror in her front hall closet to assess the damage. The lobby lighting had indeed been harsh, but there was no denying it: years of sunbathing had taken their toll, and not just on her face, but other parts of her body as well. Though she'd never gained any weight in her midsection, her stomach was soft. As she ran her hands across it, it reminded her of the shell of a tart after the berries have been plucked off and the cream licked away. What a waste: all those tans, with no one to admire the results.

She took a step back, dimmed the hall light, and mimicked the pose of the woman on the cover of the magazine. The results were much more attractive than before. Her skin looked tight and smooth. You couldn't tell that her breasts drooped and that Emma had destroyed her nipples. As she stood there, studying herself from different angles, she became aroused, which didn't make any sense—she was looking at herself—but it felt good and she couldn't help it and she didn't stop. Imagining someone else was watching, she kept doing what she was doing, periodically dimming the light even more, until it was dark.

She was getting ready to leave for work when the doorbell rang. It was a man Laura didn't recognize. He looked to be in his mid-twenties, chubby, bearded.

"Martin," he said, offering her a sweaty palm. "I live downstairs, right below you, 16A."

Martin was having some friends over that night, he explained, and the last time they were over, they'd complained he didn't have any chairs—did she have any he could borrow?

"How many do you need?" Laura asked as he followed her into the kitchen.

"I'll take what you've got," he said. "As many as you can spare."

"Is five okay?" She had six chairs.

"Five works." Martin nodded, stroking his beard. "Though if it doesn't make a difference to you, six would actually be better."

Laura, who was already running behind, helped him carry the six chairs out to the hall. She was about to shut the door behind him when he said, "Wait, I don't think I caught your name."

In her flustered rush to wrap up their encounter, Laura accidentally responded with the name she'd used in her brief correspondence with the public defender: "Liza."

LAURA MADE PLANS TO MEET the public defender for dinner on the Upper West Side. While waiting outside the restaurant, she ran into a bride she'd worked with years ago. The groom, Andrew, had been a classmate of Nicholas's, but Laura couldn't recall this woman's name. After an awkward exchange of *hello, nice to see you, how are you*, Laura, in an attempt to wrap things up, said to send her best to Andrew, and the woman laughed.

"Actually, we got divorced, and no, he didn't cheat," she said. "Turns out I'm a lesbian!" With a nod and a quick farewell, the woman turned and entered the restaurant.

Laura felt terrible, but she couldn't carry through with it, not with this woman whom she knew, and so she left. Or "stood her up," as the saying went.

LAURA DIDN'T MIND EATING BREAKFAST standing at the counter, but dinner was another thing. She wrote Martin a note and slipped it beneath his front door.

Five minutes later her doorbell rang, and it was Martin, holding a chair. "Dude," he said, handing it to her. "I'm so sorry. Things have been really busy—I got this new job repairing voting machines and I completely forgot." He shook his head remorsefully. "That's no excuse, though, I feel like a jerk."

"Don't worry," Laura told him. Martin asked if he could hold on to the other chairs until Wednesday.

"I think that's all right," Laura said. "Yes, I don't think I'll be needing them before that."

"When, exactly, will you be needing them?" Martin inquired.

When she hosted her next dinner party.

Were there any on the calendar?

No, there weren't.

In that case, could he just hold on to them?

He hosted this meeting every Tuesday evening, Martin explained, anywhere from one to two dozen people showed up, it was hard to predict. Some of them were his age, they could sit on the floor, but there were also some older folks he wanted to be comfortable—last time they'd complained a little.

Was he asking to *keep* her chairs? Laura didn't know what to say; she wanted to laugh. People like this infuriated and fascinated her. The takers of the world, they felt no anxiety making all sorts of requests. In her experience of dealing with them, they also appeared unembarrassed by being told no, because it meant just that and nothing more to them. That is asking too much, you are inconveniencing me, I'm not comfortable giving you my chairs because I don't even know you— these weren't projected fears that would keep them up at night. How am I going to get chairs for free, in an easy manner that doesn't require hauling them through the streets of Manhattan—this was their concern.

"If you could return the chairs this weekend," Laura told him, "I would appreciate it."

"Candooskey," Martin said with a confident nod.

"Excuse me?" Laura said.

"No problem," Martin told her, ringing for the elevator. "Happy to bring the chairs back Sunday."

AFTER A FEW WEEKS, EMMA'S homesickness began to subside, but she continued to call every night. During the day Laura would make a mental inventory of amusing or interesting tidbits to tell her. At first they weren't terribly amusing or interesting to Emma.

"Hmm," Emma said after Laura relayed a client's demand to have her cake decorated with edible gold foil. "That's gross."

But when Laura told her later about an exchange she'd overheard between a young boy and his mother on the subway (he'd whispered in her ear and she'd loudly replied, "What? Your balls hurt?"), Emma laughed—her first real laugh since she'd left home, it seemed. Laura began tailoring her anecdotes to her sensibility.

And so they became two people who talked on the phone, like friends.

LAURA'S FRIENDSHIP WITH MARGARET WAS one of the constants in her life. There had been times when she'd taken it for granted, or thought less than generously of her, but now more than ever she took comfort in knowing that for better or worse, Margaret would always be there.

For Laura's forty-fifth birthday, Margaret wanted to throw her a dinner party, but upon seeing the guest list and thinking of all the enthusiasm she would have to manufacture for the evening, Laura demurred. "I think it would be more fun just the two of us," she said.

"Okay, but I insist you let me take you somewhere fancy for once."

They made a reservation for two at Tavern on the Green. The morning of Laura's birthday, Margaret called to ask if they could switch it to lunch.

Laura hesitated. The food at Tavern on the Green wasn't anything special; the whole point of going was for all the lights on the trees, which could be seen only at night.

"I'm sorry," Margaret said. "I know it's not the same in the daylight."

"No, no," Laura said. "It's fine. Lunch is actually better for me."

It was a beautiful Indian summer day. Short-sleeves weather—maybe the last of the season. An hour before they were supposed to meet Laura called to propose they scrap their plan and pick up sandwiches and eat on the lawn in the back of the Met.

"How's Emma liking her school?" Margaret asked, flapping out the blanket she had brought on the grass and taking a seat.

"She's actually doing really well," Laura said.

"I'm so glad," Margaret responded. "*Charlotte*, as I'm sure you've heard, has been suspended."

Laura shook her head. "I'm pretty much out of the Winthrop loop," she said, realizing it as she spoke it.

"For two weeks," Margaret added.

Winthrop rarely suspended students. Laura tried not to look shocked.

They sat facing the road that ran through the park. Behind them was a wall of glass—the windowed façade of the Egyptian Wing. Across the lawn, a woman in her twenties stripped down to a bikini and lay on the grass with a book.

"*Well*," Margaret said, "aren't you curious to know what she did?"

"What did she do?"

"My wonderful daughter, in her infinite wisdom, coerced a classmate into flashing the hot dog man. It was part of an *initiation ritual*." She made air quotes with her fingers.

"Initiation to what?" Laura asked.

"The Funny Pink Bunnies."

"*The Funny Pink Bunnies?*"

"The Funny Pink Bunnies," Margaret said authoritatively. "It's the name of their group."

"So she's at home right now?"

"*Oh*, no," Margaret said with a smirk. "She's on her *hands* and *knees* planting daffodil bulbs in Morningside Park."

"Of her own accord?" Laura was impressed.

"You kidding?" Margaret made a face. "I made some calls, signed her up with a program that works with juvenile delinquents from Harlem."

"That should be interesting for her," Laura said.

"It's not a punitive boot camp thing," Margaret explained. "It's about self-esteem. It helps kids feel good about themselves through work."

Laura nodded. "That makes sense."

Margaret unwrapped her sandwich. "Trip began acting up at this age. Took him years to get his act together as an adult, and he realizes now, it was because he didn't feel good about himself, because he never had to work for anything."

"That makes sense," Laura repeated, because she couldn't think of what else to say.

A man with a lizard draped over his shoulder strolled by, catching the attention of the sunbather, who looked up from her book to stare.

"In other news, I'm pregnant," Margaret said.

She laughed at Laura's bewildered expression. "Twelve weeks."

"You're not kidding," Laura said, as Margaret pulled her shirt back to reveal a little bump. "Did you use . . . how did this happen?"

"The old-fashioned way," Margaret said. "Don't ask me why it worked, now, when I'm forty-four years old. It was an accident. Or a *surprise*, Janet says I'm supposed to say. My ob-gyn says I'm a medical miracle."

"Oh, Mags," Laura said. "This is wonderful news. Have you told Charlotte yet?"

Margaret took a bite of her sandwich and shook her head. "She's about to find out," she said, holding a hand over her mouth as she chewed. "That's actually why I had to change our plans. We'd been holding off until I made it through the first trimester, but I just saw my doctor and he says everything looks good." She swallowed. "Trip's been in Houston for business and I wanted to wait for him to get back so we can tell her together tonight."

"How exciting for her," Laura said.

"I hope so," Margaret said pensively. "Yes, I think it will be."

"So Janet knows," Laura said.

Margaret nodded.

"What about Edith, does she know yet?" Laura's cheerfully casual tone rang false.

Margaret took another bite. "Mm-hmm."

"Well, this is very exciting," Laura said. "I'm very, very happy for you." She took a tiny bite of her sandwich but had trouble swallowing. "I'm fine," she said, realizing Margaret was looking at her. "I truly am happy for you. It really is a miracle. A miracle baby. I don't know why . . ." She dabbed her eyes.

"Maybe I'm a little upset I'm not the first to know." Laura mustered a smile as she blinked back tears. "I know it's silly, it's just that . . . well, when something happens to me, you're the first person I tell. Usually the *only* person."

Margaret looked distressed and unsure of how to respond.

"You know, I think it's a birthday thing," Laura told her. "I've always been a bit of an Eeyore on my birthday."

Margaret rested a hand on her shoulder. "You know I love you, Laura."

"Thank you," Laura said. She was caught off guard by the pronouncement. "I do, too," she said quietly a moment later.

Neither of them spoke for a little while.

"That's what I'll look like at my poor child's high school graduation." Margaret pointed to an elderly, slumped-over woman being pushed in a wheelchair.

"Look at this thing on my arm." Margaret held up her wrist. "I noticed it just this morning. Do you think it looks suspicious?"

"It looks like a freckle," Laura said.

"But freckles don't just grow overnight."

"You've always been afraid of death," Laura reflected. "Ever since we were little."

"Isn't everyone?" Margaret asked.

"I'm more worried about the Earth," Laura said. "I don't want it to be destroyed from global warming."

Margaret made a skeptical *pffft* sound.

ONE EVENING, JUST AS THEY were about to say good night, Emma said, "Oh, yeah, Mom, I need you to do me a favor that involves doing your least favorite thing."

"What's my least favorite thing?" Laura asked.

"Shopping," Emma replied. "I need you to send me a new pair of jeans."

"Okay. But what's wrong with the pair we just bought you before you left?"

"They don't fit me anymore."

"Oh, no," Laura said. "Shit." Emma wasn't eating enough; she was running too much. Dr. Marks was right—she wasn't able to keep tabs on her in Vermont.

"What's wrong?"

"You were a size two when you left," Laura said.

"Well, I'm not anymore."

Emma's tone was curt. Whatever Laura said would further irritate her; to comment on the matter was to risk being hung up on. It was like trying to grasp the end of a chain that had slipped down the drain of the sink. There was no other way to retrieve it, but touching it might send it into the abyss.

"I'll see if I can pick up a size zero tomorrow," Laura said.

"*Mom.*" Emma groaned. "I'm not *anorexic*—my jeans don't fit anymore because they're too *tight*."

"Oh." Laura tried to hide the excitement in her voice. "And what size do you want me to get?"

"A four," Emma said. "The uphill trail running has made my leg muscles grow."

LAURA WAS IN THE BASEMENT putting her clothes in the dryer when she heard a voice from behind her. "What's a person like you doing in a place like this?

"Sorry if I scared you," Martin said, dumping a trash bag of clothes into one of the machines. "Always thought it would be funny to say that to someone down here. This basement's so creepy. Very *Silence of the Lambs.*"

"I never saw it," Laura said, returning Martin's smile and turning the dryer on. As she left the laundry room and headed through the poorly lit dungeon-like tunnel that led to the elevator, she heard the echo of Martin's voice: "Shit! Shit! Shit!" A moment later came the lumbering shuffle of socked feet.

"Forgot detergent," he said as he caught up to her.

"I have some upstairs," Laura told him.

"Yeah, me, too. Just annoying to have to go all the way back up and get it.

"Up and down," Martin said, stepping in the elevator. "The elevator of life. Down and up, up and down, all day long—and the fun never ends."

"Martin," Laura said as they approached his floor. "When you bring the chairs back on Sunday, could you please bring them back by nine p.m.? I'd like to go to bed early because I've been having trouble sleeping recently."

"Candooskey," Martin said.

"What does that mean?" Laura asked. "Is that Polish?"

"Polish?" Martin smiled. "No—*can, do, ski.* No worries, it'll happen, I can do it."

"Oh," Laura said. "I like that."

THE FIRST WEEK OF OCTOBER, Emma started mentioning Jill, and also a boy named Lucas. Laura couldn't tell if the latter was a romantic interest—from the stories it sounded like the three of them spent a lot of time together.

"Maybe you shouldn't come Parents' Weekend," Emma said.

"Why not?" Laura had been looking forward not only to visiting Emma, but also to seeing Vermont's autumn foliage.

"Jill's parents aren't coming, and I was going to keep her company all weekend."

"She's welcome to come to dinner with us," Laura said. "Lucas, too."

"I think it might make me sad again if I see you now," said Emma.

"I get it," Laura said.

"HEY, STRANGER!" CAME MARTIN'S VOICE down the cereal aisle of Associated Value. The excitement on his face suggested they'd just crossed paths in an international airport. He had forgotten to return the chairs on Sunday, but surely seeing her now would remind him.

"You shaved off your beard," Laura said. "I almost didn't recognize you."

"I'm joining the army!"

Laura was speechless.

"Just kidding." He laughed. "I lost a bet. But I had you. Admit it! For a second I *had* you!"

"For a second," Laura conceded.

After paying for her groceries, Laura discovered Martin waiting for her by the store's exit. They walked home together.

"Did you know the dude who used to live in my apartment?" Martin asked, squinting up at their building as they waited for the light.

"Mr. Emory." Laura smiled fondly. "He always wore a hat, even on the hottest day of the year. *Toodle-oo*, he would say when he got off the elevator."

"Did you know he croaked in the apartment?" was how Martin followed this up.

"I was aware that he died," Laura responded.

"But you didn't know that he died inside the apartment and wasn't discovered for three days?"

Laura shook her head. She had no interest in hearing the details of Mr. Emory's death.

"Don't you find that strange?" Martin said with a frown. "That a guy living ten feet below you could just die, and you'd have no idea he was just laying there *dead*."

"He was a very old man," said Laura.

They passed James in his usual spot on the corner. They both waved and James called out, "No more beard!"

"Joining the army!" Martin hollered.

"Yeah, right, man!" James cackled. "They'd never take you!"

"Manhattan apartments are a weird place to die," Martin said as they entered the lobby. "The coordinated effort to dispose of the body in the fastest, most discreet way possible, with service elevators and back entrances and unmarked vehicles . . .

"I wouldn't want to die in Manhattan, *period*," he said as the elevator arrived.

"Where would you like to die?" Laura asked as they stepped in. It was a weird question. She wasn't sure why she'd asked it.

"I don't know." Martin pushed his glasses up his nose and folded his arms across his belly as he considered this. "Somewhere in the country. A small town where everyone knows me and the mayor declares a holiday so everyone can attend my funeral and there's a kind of parade through the streets afterward."

"A parade?"

"You know, a brass band, a decked-out hearse, maybe a float with a giant papier-mâché statue of me."

Laura giggled. She wasn't entirely sure he was kidding.

"As far as my coffin, I'd like . . ." Martin rubbed his chin and shook his head. "Scratch the coffin, save the tree, I'd be, like, dressed in a tux, a baby-blue tux, and then I'd like to be . . . what's it called, that kind of puppet with the strings?"

"A marionette," Laura said.

"Yeah." Martin smiled and nodded. "I'd like to be tied up like that, strings attached to sticks that will be manipulated by the pallbearers so that I'm lowered into the grave in a way that looks like I'm dancing while everyone in the village sings 'For He's a Jolly Good Fellow.'

"What do you think," Martin said as the elevator arrived on his floor. "Do you think that's too much?"

"It's quite an image," Laura responded.

"So," Martin said, thrusting his hand out of the elevator to keep the door from closing. "How things going with you? Anything new?"

"Not particularly," Laura said, wondering if she should mention the chairs or wait for him to remember on his own.

THEIR CALLS GOT SHORTER AND less frequent. By Halloween nearly all of them were initiated by Laura. Sensing Emma was in a rush to get off, she kept her updates to a minimum, and instead of asking questions that would prolong the exchange, she'd simply affirm the gist of whatever Emma had told her.

"Well, I think Lucas sounds very nice," she said at the end of one of their chats.

"In case you're wondering, we're not a thing," Emma replied.

"He's not a boyfriend?"

"No," she said. "He's ob*sessed* with Seth."

"Your running coach?"

"For the millionth time, it's cross-country."

"*Cross-country* coach," Laura corrected herself. "Lucas is romantically interested in him?"

"Yeah," Emma said. "He's bisexual."

"I see," Laura said, impressed by how casually the term rolled off

Emma's tongue. "So he's romantically interested in both women and men."

"Yes, Mom, he's *romantically interested* in both genders. That's what bisexual means. Do you have a problem with that? Do you think that makes him a freak?"

"Of *course* not," Laura quipped. "Who do you think I *am?*"

THE SUNDAY BEFORE THANKSGIVING, EMMA told Laura she'd been invited to spend Thanksgiving break with Lucas's family, who lived an hour from the school.

"It's okay if I say yes?" Emma asked. "I know it's last-minute, I said I'd ask first. I can come home if you want."

Ten weeks had seemed like a long time to go without seeing Emma. Now it would be thirteen.

"I think that sounds nice," Laura told her. "You should go."

"But what about *you*—what will you do?"

"I'll go to one-three-six," she said. "What else would I do?"

"Yeah, but will Stephanie and Nicholas be there?"

"They'll be in Florida."

"It'll just be you and Doug-Doug?"

"And Ellen Lowe."

"Who's that?"

"Mrs. Lowe, you remember her—we used to see her on Goat Hill walking her dogs."

"The woman you said probably spent more money on her dogs' cashmere sweaters than your entire wardrobe cost?"

"I don't remember saying that, and I doubt they're actual cashmere, but yes, that's her."

"That's random," Emma said. "Why'd you invite her?"

"I didn't, Douglas did—they've become companions."

"*Companions?*" Emma repeated with disdain.

"They meet for dinner, they do things together."

"So it'll just be you three?"

"That's correct."

"Who's cooking?" Emma asked. "Are you making the turkey?"

Laura wondered why she was asking this, as though she were a coworker. "I think you know the answer to that question," she told Emma. "Sandra is."

"Well, you know what I think, Mom? I think it's a *little* ironic, not to mention *fucked-up*, to make an *immigrant* cook a Thanksgiving turkey for you."

"I'm not sure how I'm supposed to respond to that." Laura reached for the last of the peanut butter Ritz crackers she'd made herself for dinner. "I hear that you're upset, and I'm not sure what you want me to say."

"What I *want* you to say? Are you *serious*, Mom? That's what our conversations are? You wondering, 'How does she want me to answer?' 'Tell her what she wants to hear!' So basically, our whole relationship is fake! Like a game of dolls!"

"Don't be ridiculous, darling, of course it's not," Laura said. She wasn't sure where this was going; she feared she was being entrapped. "What does that even mean, a game of dolls?"

"You make the doll say what you want her to say!"

Laura sighed. Anything she said would be used against her. There was no winning in these situations.

"Mom?" Emma spoke after a staticky silence. "Are you still there?"

"Of course I am."

"Then talk to me!" Emma shouted. "Talk to me like a *real person*. Say what you're actually thinking!"

"What I was actually thinking," Laura said, "was that I agree. But you know my father."

"Your *fath-ah*," Emma ridiculed in her mock English accent.

"You know Doug-Doug," Laura said. "It's his house and he likes to do things a certain way."

Laura looked at the clock: it was almost ten. "It's getting late," she told Emma. "I should let you go."

"Not tired," Emma answered, suddenly composed.

"You want to stay on the phone and keep talking?"

There was a pause. "What are we doing right now? Why would you ask me that, Mom?"

Laura sighed. "Well," she said, "it doesn't really sound like you want to stay on the phone and keep talking."

"What does it sound like?"

Laura's hand tightened around the phone.

"To be honest, you seem a little combative, not so much interested in having a conversation, more wanting to pick a fight—and it's late, and I'm tired, and not in the mood."

"Well, *good night* to you," Emma said tersely. "So sorry for keeping you up!" She hung up.

When Laura called her back, Emma picked up after the first ring.

"Mama," she wept through the receiver. "You *can't* make me feel guilty, you have *no* right! All I'm asking for, all I ev-er wanted," her voice quivered, "all I *ever*, ever wanted, was to have a *normal* Thanksgiving, where we spent the *day* in our *kitchen* making our own food, and set our own table, like every other family in America!"

Dial tone. This time, when Laura called back, she did not answer.

"Emma," she spoke to her answering machine. "My dear, little Em . . ."

Laura looked over at their table with its lone chair at the end. "I get it," she continued. "I understand.

"I'm sorry I couldn't give that to you," she said before gently placing the phone in its cradle.

MARTIN OPENED HIS DOOR HOLDING a carton of rainbow sherbet.

"This is really embarrassing," he said, licking the spoon. "But the first time you told me your name, I wasn't really paying attention . . ."

"Laura," she told him.

"You can call me Marty," he said.

"Marty," Laura began. "I'm here about the chairs. I'd like them back."

"The *chairs*." He knocked his head with his fist. "Totally forgot I still had them. My bad.

"Place is a little messy," he said, letting her in.

In all her years of living in the penthouse of 166, Laura had never stepped inside another resident's apartment, and she was surprised by how small Martin's was—a quarter the size of hers. It felt even smaller, as it was cluttered with stacks of records and an antique phonograph, milk crates full of books, a stationary bike, a movie-theater popcorn machine, and a cactus, among other things. There wasn't much in the way of furniture—apart from her chairs, which were lined up haphazardly at the other end of the room, facing the window.

"You're up late," Martin said, clearing a path to reach them.

"Likewise," Laura said.

Martin yawned. "Actually just starting my day.

"Need help bringing them up?" he asked once all the chairs were in the hall outside his door.

"That would be nice," Laura told him.

As they waited for the elevator, Martin said, "I hope I didn't disturb you with that whole dancing-corpse business that other time in the elevator. Sometimes my mind goes to dark places."

Laura smiled and shook her head to dismiss his concern, but Martin continued in this vein.

"I get depression," he told her. "Part of my trouble following through with things."

Laura wasn't sure how to respond to this. She offered him a neutral expression and a nod, in what she hoped conveyed compassion and nonjudgment.

"Is your new job night hours?

"Fixing voting machines," she added when Martin looked unsure of what she was referring to.

"Oh, that was just a three-day gig." He yawned again, and then asked, brightly: "Know anyone looking for a banjo teacher, or a juggler for kids' birthday parties, or a really awesome screenplay about a guy who wakes up one day and has completely forgotten what language is so he has to find other ways to communicate?

"It's a comedy," he added.

Suddenly the walls that had contained Laura's irritation collapsed. She looked in his face and saw a fragility. He seemed more like a boy than a man, idealistic, full of foolish expectations of what his future would hold. She couldn't see his life unfolding accordingly, and it broke her heart to imagine his disappointment. She thought of him as an old man, and then of his mother holding him as a baby—and she couldn't bear it.

Laura shook her head. "I'm afraid I don't, Marty, but I will certainly keep an ear open."

The elevator arrived. They loaded the chairs and rode up.

"Wait, how long have I had these chairs for?" Martin asked as they stepped into Laura's kitchen.

"Don't worry," Laura told him. "It's just been me, so it hasn't been a problem."

"But when did I borrow them?"

"Maybe the beginning of October?" Laura said, though she knew it was really the end of September.

"That's over a month!" Martin shook his head in remorse. "God-*damn*, I feel like a jerk. A big fat fuck."

"Don't say that," Laura said. "No, you aren't."

"Laura, I want you to promise me something." A serious look came over Martin's face. "If something like this happens again in the future, you have to say something."

Laura smiled and shook her head to reassure him.

"I mean it," he said. "Speak up."

She smiled again.

As Martin stepped out the door to wait for the elevator, she said, "My mother had depression."

Martin nodded thoughtfully.

"It's funny, because no one knew it. When she died, all the condolence letters talked about how she was the happiest person they knew. Joie de vivre. Life of the party. Lit up a room."

The elevator arrived.

"Bipolar?" he asked, sticking his hand over the sensor to keep the door from closing.

"I believe she was diagnosed with that at some point," she said. "We don't really name things in our family."

Martin grinned. "Let me guess, you're from the Midwest?"

Laura shook her head.

"Sorry," he said. "That's kind of an insult."

Laura considered this. "I don't know why you say that," she said. "The people I've met from the Midwest I've liked very much."

"Thanks," Martin said. "I'm from St. Louis. What about you? Where're you from?"

"East Sixty-fifth Street," Laura said. "Between Lex and Third."

Martin looked surprised. "You don't seem like you grew up in New York City."

Laura had been told this before; she never knew if it was a compliment or not.

"Born and raised," she said. She thought about adding "seventh-generation," as Nicholas was fond of telling people, but thought it would sound obnoxious.

After locking the door behind her, Laura brushed her teeth, put on her nightgown, and got into bed. She read for a bit, turned off the light, and fell asleep.

*　　*　　*

THERE WAS A WORD FOR it—the anxious thoughts of the predawn hours. It was an old English word that no one used anymore, and, having recently learned it, Laura had already forgotten what it was. It began with a *U* and the rest of the letters were strange. Uticare. Something like that. Nevertheless, it comforted her—the mere fact of its existence many centuries ago—to think of waking up in the middle of the night and being unable to fall back asleep as less of a unique affliction than a universal thing. Part of the human condition.

Tonight she'd gotten out of bed and been standing by her bedroom window at the precise moment the Empire State Building went dark. It surprised her that in all her years of being awake at this hour she'd never witnessed this event. As a child, Emma had often wondered and asked about this. The light on the top of the Empire State Building, when did it get turned off? Whose job was it? Did he sleep in the Empire State Building?

I don't know . . . I'm not sure . . . I'm afraid I can't answer that.

Laura had always imagined it went off in a blink, but it was a gradual dimming. And when it was done she continued to stand by the window looking out at all the other buildings, which were mostly dark, except for a spattering of illuminated windows. She thought of the people who were still up and wondered what they were doing.

Laura returned to bed and drifted off to sleep for another hour, and this time, when she woke up to the clanking of pipes and the hiss of the radiator, she could see nothing out her window. Just a blank canvas of a color there was no word for. A metallic pink mixed with gray.

There was a flutter in her chest, as there always was upon spotting the season's first snowflakes, but this was more than the typical debut flurry. It was coming down hard; it was sticking.

Laura put a turtleneck on over her nightgown. Then she put on three pairs of kneesocks. A trick she'd learned as a child: if you put on three pairs of socks and went outside in the freshly fallen dry snow, your feet didn't get cold and it felt like walking barefoot on a beach.

As she passed by her bookshelf on her way out of the bedroom, she saw the tin box in its usual spot. She paused, took a step back, and picked it up.

She went to the kitchen, opened the door, and stepped out onto the terrace.

Laura had never handled ashes before. They were more tangible than she'd expected. She thought they would be like powder—that all she'd have to do was uncurl her fingers, and the wind would whisk them away in a whispery, vaporous tendril, as it was doing to the snow. But these ashes were chunky and uneven, like what you'd find in the bottom of a fireplace or charcoal grill.

She flung a handful over the railing. She scooped another handful, and another.

Soon she was clutching an empty tin. She had expected something more out of this moment; for something dramatic, whimsical, or amusing to happen, or for the ashes to float upward to the heavens. That Bibs did not make herself known during the scattering of her ashes, that they unceremoniously sank to the street, seemed to confirm the fact that she was really gone.

When Laura turned to go back in, the door wouldn't budge.

She pushed harder. It still didn't open.

She pushed and pushed, thrusting her full weight against it. But it remained stuck, as often happened in the hottest and coldest weather.

The windows were all latched shut and it was impossible to shatter double-glazed windows. The man who'd installed them had proudly demonstrated this to her as proof of their superb insulation.

She tried with her legs, gripping the railing for support, her kicks becoming more frantic as they continued to fail.

People didn't freeze to death on penthouse terraces in Manhattan. Eventually the snow would peter out and the yuppies of the Parkview, Normandy Court, or the Monterey would wake up and look out the windows and see her; she would catch the attention of a pedestrian, or the pilot of a traffic helicopter—someone would notice her and recognize that she needed assistance.

There was a ladder leading up to the roof. It would increase the chances of being seen.

She climbed up.

Laura had never been on the roof before. It felt unsafe. There was no railing; it was not a place people were supposed to be.

Now she was scared. She turned to go back down the ladder, but she wasn't sure what direction it was; the snow had thickened and she'd become disoriented. She couldn't see where the roof ended and the sky began. The visibility was so bad she could be anywhere: a ski lift in Vermont, a mountain in the Alps, halfway to the moon— where rogue particles barreled aimlessly through the soft, white violence of infinity.

She stood there, shivering, stomping her feet, waving her arms above her head. But it was in vain. How could anyone see her? She could barely make out her own hand before her.

She stopped waving. But she had to keep moving to stay warm.

Keep moving.

This couldn't be it.

Could it? It would be so ludicrous.

No, it couldn't be it. It wouldn't be fair to Emma.

Oh, Emma.

A gale inflated the skirt of her nightgown, stinging her bare thighs.

The unusual hush of the snow-padded city, broken by the grating echo of a plow.

She thought of Martin, of all people.

"Candooskey," she whispered.

She took a deep breath and exhaled. Then she drew another, deeper breath, and held it for longer. Deeper, longer, she kept practicing, until she had a sense of the limits of her capacity.

When her lungs were swollen with air, Laura, shrouded in snow, cupped her hands around her lips and opened her mouth as wide as it would go.

Acknowledgments

I am deeply indebted to the writing program at Wesleyan University and the Warren Wilson MFA Program for Writers. Of the many wonderful teachers I've had along the way, a special thanks to Dr. Mahoney and Mrs. Rice of Hastings High School, and Elizabeth Bobrick. Thank you to Diana Spechler. Amy Williams and Marysue Rucci, I am so lucky to have you. Thank you to Zack Knoll, Amanda Lang, and the wonderful team at Simon & Schuster. Thank you to the Moth. I would also like to thank my grandfather Bobby; my parents, Christy and Scott; and my sisters, Frances and Molly, for their love and encouragement. And finally, thank you to Teddy, for showing me a place to hang my bags.

About the Author

KATE GREATHEAD is a graduate of Wesleyan University and the MFA Program for Writers at Warren Wilson College. Her writing has appeared in *The New Yorker*, the *New York Times*, and *Vanity Fair*, and NPR's *Moth Radio Hour*. She lives in Brooklyn with her husband, writer Teddy Wayne. *Laura & Emma* is her first novel.